SARA C ROETHLE

Created with Vellum

# 1

The sensation of the plane bouncing on the tarmac woke me. It had been a trying few days, and the extra sleep on the plane was a welcome reprieve. I didn't mind lying on Alaric's shoulder either.

I still wasn't quite sure how to feel about him. Okay, I knew exactly how I *felt*. I just wasn't sure what to do about it. As much as I wanted to ignore the fact that he'd misled me about many things, and had allowed my torture, those two facts still ate at me.

Forgiveness is one thing. I'm great at forgiveness. Being an empath means I'm a seasoned pro at putting myself in the shoes of others. At some point I had relented to *mostly* forgive Alaric, but I couldn't forget what had happened, and I sure as hell couldn't trust him.

Betrayal is a funny thing. The sting of it often sticks with us longer than the thrill of love, the fire of hatred, or the emptiness of loss. Betrayal eats at us when we know we should be happy, and it overwhelms us when we're already sad.

I raised my head up from Alaric's shoulder as the plane came to a slow stop. He smiled down at me, unaware of my thoughts, and I couldn't help but smile in return. Despite everything, it felt good having him by my side. It would have felt even better if we were on a plane to some romantic destination, but we weren't.

Although, I suppose Norway *could* be romantic, given the right circumstances. The pictures I'd seen were gorgeous and fairytale-esque, and I was traveling there with a handsome man, but I'm pretty sure romantic vacations aren't supposed to include being hunted by supernatural beings while looking for a charm that's guarded by the dead. Running for your life is a major mood killer.

We waited while the rows of people ahead of us stood and un-stowed their luggage. I shifted uncomfortably, feeling trapped. Once there was enough room, I stood and glanced back toward James and Diana, wondering why each of them *really* wanted the charm, and to what lengths they would go to get it.

James pulled Diana's luggage down from the storage compartment. He had none of his own. In fact, he was still wearing the white tee-shirt he'd worn while he tortured me, just as I was still wearing a black dress with holes in it where he'd stabbed me. Luckily James had stolen me a long, black winter coat with faux fur trim around the hood. It hid my dress, but looked slightly out of place with my too-large hiking boots and thick winter socks.

Sophie waited in her seat across the aisle for James and Diana to get out of the way, pushing them closer toward me. Her original seat had been next to the unwelcome pair, but she'd managed to flirt her way into a seat trade, leaving James to sit next to a man who could have easily taken up two seats on his own. The man in question was still asleep in his seat by the window.

Squeezing past me, Alaric woke the man with a gentle shake of his shoulder, then signaled for him to move, much to the chagrin of the people behind us who would now have to wait even longer.

The line ahead of me moved and I scurried forward, eventually exiting the plane. It was a surreal feeling leaving the West Coast a few hours after dark to arrive in another country where evening had already come again. I'd never traveled such a long distance. Heck, I'd never traveled much at all. Living as a recluse with meager monetary means had prevented me from seeing much of the world.

My next shock came after we went through security and emerged into the cold night air. My coat was warm by West Coast standards, but it could not contend with the icy temperature of Oslo in late October. I clutched the meager protection closer to my body, but my bare legs still erupted in almost painful goosebumps.

James and Sophie stepped ahead of the rest of us, scanning the busy street like a pair of vengeful angels, dark and light, illuminated by the halo of a streetlamp. I could sense their nerves. We all knew Estus wouldn't let us escape so easily.

Alaric, seeming unaffected, smiled and put an arm around me.

Diana tsked at us like we were all being silly children and went to the curb to hail a cab. She clutched a modern black cape around her small form, the fabric swirling around her legs in the cold breeze like it had a life of its own. Though she was small and elderly, with perfect gray, granny-styled hair, I would never mistake her for anything less dangerous than she was.

She was the sister of Aislin, ruler of several clans, which made her old, and we're talking centuries, not decades. Though I was yet to see her do anything out-rightly scary, the threat was always there. She was twenty times scarier than James, and he'd stabbed me and tormented me for fun.

A cab pulled up, and it became readily apparent there were five of us, and only four available seats.

"We'll wait for the next one," Alaric announced, clearly referring to him, myself, and Sophie.

James smirked. "I don't think so. Madeline will come with *us*."

My heart sped at the idea of being left alone in a cab with James and Diana, but Alaric stepped forward before I could move. "*I'll* go with you, and Maddy and Sophie will catch the next cab. You can kill me if they don't show up."

My eyes widened, but I wasn't about to argue.

With a curt nod, Diana climbed into the front seat of the cab while James put her suitcase in the trunk. Alaric gave me a quick kiss on the cheek, then slid into the back-seat after James. I touched my cheek where he'd kissed me, feeling a mixture of annoyance and apprehension.

Diana rolled down her window and relayed the address of the hotel, then suddenly we were left to wait for another cab by ourselves. It was the first time Sophie and I had been alone since she'd rejoined our party after leaving me to be tortured in her place. I crossed my arms and turned away from her, half-wishing I would have just gone with the others, leaving her to catch a cab on her own. It wouldn't compare to her leaving me in the Salr to face punishment for her crimes, but it was a start.

She sighed dramatically at my back. "How long are you going to ignore me? Maya left me. I think I've paid for my actions."

I looked over my shoulder at her. "So because someone betrayed your trust, it makes it okay that you betrayed mine?"

"I said I'm sorry," she snapped, quickly losing patience.

I turned away from her again and mumbled, "Barely."

Another cab pulled up to the curb. I turned and followed Sophie as she opened the back door and climbed in. The heat inside was almost stifling, but felt good after standing on the chilly curb.

I would have been tempted to take my own cab, but one, I had already forgotten the address, and two, I had no money to pay the cab driver, so I was stuck with Sophie.

The driver barely even looked at us as Sophie told him where to go. I crossed my arms again and stayed silent as he drove the cab through a few roundabouts leading out of the airport, then onto the highway. I had no idea how far away the hotel was, but I hoped it was close. Sophie was staring at me intently, her face a pale oval in the darkness of the cab, and I wasn't sure how long I'd be able to maintain the silent treatment.

"You would have done the same," she said eventually.

I looked into her dark eyes, so similar to her brother's, and could see she really believed what she'd said.

I shook my head. "Not everyone is like you."

"Look," she sighed. "I said I was *sorry*. It's not something I say often, and I wouldn't have said it if I didn't mean it. What else do you want from me?"

Her emotions were intense enough at that moment that I could sense her frustration, and underneath it, guilt. She really did feel remorse over leaving me. It might not make up for the original act, but it was a start.

"Okay," I replied.

She narrowed her eyes at me. "Just . . . okay? Why don't you seem angry suddenly?"

I shrugged. "I know you regret leaving me. I'll get over it . . . eventually."

Sophie's eyes widened. "You empathed me! That's not fair."

I rolled my eyes. "You know I can't help it. Strong emotions leak through whether I want them to or not."

She harrumphed, then glanced at the driver as he swerved to the right and cut several people off so he could exit.

She turned back to me. "So you've forgiven my brother?"

I shook my head. "Not quite. Maybe with time."

She shook her head in return. "I don't know how you do that."

"Do what?"

"Forgive so easily," she explained. "If I were you, I'd have already tried to kill me, and Alaric would have been dead the moment I saw his face. Not that I'm not grateful that you're not attacking me . . . "

I shrugged again. "It's the empath thing. Trust me, I did

want to kill Alaric, but guilt is a very strong emotion. So is fear. It's hard to blindly judge someone's actions when you can literally *feel* what they are feeling."

It was Sophie's turn to cross her arms. "I am *not* afraid."

I laughed. "Oh please, you're terrified, and you're sad."

She glared at me as the cab pulled into the parking lot of a large, well-lit, resort-style hotel. "I don't think I like you very much."

I grinned. "And here you were just begging for my forgiveness."

The cab halted, and I quickly opened the door and climbed out, leaving Sophie to pick up the tab.

"I was not begging!" she shouted after me.

I laughed as I walked across the asphalt toward the hotel. Torturing calm, cool, and collected Sophie with my empathic abilities was far more rewarding than snubbing her.

Alaric and James, who had been waiting outside the hotel lobby for us, came striding forward to meet me. The warmth I'd collected in the cab was quickly fading, and the expanses of surrounding near-darkness made me nervous. Anyone could be out there watching us, and we wouldn't even know. I gazed at the hotel longingly as the men reached me.

"Ms. Moneybags has us staying at the most expensive hotel in the country," Alaric explained. He was still just dressed in his navy flannel and black jeans, unfazed by the cold.

"I wouldn't let Diana hear you calling her that," James chided.

Sophie reached us, then breezed on by without a word, like a tall, dark, angry cloud.

Alaric watched his sister's back, then whispered, "You *must* tell me what you did to make her so angry."

I wrapped my arms tightly around myself, fighting shivers. "You wouldn't be able to pull it off. Now can we please go inside before I freeze to death?"

Alaric placed a hand at the small of my back and guided me forward. The building rose up in front of us as we neared. I counted ten stories, the exterior done in a crisp white that matched the surrounding patches of snow on the ground.

James strode past us toward Sophie.

Alaric smiled down at me. "We have our own room," he said with a waggle of his eyebrows.

I stopped walking, though my bare legs were burning with cold. "Why?"

He shrugged, placing his hand against my back again to keep me walking. "If I didn't know any better, I'd say Diana is trying to play matchmaker, but I think she has much more nefarious plans in mind."

My stomach lurched, but I kept walking. She *was* planning something, I knew it. But why the room? "If she's manipulating us, shouldn't we, I don't know, *not* go along with it?"

"Why would I argue with plans that benefit me?" he said happily as the automatic glass doors slid open in front of us.

Some of the tension seeped out of my body once the doors slid shut behind us. The bellhop waiting inside gave us a strange look, probably due to our lack of luggage. The young man shrugged his narrow shoulders and sighed, then led us to a row of elevators. James and Sophie had already gone up, leaving us to ride up with the bellhop alone.

Alaric put an arm around my shoulders as the elevator lurched into motion.

I dutifully removed it, then took a step away, thinking that it was a really bad idea for us to share a room. Not only was Diana up to something, but I didn't fully trust myself. It had been impulsive to fall into bed with Alaric the first time, and I didn't want to be that stupid again. Of course, we still might die tomorrow. Normally it was wise to err on the side of caution, but was it really wise to make good life-choices when my life might not last much longer? Shouldn't I just enjoy being alive while I could?

Alaric could act like we weren't in danger all he liked, but I knew better. If Sophie was scared, it meant we were up a very smelly creek with no paddles, with plenty of holes in our boat. I'd seen first hand how Estus dealt with those who opposed him. If he found us and sent more of the Vaettir to capture us, we would all suffer very ugly ends.

The elevator came to a stop and the doors slid open. Without a glance in our direction, the silent bellhop led us down an extravagantly decorated hall to our room. He used a key card on the door, then handed it to Alaric as we entered. The room was bigger than my old house, with a full sitting area, king-sized bed, and a kitchenette partially obscured from view by bar-style seating, all done in delicate gold and pale blues.

My eyes scanned the room, then came back to rest on

the bed. They lingered there, then went back to the couch. It looked comfortable enough.

Alaric tipped the bellhop, then urged him out of the room. Once we were alone, Alaric walked past me to flop down on the bed. He laid on his back with his arms behind his head, watching me as I took a closer look around the room.

"So what do you want to *do*?" he asked eventually, putting emphasis on the word *do*, to make it seem dirty.

I walked past one of the cushy chairs on either side of the couch to peek into the bathroom. "I *think* we're here to find the charm, so that's what I want to do."

"Diana claims the location is very near, but she doesn't know exactly how near," he explained, "she needs time to pinpoint it, which means we have some time to *kill*."

I glared at him. "Stop emphasizing random words to make them seem sexy."

He grinned. "Is it working? Are my words . . . *sexy*?"

I shook my head and turned away from him.

In an instant he was up off the bed and at my side, moving a lock of my dark brown hair behind my shoulder to bare the side of my neck, grazing his fingers across my skin as he went. It might have been a sexual gesture if he wasn't watching me with such a concerned look on his face.

"I take it your attitude means I'll be sleeping on the floor again," he said softly.

I glanced at him, but didn't pull away. I had to audibly gulp before I could answer, "I'll take the couch this time. It's only fair since I had the bed at Diana's."

He let my hair fall from his grasp, then took my hand

into his grip instead. He kissed my knuckles one by one, then answered, "As you wish."

I slowly pulled my hand away. "Why are you being so agreeable?"

He glanced into the large bathroom that boasted a full-size jacuzzi tub as well as a glass-walled shower. "I think I'll take a bath."

I crossed my arms. "You didn't answer me."

"I don't suppose you'd like to join me?" he asked, still not answering me.

"We don't have any clean clothes," I commented. If he wasn't going to answer me, I wasn't going to answer him either.

Alaric shrugged and walked into the bathroom. "It's late. We'll buy you a whole new wardrobe in the morning."

I stayed where I was standing and glared at his back. "Some jeans and a sweater would suffice."

He began to unbutton his shirt with his back still to me. As the fabric fell to the floor, I blushed and turned away, marching dutifully over to the couch to turn on the TV. The screen came to life. The commercial that came on was in Norwegian, obviously, but it didn't matter because I was so distracted by the sound of Alaric filling up the bathtub that I wouldn't have been able to concentrate on it regardless.

"Maddy?" Alaric called out.

"Yes?" I asked hesitantly.

"Come keep me company."

My mouth suddenly went dry. I cleared my throat. "I don't think so."

"Do you really find it entertaining to watch a show in a language you don't speak?" he pressed.

I glanced at the TV screen again, then back to the open bathroom door.

"I'll be a perfect gentleman," he added. "Scout's honor."

Silently cursing myself, I stood and made my way to the bathroom. Keeping my eyes dutifully averted from the bathtub, I entered the steamy room and took a seat on the closed lid of the toilet.

I could feel Alaric's eyes on me, but refused to look. "There are plenty of bubbles," he assured. "You won't see a thing."

With another sigh, I rolled my eyes as I turned my head to look at him. There were indeed plenty of bubbles, but I could still see the top of his chest, slick with water. He'd wet his dark hair, pushing it away from his face to make him look even more ethereal than usual.

I did my best to maintain eye-contact as Alaric slipped a little further down into the bubbles. "You know, it seems like a waste of water to fill this gigantic bathtub just for one person," he commented.

I smirked. "Well you're the one that did it, that's on your conscience." Desperately wanting to change the subject, I added, "I thought Diana said she knew of the place the hearts showed me. Why does she need time to find it now?"

"Norway has changed a great deal since she was last here," he explained, "and this is not a place you can see, it's a place you have to *feel*. She's using her connections to at least get an idea of the general area so we can go there and search."

"So what do we do until then?" I questioned.

A small smile curved across his lips. "You could get in the bath with me."

I stared at him for several heartbeats, then sighed, "Fine."

His eyes widened. "Fine? I was expecting a lot of things, but *fine* wasn't one of them."

I shrugged and tried to act like my heart wasn't racing. "We're stuck in a hotel in a foreign country," I explained, "waiting for a very scary old woman to lead us to a place that you can only *feel* and not *see*. Meanwhile, we have an angry, sociopathic Doyen thirsty for our blood. Normally, I would be appalled by your offer, and I would snub you to the fullest extent, but I'm scared, and I'm cold, and I have no idea what tomorrow will bring, so I say *fine*."

Alaric raised his eyebrows in surprise. "You are a very strange woman, Madeline."

I smirked as I stood and began undressing. "Says the guy with cat fangs."

He grinned to show his dainty, pointed canines, then watched my every move as I took off the holey dress, bra, and panties. I quickly slipped into the tub on the side opposite him, inhaling sharply at the heat of the water. I let out my breath slowly as my skin adjusted to the temperature change, then settled down until the bubbles nearly reached my chin.

Alaric's smile turned mischievous, and I eyed him warily. Before I could react, he reached through the water and grabbed my arm, then spun me around in one fast movement so that my back was pressed against his. A little wave of water splashed out of the tub a moment later to soak his towel where he had set it on the tiled floor.

"I said I'd take a bath," I replied coolly, "I didn't say I was going to snuggle with you."

"Shh," he breathed as he lowered his lips to the side of my neck.

He laid gentle kisses all the way up to the base of my ear, making my chest and upper arms erupt in goose-bumps, despite the warmth of the water.

"I—" I began, but he cut me off by turning my face to the side with one damp hand so he could kiss me.

My thoughts were a jumble of emotions, ranging from nervous excitement to guilt. The guilt was all for me, like I was letting myself down somehow, but it was drowned out by the feel of Alaric's free hand making its way down my ribcage.

I pulled away from the kiss and looked up into Alaric's eyes, which looked even darker surrounded by his wet hair. "Desperate times call for desperate measures?" I questioned weakly, looking for an excuse for my actions.

He chuckled. "Something like that."

He pulled my face back up for another kiss and I gave in. I would probably regret everything tomorrow, but that was tomorrow. This was tonight, and Alaric's soapy body felt far too good against mine to just go to bed.

---

Some time later we ended up on the king-sized bed with the covers pulled partially up. Alaric was lying on my lower body with his head cradled on my stomach while I stroked his drying hair. My original plan of sleeping on the couch seemed pretty silly now, and seemed even sillier as Alaric's hand slowly slid up from my hip to the side of my waist.

His fingers found the little scars where James had

stabbed me. His entire body seemed to tense. When I didn't react, he relaxed, and began running his fingers back and forth across the scars.

I could sense he wanted to say something, but was probably afraid of opening up a can of worms since the scars were kind of his fault.

"What is it?" I prompted.

"How did you know I wanted to say something?" he asked with a hint of laughter in his voice.

"I'm an empath, remember?" I reminded him, though really I was just going off intuition.

He chuckled and ran his fingers over the scars again. "How did you heal them so quickly?"

It was a good question. In theory I knew how I'd done it, but I wasn't sure if I could replicate it, or even explain it. "I used the energy from the hearts, just like I did when I healed Sophie after the battle."

He moved his arms underneath my lower back and squeezed me tightly. "You know executioners aren't supposed to be able to heal, right?"

I smirked, but he couldn't see it. "Actually, I don't know much about executioners at all."

He lifted his head to meet my gaze. "And you know nothing of your parents?"

"N-no," I stammered, taken aback by the question. "Do you?"

He shook his head. "No. There's a chance I may have met them at some point, but I don't know who they are. Estus probably knows."

I shifted to put another pillow behind me so I could see him better. "Would they be executioners too?"

I'd gone so long without thinking about who my parents might be, I hadn't considered that they might be still be among the Vaettir. The thought was both intriguing and terrifying.

Alaric lifted one shoulder in a half shrug. "We inherit the traits of our mothers, but some lines are more specific than others."

Confused, I nodded my head for him to go on.

"Since Sophie and I are descended from a goddess of a major pantheon, we have similar gifts to our mother. Other smaller deities are simply embodiments of nature, and the gifts inherited may vary. Your mother could have been descended from a major death goddess, in which case your gifts would be similar to hers, or she could have come from a lesser nature deity. Death is a part of all things, and can be inherited at random."

"So what about my empathy?" I questioned.

He laid his head back down on my stomach, rubbing his hair across my skin to cause a delightful shiver. "I do not know," he answered finally. "It should not be, just as your ability to heal should not be. Few among the Vaettir are true healers, and they usually descend from major deities."

I sighed. He spoke like all of these gods and goddesses actually existed. I would never have believed it before, but I'd had a rough few weeks. I was willing to believe most anything now. I thought about my next question, then asked, "What would other executioners do with the leftover energy of releasing someone's life force?"

He kissed my stomach, sending another shiver up my spine. "They would keep it, or use it as a weapon."

I took a shaky breath, then decided to ask a question I'd

been wanting to ask ever since I found out what I was. Really, I'd been wanting to know the answer since the first time I'd killed. "Do you think I'm evil?"

Alaric lifted his head and looked up at me again, surprised. "How long have you been holding onto *that* one?"

I stared back at him. "Just answer it, please."

He eyed me seriously. "You're not evil, Maddy." I felt a moment of relief, but it was short lived as he added, "but you're not entirely good either."

At my horrified expression, he rolled off me so he could sit by my side and pull me close.

"I don't mean that how you think I do," he explained. "In nature there must be polarity. A forest fire may kill many trees and creatures, but it also brings new life and fertility to the land. Death is neither good nor bad, just as you are neither good nor bad. You simply *are*."

"But I'm a person with emotions and a moral compass," I argued. "I'm not simply *death*."

"Ah," he said with a coy smile, "but you were not asking me about your moral compass. You were asking if you are innately evil, because of your gifts."

I took a moment to think about what he'd said. "I guess I understand, but what about you? How could war ever be viewed as a good thing?"

He pulled me in a little closer, nestling me in the curve of his arm. "You are thinking of war in terms of bloody battles and rotting corpses. While that is part of what I am, that is not what war is in its purest form."

"Okay," I commented, "you've lost me again."

"It goes back to polarity," he explained. "Without one

side, the other does not exist. Without conflict and chaos, there can be no victory nor peace."

"I suppose that makes sense. Without darkness, there's no light, and so on and so forth."

He gave my shoulders a squeeze. "Precisely. Now we should probably get some rest. Come morning we will likely have work to do."

I turned, my expression utterly serious. "Well then it's probably time for you to move to the couch."

His eyes widened in surprise, and he opened his mouth to say something, but no words came out.

I snickered.

Realizing my joke, he lifted me off him and pinned me to the bed with a wicked gleam in his eyes.

"I thought we were going to bed!" I exclaimed, still laughing.

He smiled wide enough to flash fang. "Not quite yet."

My laughter died down as I gazed into his now serious eyes. He leaned down and kissed me, and as he pulled away, I smiled. I'd already made one bad decision that night, so I might as well make another.

As he kissed down my chest, I glanced over at the heavy curtains covering the window. It likely wouldn't be long until the first light of dawn edged along the corners. Early rising Diana was going to be *pissed* if we weren't up and ready when she was.

Pissing people off seemed to be fast becoming a hobby of mine, but it was better than a lot of the alternatives.

# 2

A loud banging at the door woke me, not like someone knocking, but someone trying to break in. Alaric was already up out of bed, struggling into his dirty clothes next to the bathroom door. I held the sheets up to cover myself and rose to search frantically around the room for my dress, until it dawned on me that I had left it in the bathroom. The banging grew louder until the door slammed inward, hitting the wall with a startling *thwack.*

I froze halfway to the bathroom while Alaric faced whoever stood in the doorway. He had managed to get his pants on, but no shirt. Before I could react, a woman barreled into him, sending them both to the carpet at my feet. I caught a quick glance of her bright blonde hair and black clothing, then turned to face four more people rushing into the room.

They all wore black, like the woman, and I didn't recognize any of them. Shouts and the sound of fighting echoed through the walls from the next room over, letting me know we weren't the only ones being attacked.

Two of the intruders, both men, went to help the blonde-haired woman with Alaric, while the other two, a man and a woman, slowly approached me.

"She's the executioner," the man commented with a glance to the woman.

I looked back and forth between them, weighing my options. Sparring with Alaric was the only fighting experience I'd had, and I doubted I was any match for the pair in front of me.

One of the men attacking Alaric went flying across the room. He hit the wall hard enough to dent the drywall, then slid to the ground and was still. Five-hundred years of fighting experience had obviously done Alaric good. The man's pain was only a dull throb to me, which meant he was either dead, or unconscious.

I darted my attention back as the pair in front of me finally started to close in. My eyes shifted from side to side while I hiked the sheet up around my body like a dress. My body felt strange, like I was feeling emotions and injuries from too many people, and it all just condensed into a huge wave of pain and anxiety. It made it difficult to move or even think. I closed my eyes and took a deep breath, attempting to shut everyone else out. A measure of calm reached me, then my own emotions came flooding in. I opened my eyes just as the pair reached out in unison to grab me.

"Stop this at once!" a booming voice called from the doorway. The three of us turned to see Diana, looking a little mussed but unharmed, holding out both arms in a dramatic stance.

The two intruders that had approached me let their outstretched hands drop, then turned to face the new threat. Seeing an opportunity, and still blocking out a measure of the emotions around me, I ran to the man Alaric had thrown into the wall.

He was unconscious, but I couldn't tell how injured he was. I reached a hand hesitantly toward him, hoping that if he was near death, his spirit would reach out to me. The energy from one death wouldn't be much, but Alaric had claimed other executioners used that energy as a weapon. Maybe I could too.

I turned as one of the male intruders started shrieking to see Diana standing over his hunched form, one hand held out like she was *Darth Vader*. I searched for Alaric, but it sounded like much of the fighting was now happening in the hall. I wasn't sure what Diana was doing to the man, but he dropped to his knees and began clawing at his skin, leaving deep craters to fill with blood. I clutched at my own face, clenching my jaw against the sudden pain.

The horrifying sight was taken from my view as the blonde-haired woman that originally attacked Alaric darted around her tortured colleague and came to stand in front of me.

"I'm not going to hurt you," she assured, "but I need you to come with me."

I reached out to the unconscious man again, guiltily hoping he was near death. I could feel his life force, but it felt solid inside of him. I reached out mentally, trying to connect with the energy, but it wouldn't budge from his body, meaning he wasn't badly hurt.

With a glance at her prostrate colleague, the woman grabbed my arm and hauled me to my feet. It was all I could do to use my free arm to keep the sheet around me. I tried again to pull at the unconscious man's life force, but another answered. The energy came rushing out of the man Diana had tortured, ready to be released. It flowed through me as the woman began hauling me toward the door.

Rather than assisting me, Diana tilted her head as a strange smile crossed her face. I looked at her in panic as the blonde woman jerked me forward. She turned, raising her free arm like she was going to hit me, and I reacted by shoving the energy at her, much like I had done to Estus when I escaped the Salr with James. The woman went flying back, losing her grip on me as she shot out into the hall.

I stared at her crumpled form, dumbfounded, until James stepped into view in the hall. He was covered in soot and ash, letting me know he had probably burned a few people to death.

He looked at the woman, then over to me and chuckled. "Little mouse has some teeth after all." He walked into the room, smirked at the sheet covering my body, then walked up to Diana. "Thanks for the *help*," he said sarcastically.

"Madeline is what's important," Diana replied coolly.

Not taking the time to ponder the harsh statement from Diana, I ran out into the hall in search of Alaric. I found him being helped to his feet by Sophie, surrounded by several dead people.

Seeing me, Alaric pulled away from Sophie and closed the distance between us, engulfing me in a tight hug as soon as he reached me.

Diana came into the hall, followed by James. "Release them quickly, Madeline. We must go before the human police come."

"But they're not all dead," I argued, reluctantly pulling away from Alaric.

"They will be," she said apathetically as James crouched down and slit the unconscious blonde woman's throat with a knife.

My stomach lurched at the sight. He must have picked up the knife sometime after we landed. I looked away as the woman's blood flowed onto the fancy carpet. The rest of the hallway was utterly still, but I knew the chaos had to have been heard by others. I wasn't surprised as police sirens suddenly wailed in the distance.

Snapping into action, I gathered my sheet tightly around myself and ran past Diana back into the room, then dashed straight into the bathroom. My wrinkled, tattered black dress was on the floor where I'd left it, looking unappealing and a little damp. Knowing I had no other options, I slipped the undergarments and dress back on, cursing the fact that we were yet to get me anything but a coat.

I returned to the main room to find James finishing off the unconscious man. In total we had five victims, the blonde, the two Alaric had killed in the hall, the man Diana had taken down, and the latest one, although I still had no idea what happened in the other rooms.

The sirens grew nearer.

"There's no time," Diana barked. "Leave them."

"I can't leave them like this!" I shouted, panicking as Diana put her iron cold grip around my arm and began to drag me out of the room.

Sophie had followed us in, and grabbed my coat off the couch as Diana pushed me in front of her so she could shove me into James' grasp. I began to struggle, horrified at the thought of leaving life in dead bodies, but Sophie cut in and quickly helped me into my coat.

"They're right," she snapped. "Now *move*."

When I didn't react, James threw me over his shoulder and carried me into the hall. Alaric had been busy checking the other rooms, but as we neared him James tossed me onto his shoulder like a rag doll.

"I have to free them," I pleaded from my awkward perch, knowing Alaric would at least listen to me, but he continued walking forward as the others entered the stairwell.

"There's no time," he explained as the door to the stairwell slammed shut behind us. "Besides, you'd be doing nothing for them once the police arrested you."

I knew he was right, but I could feel the souls of the dead reaching out to me, pleading to be released. "We have to go back!" I shrieked, unable to listen to reason as the spirits cried out in my head.

Alaric jogged a little faster down the stairwell. We were five stories up, but no one had even glanced at the elevators. The sane part of me knew that we were taking the stairs so we wouldn't be entirely trapped should the police show up too soon, but the rest of me could only think about the corpses we'd left behind.

I cried in vain as Alaric took the stairs in great bounds.

If I fought to go back, I would likely get us all killed, or at least jailed, though something told me James and Diana would not go down without a fight.

We reached the bottom stairwell and continued into the lower parking garage. From my backward vantage point on Alaric's shoulder, I couldn't tell who was leading us, I only knew we were last in line. The sirens grew louder as another door slammed shut behind us, and Alaric lowered me to my bare feet, but my legs buckled. He caught me with an arm under my shoulders before I could fall. I felt like I wanted to cry. We'd forgotten my damn shoes. No one else standing in our little semi-circle seemed to notice.

"They're already outside," James stated calmly.

"We'll split up," Diana instructed. She turned her vibrant green eyes to Alaric. "Get Madeline out of here. Without her, our efforts are useless."

I had one confused moment before Alaric lifted me back up over his shoulder and started running. Everyone else ran in opposite directions. There were several exits to the parking complex that I could see, but Alaric chose one that led to the back of the hotel.

I couldn't decide whether I was happy or sad as Sophie and the others disappeared from sight. Neither I suppose. Mostly I was just worried about escaping the police, and about trusting my fate to the man running effortlessly underneath me.

---

THE DOOR THUDDED against the building's exterior as Alaric carried me outside. The cold was a sudden slap in the face, or rear, considering how I was being carried. I pushed away from Alaric's back to get a better view of our surroundings as he sped across the back parking lot. There were no police in sight, which meant that likely only one or two patrol cars had been dispatched to investigate the disturbance. They hadn't surrounded the place.

Shouts echoed in the distance, followed by loud banging then more shouts.

It was only then that I looked down and realized Alaric wasn't wearing shoes either. Without hesitation, his bare feet hit the snowy ground past the parking lot.

The commotion continued in the distance as we ran, but all I could think about was the cold and distantly, the souls I'd left trapped in their bodies.

Alaric quietly cursed under his breath as he carried me into a forested area. There didn't seem to be any businesses or other buildings around, from what I could see. Just shadowy, dense forest. Thoughts flashed through my mind of cops with well-trained dogs hunting us down in the woods. We'd all been seen by the bellhop, so the police would quickly learn how many of us there were, and what we looked like. Of course, none of it would matter if we froze to death first.

I let out a yip of surprise when someone came jogging up to our side, then sagged in relief when I realized it was Sophie. I would have really liked to run on my own, but the no shoes and freezing cold aspect kept me quiet.

"James and Diana?" Alaric asked as they ran side by side, only sounding slightly out of breath.

"I don't know," Sophie replied, "but I'm glad to be rid of them."

I sucked in a breath despite the bumping pressure of Alaric's shoulder against my abdomen. "Don't we . . . need . . . Diana's help?"

Alaric and Sophie were both quiet for a moment, then began speaking to each other in a different language, the same one I'd heard them use before we left Spokane. Great, just great. Not only was I going to either freeze to death or go to jail, I was also going to be left out of any planning involved in attempting to prevent either of those outcomes.

Alaric and Sophie continued talking like I wasn't even there. I clung to Alaric, resigned to listen for signs of pursuit. I could no longer hear the sirens, but I almost thought I could hear the souls screaming back in the hotel for me to release them. The sound would probably haunt me until I died, which given my luck, would likely be within the next few hours.

Eventually Alaric and Sophie slowed and I was let down to my feet. I hissed at the cold, tip-toeing to a snow-free spot near the trunk of a massive tree. My entire body ached from cold, and from being held over Alaric's shoulder. Along the way, I had continuously replayed the entire hotel scene over and over in my mind, and still couldn't push the disturbing imagery from my head.

By now, the dead Vaettir would have been put into body bags and carted away by the police. They would likely reanimate, and Norway would be awash with sensationalized stories about a zombie rampage.

Alaric and Sophie both paced, crunching icy pine needles under their feet. Sophie was the only one of us lucky enough to be wearing shoes, and she was fully clothed in her normal black attire. Alaric wore only his black jeans, leaving his dark hair to trail over his pale, bare chest.

I crouched down to cover my legs with my coat, then glared up at both of them.

Sophie glared right back. "*What*?"

I sighed."If you both are done ignoring me, I have some questions."

Alaric stopped pacing and came to crouch beside me. "I'm sorry," he said, wrapping an arm around me. "We didn't mean to ignore you."

Accepting his body heat, but not his apology, I leaned against him. "What's going to happen when the dead bodies we left in the hotel room reanimate?"

Sophie moved to stand beside us, her dark eyes scanning the distance. "I'm sure their clan will take care of it."

"Their clan?" I questioned.

"It's the whole reason we formed clans to begin with," Alaric explained, "and why we are supposed to stay within the Salr. It is the Doyen's responsibility to make sure things like this don't happen."

I closed my eyes against a budding headache. "But whose clan were they part of?"

"That's the part I do not like," Sophie commented. "They were not from Estus' clan, and James claimed they did not belong to Aislin, either."

My shivering increased, and it wasn't just from the cold. I didn't understand the world of the Vaettir like Alaric and Sophie did, and I was getting tired of being left in the dark.

"So what do we do now? If Diana thinks the charm is somewhere near here, should we try to find it without her?"

Alaric and Sophie both looked at each other instead of

me, like they were passing thoughts back and forth in front of my face.

Finally Alaric turned to me. "We never planned on finding the charm *with* her. We just needed her help to locate the exact area."

My mouth formed a little "oh" of surprise that soon turned into a tight-lipped grimace. "You could have let me in on that plan at some point," I chided. "Here I've been worrying over exactly when she and James would betray us all."

"We didn't want to give Diana any reason to doubt your intentions," Sophie explained, "but her obsession with you and Alaric has given us pause."

I exhaled an annoyed huff of breath, fogging the air in front of me. "Stop talking like you're the *hive mind*. What do you mean her *obsession* with us?"

Alaric gave me a tight squeeze as Sophie explained, "Her obsession that the two of you be together. She would not do it for selfless reasons, and I highly doubt she's a die-hard romantic. She somehow wants to use that bond, and I do not like it. She's more invested in this than she's letting on. When we were attacked in our rooms, she left James to go after you. She chose you over her own grandson."

"But there are other executioners out there," I countered, "Surely I'm not *that* important."

Sophie shrugged. "I have no explanation for it, but I vote we leave this place and forget all about the charm."

Alaric scoffed. "And hide forever? I've no doubt Diana will do her best to hunt us down, as will Estus. Aislin is Diana's sister, which means we'll have the two largest clans among the Vaettir scouring the earth for us."

Sophie glared at her brother. "We've hidden before . . . " she trailed off.

I shook my head. "I agree with Alaric."

Sophie aimed a venomous glare at me. "Of *course* you do. So what do you suggest, Madeline, since you seem to know everything?"

I would have been offended by her sarcasm if I couldn't feel the fear wafting off her like heat waves. "The only conclusion I can come to in regards to Diana, is that she wants us to find the charm so she can either use it herself, or claim credit for its delivery to Aislin. I vote we find the charm and give it to Aislin ourselves in return for protection. Short of killing Estus, there is no other way to stop him from hunting us."

Sophie blinked at me, then shook her head. "You don't even know Aislin. What makes you think she'll keep her word?"

"Do you have any better ideas?"

We sat in silence for several minutes before Sophie said, "Fine, but we better get moving if we're going to keep ahead of James and Diana."

I nodded and stood, though pulling away from Alaric's warmth and re-baring my legs to the cold took way more willpower than I'd like to admit.

After a few minutes of me hobbling on the cold ground like a newborn horse, Sophie even gave me her boots and kept just her socks on, proving she was a much tougher woman that me, which I was more than okay with.

I had no idea how we would find the charm before anyone else found us. My hope was that Alaric or Sophie would be able to sniff it out, but there was one fall-back option. The charm was sealed in a place guarded by the dead. If the spirits still remained within the burial mounds, I would be able to sense them . . . hopefully.

It was a long shot, but at least we would probably freeze to death before Estus or anyone else could kill us.

# 3

After several hours stumbling through the wintery woods, there was still no sign of James or Diana. There was also no sign of the place we were looking for. My borrowed boots crunched over dead twigs and patches of snow haphazardly as I forced myself onward, feeling numb from cold and exhaustion.

I glared at Alaric and Sophie's backs, moving with graceful ease through the snow. Neither had expressed worry about the implications of being lost in the freezing cold woods without food or shelter, and I had to trust that they would keep us alive. We had other more imminent worries anyhow.

Unable to contend with my burning lungs, I staggered toward a tree and leaned against it. I knew we needed to keep moving, but the cold air and altitude were making me lightheaded. It wouldn't do anyone any good if I passed out.

Likely noticing the lack of labored breathing behind

him, Alaric stopped, turned, and walked back to me. Sophie watched us with hands on hips, clearly annoyed.

Alaric moved to lift me into his arms, and I was ready to let him, but something caught my eye in the air beside his head. A slight shimmer disturbed the still scenery. I was about to write it off as a hallucination, then a faint whisper shivered across my brain. Soon, more whispers joined it.

I held out a hand to halt Alaric's progress. I couldn't tell where the whispers were coming from, but it was obvious he and Sophie didn't hear them. They both watched my changed expression warily.

"You guys don't hear that, do you?" I asked, wanting confirmation.

Alaric shook his head, still watching me cautiously.

"I hear only the birds and the wind," Sophie added, "and my hearing is likely *much* better than yours."

Alaric closed the distance between us and placed a hand on my arm. "What do you hear, Maddy?"

The volume of the whispers increased.

I crouched to the ground, pulling Alaric with me. As I suspected, the whispers grew louder still.

"I hear voices," I explained distantly, utterly absorbed.

Alaric cleared his throat. "You know, that's what crazy people say . . . "

I bit my lip, trying to think of a witty reply. I opened my mouth to speak, then the air began shimmering around us, distracting me. I inhaled sharply as I finally realized what I was feeling. *Spirits*. Or at least their energy. The air felt alive with it. It was clear Alaric and Sophie still felt nothing, even as my own sense of things increased.

I scraped my bare hands across the icy ground, clearing

soil and dead pine needles near the base of the tree. I still couldn't get a direct sense of where the voices were coming from, but I knew they were somewhere below us. I could feel their heavy presence reaching out to me.

Alaric watched me for a moment, then began clearing more of the hard soil away. Sophie stood back and waited.

The whispers became almost unbearable, seeming to egg me on. With a sigh to let us know how irritated she was, Sophie joined us in our digging. The pulsing energy was thrumming so desperately that it shook my bones as my hand ran across a small, metal ring amidst a yellow clump of grass. I dug my fingers into the grass and pulled the loop free. It hinged upward, connecting to something in the ground. I attempted to tug on it as Alaric and Sophie came to crouch on either side of me, but it wouldn't budge.

With a look of wonder on his face, Alaric took the ring from me, then gave it a pull, using his knees to lift with more force than I had to offer at the moment. When it still wouldn't budge, I wrapped my hands around his wrists while Sophie grabbed his waist, and the three of us pulled together.

A large trap door pulled free from the earth. I fell onto my butt and Sophie toppled on top of me. Quickly righting ourselves, we moved around the now open door to crouch in front of the opening. I leaned over the edge and looked down, but it was dark. Damp and rot filled my nostrils as the voices filtered back in through my mind, louder now.

"How on earth did you find that?" Alaric asked breathlessly, peering down beside me.

"I could hear them," I replied cryptically.

I reached my hand into the cavern, searching for some

way to climb down inside. The trap door was wide enough for two of us to fit down at once, but the straight drop down made it a less than practical mode of entry.

I continued patting around the inner lip of the entrance until my fingers scraped across a bar of rough wood, hopefully the top rung of a ladder. I turned around and stuck a foot into the darkness, ready to climb down, trying not to think about the dangers that might lurk within. Alaric wrapped a hand around my upper arm to stop me, worry creasing his brow.

He opened his mouth to speak, probably to suggest he go first, when a dark shape barreled into his back. Alaric and I fell with our attacker into the darkness.

I landed, *hard* on loamy earth, with a squirming weight on top of me. I'd distantly registered the echo of the trap door slamming shut, sealing us in darkness. I strained to get up, thinking I had injured my back, but then whoever was on top of me rolled off and I was able to sit up with a groan. I didn't think it had been Alaric, they weren't big enough.

Banging and shouting above us let me know Sophie was still outside. The sound of her shouting suddenly moved away from the door, but I could still hear her, like she was shouting at something, or someone, else. I wanted to call out to her, but I hadn't entirely regained my senses.

"Maddy?" Alaric whispered.

"I'm here," I groaned, wanting to stand and move toward the sound of his voice, but the darkness was so complete, it held me immobile. Plus, whoever had landed on me might still be nearby, and I didn't want to accidentally run into them instead.

I jumped as a hand landed in mine.

"It's me," he whispered.

I nodded, then realized he couldn't see it as he pulled me to my feet. Standing gave me an overwhelming sense of vertigo, and the smell of mildew and damp earth made me feel like I might throw up.

"Someone is in here with us," Alaric whispered, pulling me against his side.

"I know. Whoever it was landed right on top of me."

I became further disoriented as we began to move. Even with my free hand held out in front of me, I felt like I was going to run my face into something at any moment.

"What about Sophie?" I whispered. I could no longer hear any commotion from above ground, and I was worried something had happened to her.

"Sophie can take care of herself," he replied. "Plus, I think she's probably safer than us at the moment. Now we should probably stop talking. Try to step lightly."

I ran my hand along the damp, rough wall, feeling the varying pits and grooves of natural stone.

I knew I should be silent, but questions burned within me until I quietly blurted, "Do you think this is the right place?"

Alaric tightened his arm around my waist. "Don't you?" he whispered. "Or did you have some other reason for pawing around in the soil, then trying to climb down here without even thinking about what might lie below?"

My hands slipped across rough wood mounted in the stone corridor. A doorway. We stepped through, then turned a corner, following a faint illumination in the distance.

"What is that?" I whispered.

"There's only one way to find out," Alaric whispered in reply, removing his hand from my waist to my arm.

We crept toward the light. While the small amount of light eased some of my tension, the feeling of eyes on my back gave me chills. Why would someone push us into the cavern, only to hide in the dark?

The light intensified as we neared, revealing a hunched form, sitting in a rocking chair with its back to us. Surrounding the chair was a rather cozy room complete with upholstered furniture, and a large woven rug. The cozy scene was thrown off slightly by the surrounding darkness. I couldn't tell where the light was coming from, but it should have touched that darkness. Instead the black was like a solid wall.

At first I thought the figure in the rocking chair was an elderly woman, since all I could see was the hump of her back and the lackluster fabric of her loose clothing, but then she left her chair to turn and rise before us. At her full height, she stood a good foot taller than Alaric, and that wasn't including the antlers protruding from her skull. They were the antlers of a deer, and they somehow complimented her strange, narrow face. I wasn't quite sure how I knew the creature was female. She just had a certain femininity about her.

"She's a Norn," Alaric muttered in disbelief.

I knew that Norns were creatures of Norse myth, and that they controlled the fates, but that was about it. Suddenly I wished that I had finished the book I'd started on Norse myth in college. I might have remembered whether or not Norns ate human flesh.

The Norn blinked large, up-tilted eyes at us. It was difficult to tell in the soft light, but I was pretty sure her glistening skin was a pale shade of green.

She spoke to us in a harsh guttural language that I didn't understand. I was about to ask the creature if she spoke English, when Alaric replied in the same language. I realized with a start that it was the same language I'd heard him and Sophie speaking.

"She asked us why we're here, and in such a poor state of dress," Alaric explained. "I told her what we seek, and that we were attacked."

"Was it wise to just blurt it out like that?" I asked as the creature stared at us intently.

"Lying to a Norn would do no good," Alaric replied with a small smile.

The Norn said something else that made Alaric look over his shoulder.

"What is it?" I asked, whipping my gaze to the near-darkness behind us.

"She said that someone else is approaching. Probably whoever pushed us down here."

The Norn said something else, something that made Alaric's face go rigid.

"What did she say?" I asked when he didn't explain. When he still didn't answer me, I shook his arm, not liking the look in his eyes.

"She asked who will claim the charm after we've sacrificed ourselves," he explained evenly.

My eyes widened. "*What*?"

Someone stepped up on my other side. I stumbled away

from Diana, looking a little disheveled in her black cloak. She said something in the Norn's language.

Alaric let out what sounded like a curse word in that strange language, then grabbed my arm, pulling me away from Diana and the Norn.

"What's happening?" I gasped, stumbling backward.

"It's a trap, Maddy," he growled. "A sacrifice is needed to release the charm, and we're it. This is what Diana was planning."

The whispers started up again, almost drowning out Alaric's words. With all the excitement, I hadn't even realized they'd been quiet until then. I pulled away from Alaric and clamped my hands over my ears, but it did nothing to stop the sound, because the voices weren't coming from around me, they were inside my head.

Alaric lifted me and carried me toward the entrance. The Norn and Diana did nothing to stop us. I found out why a moment later as the darkness in front of us solidified. I could see no wall or barrier, but whatever we stood in front of was solid, as if the darkness had been given form.

"Let me down," I hissed. We weren't getting out of here, and I wanted to face Diana on my own two feet.

We both turned back to her, our backs against the solid wall of darkness.

"The least you can do is explain why it had to be us," Alaric said coldly.

I glanced at his icy expression and wanted to yell at him for just giving up, but the voices in my head were making me dizzy, especially since I couldn't understand what any of them were saying.

Diana chuckled. She looked like a dwarf next to the

Norn, but stood so confidently that she still looked imposing. A small smile crossed her aged lips. "The charm is sealed by ritual. Six of the Vaettir died to seal it. Each pair loved each other dearly, a trait rare amongst our people. The woman of each couple killed her mate, and then herself, first sacrificing her heart, and then her life. That kind of magic is not easy to undo."

The voices surged in my mind. I fell to my knees. I was doing my best to understand what Diana was saying, but I could barely hear her voice over the voices in my head. Alaric crouched beside me, but kept his eyes on Diana.

"I needed an executioner to release their spirits, so that they would no longer bind the charm," she continued.

"We had assumed that already," Alaric snapped, "but that does not explain the need for sacrifice."

Diana chuckled again, and I would have walked forward and hit her had I been able to stand. "Magic is a funny thing," she explained. "To fully undo a ritual, it must be repeated in some way. It seemed much more simple to just use the two of you, rather than finding another couple."

The voices stopped abruptly. I could sense the dead, paying close attention to us. Their apprehension was palpable. Though I saw no burial mounds, I knew the place from my vision was near. I could feel each of the corpses pulsing like I had seven heartbeats.

Alaric rose and stepped in front of me. "She does not love me. Cutting out my heart might hurt her, but it would not be akin to sacrificing her own heart. Putting us together in a hotel room for a night was a feeble plan, at best. The ritual will not work."

I was finally able to peel my eyes away from Diana at that. Alaric glanced back at me.

"Maddy?" he said weakly. "I'm right, aren't I?"

"She already loved you, you fool," Diana chided, "but another night to increase the bond couldn't hurt, now could it?"

Ignoring Diana, Alaric continued to stare at me. "Tell me she's wrong, Madeline."

Was she wrong? I honestly hadn't considered the possibility of loving Alaric. I knew that I could grow to love him, given the time, but did I love him already?

My eyes widened in horror as I realized the answer. I did love him, at least in some odd, twisted way, and now we were probably going to die for it.

The look on my face was enough of an answer for Alaric. "Find a way out. I'll hold them off."

I rose shakily to my feet and moved to his side. "I won't leave you. There's two of them and two of us. This isn't over yet."

The Norn said something else in her language, then Diana said, "Neither of you will be leaving. The room is sealed. The ritual will be completed whether you volunteer, or not."

At her words the voices in my head started anew. I crumpled back to the ground, hands covering my ears though I knew it would do no good. I watched helplessly as Alaric charged Diana and the Norn, and then my vision went black. My last thought was, *I hope I don't wake up.*

# 4

I woke lying on my back. I scraped my hands across the ground, touching damp soil. I rolled my head to the side and saw Alaric chained up to a tree, and it all came rushing back to me. The Norn. Diana. *The sacrifice.* We were still underground, so the tree supporting Alaric shouldn't have been there, yet its limbs stretched up into the darkness, covered in healthy green leaves. Candles surrounded the tree's base, holding back the darkness.

I rolled onto my stomach and pushed myself up to my knees. More candles lined the cavern walls. I staggered to my feet. I needed to get to Alaric.

I stumbled as I realized I was right next to one of the burial mounds from my vision. The mounds were unmarked, and covered in dark soil. The same soil now covered much of my skin. The only reason I even knew that the mounds were graves at all was because I could feel the dead below. They were all silent. *Waiting.*

I looked back to Alaric, who appeared unconscious,

hanging limply from his bindings, then hurried toward him, praying to whatever forces might be listening that he was just unconscious and not dead.

I reached him and placed a hand on his pale neck, searching for a pulse. It was there, but faint. I pulled my hand away, leaving a mark of black soil on his skin, then turned to search the rest of the room for a way to free him. The chain that held him was composed of dark steel with no lock that I could see.

At the edge of the cavern, the Norn stepped out of the darkness with Diana a few steps behind. I could have sworn there had been a solid wall where they stood just moments before.

"I won't do it," I stated, sounding much stronger than I felt.

Instead of replying, the Norn raised her hand and the voices started up again. She blinked her strange, large eyes at me, completely devoid of compassion as the spirits called out. I couldn't understand their language, but being this close to them broke down other barriers.

Images flashed through my mind of their sacrifice. There had been so much blood when the men's throats were slit that it seeped into the soil, enriching it, though nothing would ever grow in such a place. Nothing but the tree in the center, because it was composed of the magic of sacrifice. I saw each of the women falling to the ground, having slit their own throats, and then my view was from the ground as well, looking out from the eyes of the final woman as she died. The images faded and I was left with nothing but a sense of time. The spirits had been trapped there for centuries, alone and in the dark.

I opened my eyes without even realizing I had closed them to find myself kneeling on top of one of the mounds, my hands pressed against the dirt. The woman inside had been the one to show me the images. I recoiled instantly with the realization that I had been only moments away from releasing her spirit.

At my hesitation, the images started again, taking away my other senses. I saw war. I tried to push away images of rotten corpses strewn across vast battlefields, and women and children burned alive for living along the wrong trade-route, but it was like watching a movie inside my head. I couldn't just close my eyes to shut it out.

My mind reeled away from the memories, but they stuck with me as if they were my own. I was back on the mound, with my hands buried in the black dirt. I could feel the soul within begging for release. She had died for a cause. The charm was evil, and had to be locked away, lest her children and her children's children suffer the same fate as their elders. Yet she was tired, and her children were likely dead. Why should she have to protect the charm any longer? Hadn't she sacrificed enough?

I shook my head as I reached out toward her spirit. My mind was warning me to stop, that if I set her free I would have to help the others, and then Diana would try to make me kill Alaric.

The other corpses pulled at me as I hesitated. It wasn't fair for them to stay trapped while I lived. I shook my head, knowing that last thought was not my own.

"Get on with it," Diana demanded impatiently, snapping me back into reality.

My hands felt glued to the earth, like the woman's soul

would not let me go. She would hold me there forever if I made her. The connection deepened the longer I knelt there. Suddenly I could feel not only her memories, but her body, withered and decayed, and I could feel the pain of her brutal death. The pain seared through my body, but it was nothing compared to the pain of killing the one I loved. I shook my head. The one *she* loved. My thoughts were blurring together with hers. Unable to bear the pain any longer, I released her, then fell sobbing to the ground as I felt the other dead shift in anticipation.

All I could think as the woman's energy rushed through me was, *fuck this*. I would not die like this woman had, and I would not let her sacrifice be in vain. If I let Diana have the charm, those in the earth below me would have died for nothing.

Not really knowing what I was doing, I took a deep, shaky breath, then shoved the woman's energy back into the ground through my hands. The power ignored the woman's now-empty corpse and forced its way through the ground until it found the others.

I stumbled to my feet as the ground began to shake. Diana no longer looked cocky, she looked terrified. "What are you doing!" she cried. "Release them!"

I could no longer hear the voices of the dead, but I could *feel* them. They were rising to the surface, animated by the energy I'd given them.

I ran back to Alaric, unsure of what I had just released, and clung to his limp hand. The soil of the nearby mounds began to shift. First came their skeletal hands, clawing at the air. Decayed corpses pushed their way up through the soil, pulling free to rise slowly to their feet. Most were just skeletons with tatters of cloth and a few dried ligaments, but some had retained a measure of dried skin.

Something squeezed my hand and I flinched, then I realized that Alaric had regained consciousness. I glanced at him, but he had eyes only for the dead.

I turned back to the corpses, all facing me. Having their eyeless skulls staring at me should have been the most horrifying sight I'd ever seen, but I wasn't scared. Though they did not speak, I could sense their emotions. They were still not free, and they would do anything if only I would just release them.

I smiled as inspiration hit me. I would let them go, but they would have to do me a favor first. I squeezed Alaric's hand. "Tell them to kill Diana and I'll release them," I ordered.

"What?" Alaric asked, confused.

"I don't speak their language, tell them."

With a shriek of frustration Diana began marching toward us, leaving the Norn to wait by herself.

"Tell them!" I pleaded.

Alaric spoke quickly in the strange language.

The corpses turned toward Diana in unison, freezing her in her tracks.

"No," she breathed, realizing her predicament.

She backed away, pleading with the corpses in their language. They shambled toward her, backing her into a corner until she reached the Norn. Diana reached out her hands, and I knew she was trying to harm the corpses like she had harmed the man back in the hotel room, but nothing happened. These Vaettir had already felt all the pain they would ever feel.

Diana turned wide eyes up to the Norn. "Stop them!" she pleaded, but the Norn only glanced down at her, then turned her gaze back to me.

I couldn't be sure from the distance, but I thought I saw a satisfied smile creep across the Norn's face.

Diana screamed as the dead reached her. Her fear was more palpable than any other emotion in the room. It stabbed me in the gut like a knife.

"You'll feel me die, Madeline!" she threatened as skeletal hands clamped down on her aged skin.

She was right. I could feel people's wounds like they were my own, and even muted, Diana's death was going to be a horrible one. Alaric squeezed my hand hard enough to make my knuckles pop and I was able to look away from the scene.

"Focus on me," he whispered.

There were tears in my eyes as I nodded, and then the dead began their work, tearing Diana limb from limb. I fell to the ground with the pain of it as she continued screaming in vain, but Alaric kept my hand gripped tightly in his.

I focused on him, and felt a measure of calm, but Diana's emotions of pain and fear were much stronger than calm, and they leaked through until I was screaming with her. I curled up into a little ball, with one arm raised above to retain my hold on Alaric.

Suddenly her screaming stopped, and mine cut off just as abruptly. The only sounds that could be heard were the thuds of Diana's body parts dropping to the ground.

My entire body trembled as I staggered to my feet, still holding onto Alaric.

The corpses turned empty eye-sockets to me. The Norn, still smiling, was motionless behind them. I noticed blood on skeletal hands and tatters of clothing as the corpses began to shamble in my direction. They had done their part, now it was time to do mine.

I swallowed the lump in my throat and kept my eyes averted from Diana's remains, which wasn't really difficult with what equated to mostly decomposed zombies filling my vision. I pulled away from Alaric as the first one reached me. It was a man's corpse, and I wasn't just judging by the size of the skeleton. I could still feel the energy of who he once was, trapped inside his bones.

Sick curiosity got the best of me, and I leaned down and forward to look through his ribcage. Sure enough, a perfectly preserved heart gently pulsed inside, long since abandoned by the other organs. Estus had once told me that the heart was the key to it all. Release the heart, and the spirit could fully move on.

I reached out and placed my palm against the man's ribcage. As I did so, the heart within reacted. Instead of the fear and rage I was used to from Estus' victims, I felt an overwhelming exhaustion, tinged with sadness. My knees almost buckled at the sensation. Without thinking about it, I released the heart, willing away its melancholic hurt. The bones crumbled to the ground, no longer possessing whatever magic had held them together.

The expected rush of energy wiped away my fatigue, then the next corpse stepped forward. I released each of them, the energy building inside me as each set of bones fell to the dark earth. The Norn watched it all impassively, making no move to interrupt.

When I was done, I turned back toward Alaric, feeling almost drunk on extra energy. It was even more of a high than what I'd felt after releasing all of Estus' long tortured hearts, letting me know the people who'd died to keep the charm in place had been very powerful indeed.

He looked down at me with a mixture of awe, and maybe a little bit of fear as I touched my fingers to the chains binding him. They fell away at my touch, and I had to help steady him as his feet hit the ground.

He wrapped his arms around me and held me for several seconds, tight enough that it was hard to breathe, not that I really minded.

"You are a little bit amazing," he whispered against my hair.

"Just a little bit?" I whispered back, still feeling giddy.

We turned, hand in hand, to face the Norn. The tall creature inclined her head in our direction, then said something in her strange language.

I looked to Alaric for a translation.

His expression was thoughtful as he said, "She asks that you approach her, *alone*."

I oddly wasn't afraid. I was still riding on waves of stolen energy. It was dizzying, yet made me feel safe, and maybe a little bit powerful. I let go of Alaric's hand and approached the Norn, maintaining eye contact with her as I went. Once I reached her, I had to crane my neck upward to still be looking at her face.

She smiled and reached her long fingers toward me. It was only then I realized she only had four of them, and her hand was actually shaped more like the talons of a hawk with three fingers in front and one in the back, each ending in a gleaming black point.

Three talons came to rest on the side of my face, finally causing my pulse to quicken. I only had a moment of fear, though, as images began to flash through my mind. She might not speak my language, but she could communicate in pictures, just like the corpses.

The images flashed so quickly, I couldn't make out half of them. I saw many faces I didn't recognize, violence, and scenes of ritual. At the center of the chaos was a tiny key. *The charm.* Releasing it would bring its chaos upon the world, but it could no longer remain sealed away. It had to be destroyed, and it would take magic like mine to do it. Finally the images stopped to rest on a gathering of other Norns like the one standing in front of me. They were the guardians of the key.

As the final image faded from my mind, the Norn pulled her talons away and moved past me toward the tree. I turned to watch as she stopped in front of it, looking much like a tree herself with her tall, narrow form, and loose, shape-stealing robes.

I made my way to where Alaric had gone to stand, close to the wall and off to the side so we could see the Norn's face as she reached her talons out to the tree, caressing the bark. My breath hissed through my teeth as her other clawed hand dove suddenly into her lower chest, the talons cutting easily through her skin and clothing. She staggered against the tree, her spindly arm contorting to reach underneath her rib cage.

Alaric and I watched in horrified silence as she withdrew her hand to reveal her still-beating heart, perfectly removed to remain whole. Blood seeped into her robe as she fell to her knees, then extended the heart in our direction.

I rushed to her side with Alaric following on my heels. I had no idea how she was still alive, but the Norn blinked up at me, pain furrowing her brow.

Her pain shot through my chest, stealing my breath. I would have fallen, but Alaric caught me.

She held the heart up, then bowed her head. Understanding what she wanted me to do, I clung to Alaric with one hand while I stroked trembling fingertips across the heart, releasing it.

The antlers on her head touched the soil as she slumped to the side, dead, then I was hit with energy like I'd never felt. Alaric released me with a hiss of breath and I fell to my knees by the prostrate form of the Norn. Her pooling blood dampened my bare knees, but I barely noticed as I looked around frantically for some way to release the energy.

It felt like it was scorching my brain, and filling my lungs with hot steam, far too much for me to hold. Seeing no other option, I placed my hands against the nearby tree and willed the energy away. I didn't picture something happening like I normally would, I just *pushed*, desperate to feel normal again.

The energy left me in a steady current, and we had just a moment of stunned silence before the world started moving again. The tree shot upward with new growth, twisting like a serpent as its bark expanded, too fast for the eye to follow. I collapsed in a panting heap beside the tree, too tired and delirious to move away.

Suddenly Alaric was there, pulling me into his lap and wrapping his arms protectively around me as we both stared up in awe. Where the branches reached the ceiling of the space, they diverged away from each other and began curving back down toward us.

Thoughts of being impaled by the tree hit me just as Alaric rolled me closer to the trunk, sheltering me on my back with his body, but the branches slowed and stilled, all except for one. One tiny, hair-thin branch reached down until it was mere inches in front of my face. At its end was a small, black metal key.

Alaric and I reached out together. His hand closed around mine, as mine closed around the key. It pulled away from the branch easily, and our hands came back down. I observed the key in my palm. It felt so small and mundane in my hand, but I was pretty sure we'd found the charm everyone was searching for, far more dangerous an item than I could have imagined.

Alaric stared down at it. "Now that we have it, what on earth are we going to do with it?"

I glanced over to the Norn who had given her life to release the key. Her sacrifice had shattered the ritual binding it to smithereens.

I gripped the key so tightly the edges cut into my skin, thinking of the images the Norn had shown me. "We destroy it."

"As my lady wishes," he replied, half-joking, though I knew he meant what he said. He pulled me in a little closer, cradling me in the cool soil, surrounded by bones.

I knew in that moment that this whole ordeal had only just begun. It would have been easy to use the key as a bargaining chip for our own lives and freedom, but after what first the corpses, then the Norn had shown me, I couldn't just give the charm away. The tiny key had the power to cause massive wars and chaos. So much death.

Destroying it would not be easy, but I knew it was possible. That was why the Norn wanted me to have it. My particular brand of magic was needed, but I'd need power. I'd need many, *many* deaths. I paled at the thought, but those deaths would be nothing compared to what would happen if the charm fell into the wrong hands. It was a tool of chaos, and needed to be destroyed. The only question was, did I have the heart to do it?

Alaric kissed my cheek, his lips lingering against my skin. "How will we destroy it?"

I pulled my head back so I could look up at him. "We're going to start a war."

He grinned, and it was a little frightening given the context. "Why Maddy," he said mischievously, "that just so happens to be my specialty."

"War and Death," I breathed. "Partnership at its best."

I rubbed my thumb across the key in my palm as I considered the possible consequences of such a plan, and all I could think was that things looked bleak, but . . . didn't they always?

# 5

"I break all of my nails getting down here, and you two are just lying in the dirt!" Sophie stood at the edge of the cavern, hands on hips.

I sat up and pulled away from Alaric, but still didn't feel steady enough to stand. I gripped the charm in my hand, feeling oddly protective over it, and not liking the feeling one bit.

Alaric laughed. "It's about time you came to the rescue. Maddy nearly killed me."

Sophie sighed as she glanced around the room, undisturbed by the piles of bones that had once been Vaettir. Her eyes came to rest on the Norn.

"Is that what I think it is?" she asked.

"It *was*," Alaric corrected.

"*She* was," I corrected on top of his correction.

I felt oddly sorry for the Norn, even though she had nearly let Diana sacrifice us. I was pretty sure the Norn knew all along what would happen. Norns were supposed to be weavers of fate, after all. Maybe she knew I would come, and knew I cared enough about the world to not want such a horrible magic to be released once more. Hopefully that meant I actually stood a chance of destroying it, since the Norn had given her life for that purpose.

"Can we please get out of here?" I asked weakly.

Alaric stood, then helped me to my feet.

"Where's Diana?" Sophie asked, eyeing us both expectantly.

Alaric gestured with the hand that wasn't around my waist to the bloody pile in the corner of the room.

Sophie's lip lifted in distaste.

"Any sign of James?" I asked.

She looked back at us and shrugged. "I left him unconscious up above. When you guys fell in the hole, the door slammed shut and wouldn't budge. I had to dig the damn thing out and rip it off its hinges."

Well that explained the broken nails. "Can we *please* get out of here?" I asked again.

"Did he attack you?" Alaric questioned, ignoring my question as well as Sophie's griping about the door.

Sophie snorted. "No. He actually acted like he wanted to help me, but I wasn't about to leave him at my back."

Alaric smiled knowingly at his sister. I wasn't sure what the smile was about, and at that moment, I didn't really care. I looked at them both expectantly, hoping we could finally leave.

Sophie kicked a nearby bone. "We should search this place for supplies first," she glanced at me, "unless you care to give me back my shoes?"

I cringed. Supplies would be nice, but I wasn't sure it was worth it if it meant I had to stay there a moment longer. I was rather disturbed by the whole ordeal, especially with the part I'd played, and what it meant for me in the near future.

I finally really *looked* at Sophie and realized with a start that there was now a way out of the room, since she had walked in so easily. I looked behind her to see a shadowy doorway, previously solid wall. The Norn's death must have unbarred the room.

"Let's go," I instructed.

Sophie turned and led the way out of the room, but I gestured for Alaric to help me over to the bloody pile that was once Diana instead of following Sophie out.

His eyes widened when he realized my intent. "Are you sure she deserves to be released?"

I shook my head, thinking of the souls that had guarded the charm for far too long. "No one deserves that fate."

With a nod, Alaric helped me to kneel beside Diana's remains. Her limbs and head had all been ripped free of her body, but her torso was still mostly intact, wrapped in the bloody fabric of her clothing and cloak. My limbs ached with the pain of her death, but it was a subtle pain, as most of her life was gone. Only the energy within her heart remained. I reached my hand out toward where her heart should be, but stopped as I felt something tickling at my bare leg.

I looked down in horror, hoping to whatever I should hope to that a mouse or some other creature had made its way into the underground lair.

My hope was dashed as Diana's hand, still attached to

most of her petite arm, wrapped its fingers around my leg right above my boot and dug in. In an instant, Alaric was on my other side, prying the fingers off my leg one by one, face calm. Resisting the urge to vomit, I ignored what was happening to my leg and turned back to Diana's torso.

Her emotions coursed through me as I reached my hand out toward her chest again. I had expected anger and hatred, but all I felt was fear and confusion. She had been alive a very, very long time, and had not expected to die, especially in such a simplistic way. She didn't want me to release her soul, because she was still clinging to whatever life she might have. Alaric pried the last of her fingers away, freeing my leg from her grasp, but I barely noticed.

I shook my head, wondering how I could read a dead woman's emotions so clearly, while at the same time hoping that this increased feeling of empathy wasn't permanent. It was bad enough feeling someone's wounds as they happened, did I really have to share in their darkest fears?

Gritting my teeth, I released her spirit, and was relieved of her emotions simultaneously. Part of me felt a little smug that even in doing what was right for her, I was able to go against Diana's wishes, but most of me just felt confused and afraid. Maybe I had only felt Diana's emotions so strongly because they so closely mirrored my own.

I stared down at the now lifeless corpse pieces, feeling melancholic about the whole ordeal.

Alaric touched my arm to get my attention, and I turned to him, feeling as if I'd just woken from a dream. "We should prepare to leave," he said softly. "Estus' people are still out there looking for us, and the human police may be as well."

I nodded and stood as all of our future concerns came rushing back.

We left the dark room, and I ended up waiting in the Norn's comfortable sitting room while Alaric and Sophie searched for clothing and supplies. The entire scene from the attack in the hotel room all the way up to the Norn's death played over and over in my head. For some reason, the scene that stuck out most to me was Alaric finding out that I maybe loved him, and him begging me to not let it be true.

The rational side of me assured that his fear and astonishment came from the fact that the revelation meant Diana would force me to kill him, but some small, scared part of me said he was afraid for other reasons. Reasons like me being a cursed death machine. I couldn't even begin to think about the idea that I might be in love with him. I didn't have time for love, especially when it could easily be ripped away at the flick of Estus' hand.

The supply search didn't take long, fortunately, as the underground complex was small. Alaric and Sophie returned to save me from my thoughts, and they saved me from the cold as well with a pair of roughly made pants and too-large winter boots. The clothes seemed like they came from a different century, and smelled like they had been stored for just that long. It was a marvel that they even held together, but I wasn't going to turn my nose up at anything that would protect me from the harsh weather above.

There was no food to be found, even though the Norn had likely stayed in that little sitting room alone for ages.

Perhaps Norns didn't have to eat, but I did. My stomach growled painfully as I put on the offered clothing and followed Sophie and Alaric back to the trap door, then climbed the ladder out into the daylight.

James was still lying unconscious in a patch of snow above. The three of us stared down at him.

"Leave him," Alaric suggested. "I'm sure he'll find his way back to civilization."

"That's what I'm afraid of," Sophie countered. "He'll likely realize we have the charm, and he'll run to tell Aislin, or perhaps even Estus. The search for us will quadruple in strength."

"Do you suggest we kill him?" Alaric asked with a smirk.

Sophie looked down at James with an odd mixture of emotions on her face.

"Or was there a reason you left him alive up here to begin with?" Alaric added like he already knew the answer.

I hoped Alaric had some idea of what was going though Sophie's mind, because I sure didn't.

"Not that you guys ever listen to my opinion anyway," I said sarcastically, "but I really don't want to be around when he wakes up and discovers I killed his grandmother."

Sophie blinked rapidly and shook her head as if coming out of a dream. "He's our only *in* with Aislin. Perhaps we might need him."

I twisted my lips at her logic. "Diana was also Aislin's sister. I think that option is lost to us. Besides, weren't you the one who suggested we remain clan-less?"

Sophie glared at me. "And what of the charm? I imagine you have it?"

"We're going to destroy it," I replied, not taking a second to think about it.

Sophie crossed her arms. "What if we could use it to protect ourselves? If it could grant one of the Vaettir the power to rule, could it not grant us a little diplomatic immunity?"

"We destroy it," I said again, unable to put into words what the Norn had shown me. "Now back to James."

I could tell she didn't fully accept my answer, but she did turn back to the man in question. "We take him with us," she stated.

Alaric and I both looked at each other in surprise as Sophie continued to stare down at James.

"Do you really think that's wise?" Alaric asked, turning back to his sister.

Sophie didn't look up. "We can't have him telling anyone we have the charm, or leading them back to this place," she explained.

"And you can't kill him," I said with a soft smile.

She snapped her eyes up to me and practically snarled. "I *could*," she argued.

"But you *won't*," I finished. "And here you all were thinking *I* was the cream puff of the group."

Alaric held a hand up to his mouth to hide his grin.

A low growl trickled out of Sophie's throat.

I grinned wider. "I'm sorry, you're not a cream puff. You're a sweet, cuddly little kitten."

Alaric snickered.

"If you're done being comedic," Sophie growled, "you could make yourselves useful and help me carry him."

Alaric did as his sister bade him, still laughing as he went. I watched as they lifted James to standing.

The three of them looked an odd picture. Alaric had found a shirt that was the same old-fashioned style as my pants and similar boots to mine. They clashed with his modern jeans and the modern clothing Sophie and James wore. The scene was made even more odd and slightly humorous by James' head lolling around as they moved him.

I was dreading the moment when I'd have to explain to them everything the Norn had shown me, though they would likely be more practical about it than I wanted to be. Alaric and Sophie were descended from a goddess of war, after all. What were a few more corpses for the greater good?

# 6

TWO DAYS LATER.

I shifted from foot to foot in my brand new, low-heeled boots. My leather pants creaked softly, making my pulse quicken since I was supposed to be quiet. I was *never* letting Alaric choose my clothing again. The simple, long-sleeved black top was a little more practical, but it didn't matter since it was covered by my stolen, knee-length black coat.

My long hair threatened to come loose from the braid I'd put it in as the chilly, Norway wind buffeted against me. I glanced over my shoulder, anxious for Alaric and Sophie to finish *procuring* whatever final supplies we might need so we could head back to the woods where we'd left James.

My anxiety doubled as I thought about James. Sophie had knocked his head too hard, because he didn't remember a thing. While his amnesia complicated things, I guiltily hoped his memory would remain lost, then I wouldn't have to tell him that I'd killed his grandmother.

On the other hand, I didn't enjoy acting as though I actually liked him.

He'd been so confused when he woke, knowing who and what he was, but little else, that we'd all agreed a little bit of pretend was in order. His most recent memories occurred over thirty years ago, so he wouldn't understand if we all just let our hatred shine through.

I braced myself against a particularly forceful gust of wind, thinking that maybe it would be nice to lose that much memory. James didn't remember killing Sophie's lover, and he didn't remember all of the people he had tortured. Heck, he didn't even remember torturing me.

I jumped as two dark shapes appeared on either side of me, then tried to quiet my breathing as Sophie and Alaric hurried me away from the store they'd just robbed. They each had brand new black backpacks slung over their shoulders.

"You know," Sophie whispered, "the *look-out is* supposed to *actually* pay attention."

"I was," I whispered back. "It's not my fault you two move as quietly as cats."

I glanced at Alaric to see his pale face grinning in the moonlight. He was like a kid in a candy shop any time he stole. I guess after living five-hundred years, you had to take your thrills where you could find them.

I looked down to hide my frown as we made our way through the quiet streets. We still hadn't talked about the possibility that I might love him, and I wasn't sure if I wanted to. I hadn't yet concluded the notion. I reflexively reached up to fondle the key at my throat, secured by a length of leather cord.

I felt oddly attached to the little black key, my own little tool of chaos. It wanted war and conquest. I was going to give the charm what it wanted, if only to ultimately destroy it.

The charm seemed to pulse with energy, as if it had read my thoughts, then we reached the edge of civilization, and it was all I could do to keep up as Sophie and Alaric began to run.

They darted over the snow and around trees. To anyone listening, they would only hear my clumsy footfalls, as my companions were as quiet as they were quick.

After a time I slowed, then stopped and hunched over, trying to catch my breath. Alaric circled back around to me as Sophie continued on. Within seconds, she was out of sight.

Alaric grinned down at me, flashing his dainty, feline fangs, then scooped me up in his arms. He began to run effortlessly with me in his grasp.

Heat radiated from my body despite the cold, making my usually useful heavy coat a bit of a hindrance. I looked up at Alaric's face, which didn't appear strained or flushed at all, and suddenly felt greatly inadequate. Sophie, Alaric, and James were all unnaturally strong, with way more endurance than I'd ever have.

"How do you do that?" I asked.

"What?" he replied, his voice not hitching in the slightest.

"Run without tiring, even while carrying me. James can do it too, but I'm stuck with sucky human speed."

He grinned, his eyes remaining on the path ahead. "My gifts are mostly physical. I have little innate magic, except for my ability to shift my hands, teeth, and eyes. Those with more obvious magic usually tend to be physically weaker. Estus is like you."

"So some get to be scary in the magic department, but in a fist fight, shit out of luck?"

He snorted. "Something like that."

He slowed as we reached our campsite where Sophie was already waiting with James, then let me down to my feet. What I could see of James' face by the light of the campfire was morose. His elbows were on his knees, hands propping up his chin. He sighed as he rolled his near-white eyes up to us, then let his chin-length, golden hair fall forward in defeat.

Sophie grunted in irritation, then unrolled her previously stolen sleeping bag. Her new black backpack rested beside her, and I couldn't help but wonder what it contained. We had already stolen clothing, camping supplies, and food. What else was there?

Alaric nudged me playfully with his shoulder. "Let's go find some firewood."

I nodded and followed him as he walked away. I eyed the backpack still slung over his shoulder with interest, then caught up to his side. The backpack blended in with the black of his clothing, but still looked somehow out of place. It made him seem younger, like a teenager on his way home from school, only most high schoolers weren't 6'2" and well muscled, and they didn't look at you with their dark eyes like they were thinking about eating you.

"So," I began as we ventured further into the darkness, "about what happened with Diana . . . "

"You're regretting killing her?" Alaric joked, avoiding the actual subject I was attempting to broach.

I rolled my eyes. "I'm referring to what happened *before* that."

He crouched down and snagged a few fallen branches.

I suddenly wished I hadn't brought up the subject at all. I took a deep breath as I looked down at his dark hair. I knew it was unbelievably soft, and had the sudden urge to run my fingers through it, but I resisted.

"When I said that I loved you, I was put on the spot," I grumbled. "I'm not really sure how I feel. I'm not even sure how much I *like* you. You did let me get tortured, after all. I just don't want the idea of love hanging in the air like some big, foreboding thing that we're both avoiding talking about." I let out a harsh breath. I hadn't expected my words to tumble out so haphazardly, and now my pulse raced as I waited for him to reply.

He smiled and stood back up, firewood in hand. "I see you've been holding on to some things," he joked. "Has it really been bothering you?"

"Yes," I answered quickly, "or no." I took another deep breath, then explained, "I just thought we should talk about it."

"And you want to know if I love you back," he finished.

"No!" I exclaimed, though really I did. "I just want to be clear on the fact that if I love you, it's in some weird, twisted, *Stockholm Syndrome* type of way."

He quirked an eyebrow at me. "Isn't that the one where captives begin to love their kidnappers?"

I blushed. "Well you *did* kidnap me."

He frowned. "I was acting on orders."

I shook my head, then started walking. "Be that as it may, I'm not about to just blindly love you without taking into account everything we've been through."

"So you *do* love me?" he asked from behind me. Before I could answer, he caught up to my side and tugged on the end of my braid playfully.

He let go of my hair and brushed my shoulder as he walked ahead of me to where I assumed there was more firewood. I, for one, couldn't see anything. Night vision must have been another perk of physical magic.

I reached his side again and stopped while he picked up more wood. "That's not what I meant. I just meant that I'm not some silly, naïve girl that falls in love despite all the evidence the guy might not be good for her."

Alaric stood and looked down at me with a strange expression.

"What?" I asked, when he didn't speak.

He sighed. "Have you ever stopped to consider that maybe *you* might not be good for *me*?"

My jaw dropped. When I managed to close it I asked, "How so?"

"Well, Madeline," he began in a lecturing tone. "Since we met, I abandoned my home, became a fugitive, almost got sacrificed *by you*, and now I'm about to risk my life to start a war because *you* want to destroy that little key around your neck. I think you've been much worse for me than I have for you."

My stomach churned. I knew that most of it hadn't been my fault, at least not directly, but he *had* gone through a lot by simply being associated with me.

He began walking again, and I had to jog to catch up with him. "Then why even pursue me at all?" I asked weakly.

He stopped and flashed a lascivious smile. "Because I *like* things that are bad for me."

My mouth went dry as he dropped the firewood he'd been carrying and closed the distance between us.

"But do you love them?" I managed to say.

"Perhaps," he said slyly as he reached his hand up to cradle my jaw, "but I would be loathe to admit it, especially after they've worked so hard to convince themselves that they don't love me in return."

He leaned down and kissed me before I could say anything in reply. I kissed him back, not sure if our conversation had actually accomplished anything. I had a feeling that it hadn't, but at the moment, I didn't really care.

Alaric pulled one hand away to unzip and reach into the backpack behind him. A moment later his hand returned to hook something onto the side of my belt.

I pulled away from the kiss and looked down to find a *huge* hunting knife at my hip. I looked back up to meet his eyes. "Are we planning on stabbing people?"

He quirked his lip into a crooked, half-smile. "Hopefully not, but as the saying goes, 'Speak softly, and carry a big stick.'"

I raised an eyebrow at him. "Or in this case, complain loudly, and carry a big knife?"

His expression turned thoughtful, then he nodded. "Something like that, now come here."

He wrapped his arms around my waist and pulled me against him. Sophie and James were probably running out of wood for the fire, but my concern over the situation was minimal. My greatest concern at that moment was the man holding me close, looking devilish with his long, black hair, and eyes that had at some point shifted to feline.

# 7

I pulled away from Alaric at the sound of shouting. Sophie's voice rang out clear in the night, while James' was a mere murmur in reply.

Alaric rolled his eyes. "Even with his memory gone, they're still fighting."

I took a step back, feeling silly for getting absorbed in a makeout session literally seconds after trying to explain to Alaric that I didn't love him.

"We should probably get back before their arguing alerts the police and any Vaettir looking for us," he continued.

I didn't argue, and instead waited while he regathered his firewood, then followed him as he led the way back to our campsite, glad that he couldn't see my blush.

We still had no idea if the cops were even after us, but we'd decided to play it safe and stay out of sight. The hope was that the local Doyen had cleaned up our crimes. It was standard protocol for the clans, but we weren't banking on it.

I might have been more skeptical than I was if I didn't already know what the clans could accomplish. There should have been questions when I accidentally took the life of one of my foster parents, but the questions never came. Estus had covered it up.

However, this time there were multiple bodies instead of one, and we had no idea what had happened between Diana, James, and the police when Alaric, Sophie, and I had made a run for it. We likely never would know, unless James regained his memory or Diana miraculously came back to life.

I stumbled across felled branches and rocks as we went, feeling tired and hungry. I'd been so worried about getting my convoluted point across to Alaric that I hadn't realized how far we'd walked to find firewood.

I breathed a sigh of relief when the campfire came back into view, a tiny beacon of light in the darkness. I could no longer hear Sophie and James arguing, and as we approached I saw that they now sat on opposite sides of the fire, not meeting each other's eyes.

Alaric walked ahead of me to dump the extra firewood near James, then went to sit by his sister. Feeling embarrassed about how long we'd been gone, and a little bad for James in his current state, I took a seat next to him instead of the others.

He turned and gave me a sad smile. I *almost* reached out and patted his shoulder in encouragement, then reminded myself that he was still *James*, the man who had stabbed me and enjoyed it, even if he didn't remember it. He didn't deserve my sympathy.

Feeling uncomfortable, I scooted a little bit away from him.

Alaric turned to his sister. "Was there a reason you were trying to alert anyone within a five mile radius of our presence?"

Sophie scowled, then gestured at James with a sharp nod. "Mother Theresa over there thinks that we should make peace with the local clan so we can all live happily ever after."

James frowned and looked down at the fire, obviously not wanting to argue with Sophie any further.

I pushed my boot-clad feet a little closer to the fire. "It's not the most absurd idea, especially for someone who has no clue what's going on."

"*If* he has no clue what's going on," Sophie added.

I stared back at her, confused.

"She thinks I'm faking," James explained.

"Ah," Alaric cut in. "Well that explains the yelling."

I shivered. Even though the area we'd chosen was well-sheltered by trees, the earth was still damp from residual snowfall. The moisture was yet to soak through the leather pants, but it was still cold.

"It's something he would do," Sophie muttered.

Everyone went silent.

"It doesn't change our plan either way," I said finally. "Tomorrow we contact the local Vaettir, and we take them by force."

"You say that so casually," Sophie replied hotly, "like we

aren't about to all risk our lives on the slim chance that you can make the charm work to your advantage. That's if we can even get the locals to talk instead of jumping straight to killing us."

"Do you have a better plan?" I sighed, knowing for a fact that she didn't.

She crossed her arms and glared at me. "No, but I'd like you to take things seriously."

"You're not my case worker anymore," I snapped, "and I'm no longer a scared teenager hoping for some worthwhile advice. I know you're unhappy with this whole situation, and I know you're hurt that Maya betrayed you after you risked your life for her, but neither of those things are my fault. Stop taking your bad mood out on me."

Alaric grinned as he watched our exchange, but made no move to cut in. James looked down at his feet miserably.

Sophie took a deep breath. "You're right, I'm sorry," she replied, sounding pained. "We will contact the natives, and meek, little Madeline will assert herself as their omnipotent leader."

I bit my lip at her sarcasm, but let it go.

"The natives are already here," came a heavily accented female voice from behind where Alaric and Sophie sat.

All of us except for James jumped to our feet. James remained seated, terror clear on his face. Either he wasn't faking his memory loss, or he was an exceptional actor, because the James I knew never looked scared.

Three people stepped forward out of the darkness. Two stood beside Sophie, and the third beside Alaric. I assumed the person standing beside Alaric had been the one to speak, as she was the only female of the group. At first I thought we might stand a fighting chance, then several more shapes came into view.

"I assume you are the ones who killed our people at the hotel, though I was told there were five of you," the woman who'd initially spoken continued.

She seemed confident even though we had killed several of her friends just a few nights before, or maybe it was just her height. It was hard *not* to look confident when you were around 6'4" with a mane of pale blonde hair and a perfect, creamy complexion. She had a warrior's body, all muscle, but lithe enough to move quickly.

Her light eyes flicked to each of my companions, then settled on me. "Am I to assume that you are the one who will be swooping in to take us over?" she asked as a smile curved her lips.

"Well there's a long story behind that," I began, but she held up her hand to cut me off.

"We've been searching for you, Madeline," she explained. "I'm to bring you to our Doyen."

"She goes nowhere without us," Alaric stated, sounding more serious than I was used to.

The woman glanced at him briefly, then turned her gaze back to me. "*Fine.*"

She gestured with her hand and the rest of her people moved forward. As they came into view, I noticed that many of them were extremely tall and blond, just like their leader. It felt like we were being taken captive by a Viking clan, and the effect was increased by the large amounts of leather and fur most of them wore.

Two hulking men who looked like twins each tried to grab onto Alaric and Sophie, but their hands came up with empty air. Moments later Alaric was at my side, and after glaring at her would-be captor, Sophie joined us.

James allowed one of the few dark-haired people, a woman, to help him to his feet. The blonde Amazon calling the shots watched the whole display like it was the most amusing thing she'd ever seen. Since the Vaettir aren't exactly a cheerful people, maybe it was.

She turned and walked back the way she'd come, confident that we would follow. Alaric and Sophie both stopped to pick up their backpacks, which I presumed held more weapons like my knife, then sandwiched me like bodyguards. In a way they were, since I was fairly helpless until someone died, and the knife at my hip would do little against a trained attacker.

The cold seeped in as we left the heat of the fire behind, and the light touch of Alaric and Sophie's shoulders offered no warmth. James followed behind us like a dejected puppy as the rest of the Vaettir fanned out around us, many of them disappearing from sight in the dark woods just as suddenly as they'd appeared.

The blonde's tall form walking in front of us was little more than a shadowy silhouette in the dark forest. I tried to catch Alaric's eye as we walked, hoping for an explanation to why we were following the blonde's orders so willingly, but both he and his sister kept their expressionless gazes ahead on our captor.

After a painfully cold ten minutes trudging through the woods, the blonde stopped in front of a massive tree. I stopped and waited, confused. The only way I'd ever entered a Salr was by way of magical vines, but I didn't see any vines in the snowy landscape.

The blonde hadn't moved that I could see, but suddenly the earth began to tremble. I watched in awe as the tree in front of us shimmered like a mirage in the hot sun, only it was nighttime and freezing. The shimmer dissipated, revealing a dark doorway in the middle of the tree, tall enough for the blonde to walk through comfortably, and wide enough for two people to walk side-by-side. Alaric and Sophie did not appear impressed, but I sure was.

The blonde disappeared into the darkness within, while our other captors waited for us to move forward. I resisted the urge to clutch the charm near my throat as I took a hesitant step. Sophie dropped back behind us, leaving Alaric to walk by my side into the tree. Unable to help it, I reached out and touched the rough bark of the doorway, needing to reassure myself that it was real. The bark was cold, and left my fingertips damp.

I took another step forward, disoriented by the act of walking into a tree and not hitting the other side. The darkness remained solid as we walked further

Alaric abruptly grabbed my arm. I froze in alarm, but then he moved and I realized he was just signaling that there was a step down in front of us. I followed Alaric's lead down several more steps, blind in the darkness, until we reached the landing and the gentle lighting of the Salr.

This new Salr was startlingly similar to Estus'. There was no apparent source of lighting, yet the hall was filled with a dim glow, illuminating the same gray stone that composed the other Salr.

The blonde had gotten several steps ahead of us as I stumbled on the steps, and now turned to wait further down the hall. Alaric held out his arm to me. I stared at his arm, not sure I understood the gesture, but it became clear as his other hand guided my arm through the bend of his elbow. He then moved his guiding hand to grasp my fingers, placing them delicately onto his forearm.

The blonde chuckled, then turned and started walking again, boot heels clacking on the stone. The other Vaettir shifted impatiently behind us, and I quickly hopped forward then started walking.

I felt awkward being escorted rather than walking on my own, though I would have taken other forms of closeness. I was part of the hand-holding or arm around the shoulders generation, and being led around like a *lady* felt weird.

"Why all of the formality?" I whispered, keeping my gaze forward.

"Shh," Sophie warned from behind us.

I bit my lip, wanting to argue. We'd had no time to plan, and I had no idea what courtesies we were supposed to observe when going into a foreign Salr. Then again, we were there to take them over, so maybe we weren't supposed to be courteous at all.

I glanced over my shoulder to see Sophie and James walking side-by-side, and the rest of the Vaettir walking in pairs behind them. Perhaps we'd be observing some ceremonies after all.

We were led though multiple twists and turns, until eventually we came upon a large throne room, similar to the one in Estus' Salr. It seemed odd that a place of refuge, which was what the Salr were, would come with a throne room, but it also seemed odd that they came with dungeons, unless the features had been added once the Vaettir began to live in them full time. Maybe the Salr shaped itself to suit its inhabitant's needs. I'd seen enough crazy stuff lately that anything seemed possible.

Unlike Estus' throne room, which held a dais, but was barren of decor, this one was accented with heavy tapestries done in rich colors, and thick, Persian rugs. The Vaettir who'd escorted us went to stand on either side of the room in orderly lines, while the blonde went to stand by the simple, wooden throne. At first I thought she might sit in it, but then a man emerged from a nearby doorway and stole the show.

He looked just as Viking-esque as the rest of them, except with rich, chestnut-colored hair instead of blond. His roughly 6'5" frame was covered by a heavy robe done in gold and garnet red. Our eyes met, and he smiled, then he moved his gaze to the blonde by the throne. His eyes had been a startlingly bright reddish brown that contrasted interestingly with his armpit-length hair.

The Vaettir surrounding us knelt as he walked past them. I watched them stupidly until Alaric tugged me down to my knees. I glanced at him, but his expression was unreadable, so I turned my eyes to the reddish-haired man instead.

He lowered himself onto the throne, seeming somewhat out of place in the regal setting, likely because he looked around thirty years old. I had expected an older person as Doyen, just like Estus, but it was a silly expectation. The more powerful the Vaettir, the less they aged. To have become Doyen, this man was likely old, and to look so young bespoke his power. Estus was scary powerful himself, but not powerful enough to halt the aging process as much as others.

Of course, he might just be descended from a major deity, like Alaric. Less power, but no aging. The man gestured for us to stand, but stayed seated himself.

"I am Mikael," he announced as we stood, "Doyen of this clan. You must be Madeline."

I realized with a start that he was talking to me. I had expected him to start with Alaric or Sophie, or anyone else who actually might know what was going on.

"Y-yes," I stammered. "That's me."

He cocked his head and raised an eyebrow at me. "I'm told you've come to take over my clan. Forgive me, but you don't seem well-equipped for such a task."

I bit my lip. The blonde had been with us the entire time, so someone else must have raced ahead to rat us out.

When I didn't deny nor confirm his accusation, he asked, "Do you have the *lykill*?"

My eyes narrowed in confusion. The word was pronounced *ley-kik,* and sounded like the language I'd heard Alaric and Sophie speak.

"The ley-what?"

"It means *key*," Alaric whispered, finally deciding to be helpful.

He didn't elaborate any further, which made me think we didn't want Mikael to know we had the charm.

"I'm not sure what you mean," I replied loud enough for everyone in the room to hear.

"She's lying," the blonde stated immediately.

Mikael smiled, and it was a bit unnerving. "I cannot let

you take my clan from me," he announced, "but I can offer you sanctuary from your pursuers."

"But why?" I asked at the same time Alaric said, "I don't think so."

I had been so focused on Mikael, I only then noticed the anger emanating from Alaric.

"I could simply take the key from her," Mikael commented as his gaze moved to Alaric. "Your choice."

The charm in question was pulsing at my neck like something alive, as if it sensed all the excitement. Before I could think better of it, I reached my hand up to my throat to touch the little key through the collar of my shirt.

Mikael turned his gaze back to me, quirking the corner of his mouth into a half-smile. "Unless she knows how to use it . . . "

I could have cut the tension around us with a knife. All the Vaettir had gone rigid, waiting for their Doyen to signal the attack. The only person who appeared calm was Mikael, still slouched on his throne with one leg now dangling casually over one of the chair-arms.

I continued to clutch at the charm, unsure of what to do. I had no idea how to use it, but Mikael didn't know that. I flicked my eyes to Alaric, hoping for some subtle advice. What I got was not subtle at all.

"I hope you can figure this out quickly," he began, his eyes only for me, "because I won't be able to hold them off for long."

At a sudden flick of Mikael's hand, the Vaettir surrounding us surged forward. Alaric and Sophie were nothing but blurs as they darted around me, flinging our attackers aside like rag dolls. I smelled burning flesh somewhere behind me and knew that James had joined the fray.

I stood frozen as I clutched the charm. I briefly thought about the knife at my waist, but dismissed it. My eyes found Mikael, who still sat casually upon his throne. He gazed at me with his head tilted downward in challenge, daring me to act.

Feeling like I was in a trance, I untied the cord that held the charm, removing it from my neck, then dangled it out in front of me. Accepting the taunt, Mikael stood, then strode confidently toward me. Somewhere in the back of my mind, my thoughts raced, asking me what the hell I thought I was doing, but the front of my mind was calm, and didn't feel like it belonged to me any longer.

A part of me knew I should be sensing the pain of those getting injured around me, but it was somehow blocked out. All I could focus on was the charm in my hand, and Mikael's determined gaze as he neared me. Distantly I knew his people were attempting to capture, not kill my companions, as we were greatly outnumbered, but remained unharmed. Whatever had taken me over rejected the idea of capture. It was not an option.

I didn't feel in control of my own limbs as I yanked the cord up, then caught the charm in the palm of my hand. The charm's pulsing grew stronger. The distant back part of my mind realized the charm was feeding on the chaos around me. I could feel it sucking the energy in, much like I did when I released a soul, except I only took a portion of the energy, the charm was taking all of it.

Alaric flashed for a moment in front of me, then was gone, tumbling to the side as he kept another one of our attackers away from me. We were extremely outnumbered, but having two five-hundred year old embodiments of war fighting on our side helped to even the odds.

Mikael reached me, and it was like everything around us went still. I knew that mere seconds were passing, but the scene was playing out before me in slow motion. The charm's stolen energy began to trickle down my arm, filling me up with more power than I would get from one hundred simultaneous deaths.

Mikael reached out, just as the charm's consciousness suddenly ripped through my mind. It didn't want to go with him. Our powers were the same, and I would be able to use it to its full potential.

Energy shot from the fist I'd closed around the charm. I wasn't sure if it was my doing, the charm's, or a mixture of both, but it brought Mikael to his knees. He gritted his teeth against the force of it, but was unable to regain his feet.

Words trickled out of my mouth that I didn't quite understand. "You will kneel until I tell you to stand, Mikael Agnarsson."

"I . . . did not . . . expect this," he spat through gritted teeth.

Finally he bowed his head, and the torrent of energy stopped, just as the key's consciousness left me all at once. I looked around the room, truly freaked out, having no idea how I'd known Mikael's surname.

Those who still stood were silent. Alaric and Sophie both waited within arm's reach, but neither reached out to touch me.

I looked back down at Mikael, who had raised his head

to glare at me. "I suppose this alters my plans," he stated calmly. I was pretty sure he could have stood then if he wanted to, but he stayed kneeling. "What would you have of me, *mennskurð*?"

I glanced at Alaric and whispered, "What is *mennskurð*?"

He looked a little green as he answered, "It means *the lady*, but refers to a woman of high standing, sometimes a seeress."

I looked back to Mikael, who waited patiently with an odd smile on his face. The smile wasn't exactly bitter or unhappy, maybe *rueful,* or . . . calculating?

All of the Vaettir waited with their eyes glued to me. Some looked worried or confused, some angry, and some apathetic.

"What should I say?" I whispered again.

"You know, I can hear you," Mikael teased. For someone who was losing control of his clan, he didn't seem terribly upset.

A catty remark froze on the tip of my tongue. It probably was a bad idea to antagonize even a fallen Doyen while his people waited ready to pounce.

"I would like to hold a private audience with you, *and my advisors*," I added quickly. "We have delicate matters to discuss."

Mikael's smile widened, a hint of challenge in his reddish eyes. "Wise choice, *mennskurð*. May I stand?"

"Yes," I replied as I took a step back, "and please, just call me Madeline."

He rose, taking a step forward to close the space between us, then offered me his arm. "Shall we?"

I looked down at the offered arm, then to Alaric, who nodded. Sophie was paler than usual, but fully determined as she kept her eyes trained on the other Vaettir around us. James just looked scared.

I looped my arm through Mikael's and allowed him to escort me, much like Alaric had done earlier. The fabric of his ornate robe was scratchy underneath my palm. He led me toward the door he had originally emerged from, and had to hold up his free hand to stop the blonde from following us. She did *not* look happy.

We went through the door unhindered, with my three companions following behind us. James shut the door, and I felt instant relief, even though it was still uncomfortable to have Mikael at my side. The room we entered was done up like a sitting room, with large, cushy chairs and a gleaming coffee table in the middle. It seemed like a good place for a private meeting, but Mikael kept walking.

We went through another door, down the hallway for a while, then through a final door into a room with a large table and chairs all around. It would have looked like any other conference room, except the walls and floor were made of stone, and the table was made of rough-hewn planks of wood as thick as my torso.

Mikael dropped my arm, then pulled a chair out for me. After I sat he went around the table to sit across from me, leaving everyone else to get their own chairs. Alaric took the chair to my left, then Sophie and James took the next ones down. I was glad they still wanted to sit near me after what had happened with the charm. I wasn't sure if *I* even wanted to sit near me.

"That was quite the display," Mikael stated, breaking

the silence. "I have a feeling things will be much more interesting this time around."

"This time around?" Sophie questioned.

Mikael grinned. "Yes, my dear, last time the *Lykill* surfaced, it fell into the hands of an earth spirit. She caused a great deal of destruction, but earthen spirits at their core embody stability and patience. Really, she had no business wielding a tool of chaos. Executioners, or simply *Dauðr* in the old tongue, can control massive amounts of energy, the same type of energy controlled by the charm."

His gaze landed solely on Alaric and Sophie as he said, "The only thing more interesting would have been if the charm had chosen one of you. A being of chaos and war to wield a powerful tool of, well, chaos and war."

"So let me get this straight," I interrupted. "You were around when the charm was last used, when all of those terrible scenes of bloodshed and misery occurred?"

Mikael raised an eyebrow at my question. "You speak as if you witnessed those scenes with your own two eyes."

"One of the women who gave her life to seal the charm away showed them to me," I explained, feeling suddenly angry, though I wasn't sure why.

He steepled his fingers together in thought. "Interesting, very interesting," he mused.

I glared at him. "You didn't answer my question."

"He was there," Alaric answered for him.

I looked back and forth between the two men. "You two know each other?" I asked, perplexed.

Sophie met my eyes as I scooted back so I could view everyone at once. She looked just as confused as I felt.

"We've *met*," Alaric replied, clipping his words in irritation.

"But that's a tale for another time," Mikael finished for him, then turned back to me, "What is it you plan, *mennskurð*?"

Unsure of whether we were divulging our actual plans or not, I turned to Alaric.

His jaw was clenched in irritation. It reminded me of how he'd looked when he allowed James to torture me. I was beginning to realize that look was reserved for situations where he was forced to follow decorum when he really, *really* didn't want to.

When it became apparent that I wasn't going to get any advice, I turned back to Mikael. "We're going to start a war, and I need you to instigate the first battle."

Mikael chuckled. "And for this task, you've chosen one of the smallest clans in existence?"

My mouth opened into an *oh* of surprise. "It was kind of a choice of convenience," I said weakly. I glanced at Alaric again, then back to Mikael.

"Who were you hoping to start a war with?" he pressed.

I eyed him suspiciously. "Why are you being so cooperative? Just a short while ago, you were threatening to take the charm away from me."

His slight cringe was the only sign that he'd minded the exchange. "You quickly proved that it was not an option," he explained. "The key has chosen you as its wielder, and will protect your right to it."

"You speak like it has a mind of its own," I accused, feeling uncomfortable in the hard, wooden chair.

He laughed so suddenly that I jumped in my seat. “Would you argue with such a claim?”

I thought back to the energy flowing through the charm, and the foreign thoughts and emotions that had raced through my head. “I guess not.”

“We will start a war among the two largest clans of the Vaettir,” Alaric cut in, saving me from Mikael's calculating gaze.

Mikael's smile was wicked as he turned back to me with a look of excitement in his eyes. “Well then,” he replied. “This shall be very interesting indeed.”

Interesting wasn't how I'd describe it. I'd go with terrifying, sad, or maybe guilt-inducing. I'd have no qualms if Estus died in the process, but many others would die too. Innocent people with no choice but to follow orders would be sacrificed unwillingly for our cause. Now to add to everything, we were going to do it with one of the smallest clans around. If we made one wrong move, Estus or Aislin would wipe us out.

I looked around the table, doubting everything. It was obvious that Mikael didn't share my sentimentality, and I doubted Alaric or Sophie would either. Maybe James and I could cry together about it over a shared bottle of wine. Now *that* would be interesting.

# 8

We were given rooms and food. Everyone was extremely courteous, and I didn't trust it one bit. My empath abilities allowed me to sense the confusion and fear wafting off any Vaettir who neared us. They had no idea what was going on, or why their leader was catering to the people they'd taken prisoner.

Alaric, Sophie, and James all currently occupied the room I'd been given, though they'd each been allotted rooms just as grand. They looked out of place in their black clothing against the royal blue and gold decor. The artfully carved oversized furniture, colorful tapestries, and thick, cozy bedding must have cost a pretty penny.

I sat on said bedding, waiting for someone to tell me what we were supposed to do next, but all they could do was argue.

"Why have I never heard of Mikael?" Sophie snapped at Alaric as she stalked back and forth across the carpet. "How do you know him? We would have planned this whole thing differently."

"Sophie," Alaric replied calmly. "We didn't plan any of this. It's not like we were taken prisoner on purpose, and I had no idea Mikael was Doyen here."

"Well tell me how you met him, at least," she said, somewhat deflated.

Alaric glanced back at James, still uncomfortable divulging information in front of him, even though James likely wouldn't think twice about any of it.

I raised my hand to speak. Sophie glared at me, but Alaric gestured for me to proceed.

"While I'd like to know more about Mikael, and what it means for us that his clan is so small," I began, "what I'd most like to know, is what the hell happened to me when I used the charm? How did I know Mikael's surname?"

Sophie's glare softened. "I'm not sure," she replied.

"But Mikael likely knows," Alaric finished for her. "Not that he'll tell us."

"Yes," Sophie growled as her gaze turned once again to her brother, "back to *Mikael*."

"Because it felt like I was possessed," I went on, not willing to let the subject drop.

The charm began to pulse gently against my throat, like a cat purring. Feeling uneasy, I pulled the little key out from my collar to rest on top of my shirt. It continued to pulse, but at least now the feeling was slightly dampened.

James looked at the charm like it might jump off my neck and bite him. "Maybe you should take it off," he suggested.

"She can't take it off," Sophie chided before I could

respond. "Mikael would have taken it if he could, and I've no doubt he's still after it."

"Now *you're* talking like you know him too," I observed.

"I'm just not an idiot," Sophie grumbled. "I saw the look on his face when you went all creepy and pulled the charm out. He wants it."

"I'm going to bed," James announced solemnly, obviously hurt by Sophie's reaction to his suggestion.

I started to say "good-night" but only got out a "goo—" as he stood and let himself out of the room, shutting the door behind him.

I gave Sophie a tired look. "Do you have to be so mean to him?"

"He's still *James*," she argued.

"And you're still the one who made us keep him," Alaric argued back.

Sophie crossed her arms and looked back and forth between the two of us. With a final huff, she left the room without another word.

I looked to Alaric with an eyebrow raised. "Are you off to bed now too?"

His lips curled into a smile. "If you think I'm about to leave you alone with Mikael lurking around, you are sorely mistaken."

"So how *do* you know him?" I asked as he took a step toward me.

He stopped short, his shoulders hunched in defeat. "You just *had* to ask, didn't you?"

I nodded excitedly as he took a seat next to me on the bed.

"He knew my mother," he admitted, "and he inadvertently caused her death."

My eyes widened in surprise. "That's why you didn't want to tell Sophie?"

He nodded without looking at me. "She would have marched right out of this room to kill him."

"But you said inadvertently," I replied softly. "She'd kill him for an accident?"

At that, he turned his dark eyes up to regard me. "Wouldn't you want someone to pay for your mother's death, even if it had been an accident?"

I waited for him to remember the little detail he had forgotten.

Almost immediately he cringed. "I'm sorry, Maddy. I forgot you never knew your mother."

I shrugged like it didn't matter, and in many ways, it didn't. It was a pain I had dealt with long ago. "I guess I'd still probably want to avenge her . . . "

Alaric sighed and looked back down at his lap. "I tried to avenge my mother, but I was rather young and stupid at the time."

"What happened?" I prompted when he didn't continue.

He glanced at me with a rueful smile. "You're not going to let this drop, are you?"

I gave him my most innocent look. "If you don't want to talk about it . . . " I trailed off.

He gave me a playful look that said, *I know you're manipulating me, but I'm just going to go with it,* then he put an arm around my shoulders and pulled me backward. Our backs hit the bed, then I turned to nestle into the curve of his shoulder, pulling my feet up to curl against him while his legs remained dangling off the edge of the bed.

"It was during the *Thirty Years War*," he began.

"So in Central Europe?" I questioned.

He patted my shoulder. "Yes, now no more interruptions."

"I was just a child of roughly one hundred years," he went on.

"That's not exactly a child," I cut in incredulously.

He playfully put a hand over my mouth, then continued, "It was a time before the Vaettir had fully withdrawn from the world, though many had started living full time within the various Salr. We would often become involved in politics to better our financial standing. As a descendant of *Dolos,* Mikael was an expert at such politics."

"Dolos?" I questioned against the hand that still gently covered my mouth. The name sounded somehow familiar to me, but I couldn't remember where I'd heard it before.

"The god of deceit and treachery," Alaric explained, finally removing his hand.

The wheels began to turn in my head, but I kept my thoughts to myself.

"It is due to Mikael's nature that he was able to remain among the humans much longer than the rest of us. He's an extremely difficult man to pin down," he continued.

"Or so you found when you tried to avenge your mother?" I guessed, attempting to lead him back to the point of the story.

Alaric pulled me a little closer, then took a deep breath before continuing, "When Christian IV invaded Germany, Mikael was by his side. Christian IV had been a successful ruler, and had amassed a great deal of wealth for Denmark. Even so, the incursion into Germany was funded by the French Regent Cardinal Richeleau. Mikael betrayed Christian to the Germans, and the Danes were defeated."

"And Mikael got rich?" I questioned, finding the story fascinating, but not seeing what it had to do with Alaric's mother.

"And the money was supposed to go to Mikael's Doyen," Alaric added, "but Mikael was not fond of the idea of serving someone else. He fled, and my mother helped to cover his tracks."

I scrunched my face in confusion. "Why would she help him?"

Alaric shrugged. "He and my father had been old friends. I think she did it because my father would have wanted her to, had he been around. My mother was blamed for his treachery, and she was beheaded."

I gasped. I knew where the story was leading, but I hadn't expected the telling to be so . . . blunt.

"I could not stop my mother's death," Alaric stated, voice void of emotion, "but I thought I could avenge her. I went after Mikael, and found him even. I never told Sophie, and neither did the few who knew the truth. She believes our mother died in battle. I knew Sophie would have gone after Mikael herself, but if he had bested me, he would best her as well."

"He bested *you*?" I asked, slightly shocked. I'd seen Alaric fight, and I didn't think anyone stood much of a chance against him. He was an embodiment of war, fighting was an innate part of him.

He sighed. "I told you, I was but a child at the time, and

Mikael was many centuries old at that point, now he's positively ancient."

My pulse raced at the very thought of someone even older than Estus, or Sivi, the frightening water elemental who wanted to kill, well . . . everyone. "Just how old?" I asked weakly.

"He was a Viking led by Ivar the Boneless in the 800s," Alaric explained, "though I do not know when he was born."

With that information, my heart nearly stopped. He was a 1,300 year old Viking . . . and I had forced him to kneel. How stupid could I be? Or really, how stupid could the charm be? Why on earth would it choose me when it could have an ancient Viking as its host?

"So is there a reason why he hasn't killed us all yet?" I asked, my voice barely above a whisper.

"In Greek Mythology, Dolos was an apprentice to the Titan Prometheus," Alaric began in a lecturing tone. "He was not particularly powerful, but he was clever. While Prometheus was sculpting *Veritus,* a being who would influence humans to tell the truth, Dolos secretly replicated the sculpture, only he ran out of clay for the feet. Prometheus happened upon Dolos' replica, but thought it so perfect that he wanted to take credit for both statues. He fired them both in his kiln, and Dolos' statue became *Mendacium,* or lies, while Prometheus' became truth. In effect, Dolos created lies, and became the god of trickery and deceit."

The explanation made my head hurt. "That doesn't tell me why Mikael hasn't killed us yet," I groaned.

"Because you don't kill your pawns," Alaric said coldly,

"you use them to your advantage, then let your enemies kill them."

Suddenly I felt cold. I pressed my body more firmly against Alaric's, but his warmth didn't help. It wasn't *that* kind of cold. "Do you think what happened with the charm was a trick? Did he willingly kneel?"

"No," Alaric replied, "but if anyone can find a way around something as powerful as the charm, Mikael can."

"Then why are we still here?" I whispered as I lifted my head up to look at him. "Why aren't we trying to find a way out?"

Alaric smiled wickedly, surprising me. "Because this is my chance to finally best him, and I am no longer *any* man's pawn."

My eyes widened as I stared at him. Alaric might not be a pawn, but I sure was, and I'd never been very good at chess.

# 9

After Alaric's little revelation, I had definitely wanted to discuss things further, but we were interrupted by a knock on the door. We both rose to answer it, but Alaric beat me to it.

The tall blonde whose name we still hadn't learned stood framed in the doorway. She wore the same outfit she had earlier, only minus a few layers. The muscles of her bare arms flexed imposingly as she regarded us.

"The Doyen would like to invite the Executioner for a nightcap," she announced.

Alaric feigned a hurt expression, then said, "And no invite for little old me?"

The blonde smirked. "Not quite."

"But I imagine you'll be standing guard at the door?" Alaric asked.

The blonde answered with a curt nod.

Alaric smiled. "Then so will I."

The blonde glared, then turned on her heel and walked away, obviously expecting us to follow.

Alaric followed her, and after standing shocked for a moment longer, I hustled to catch up to his side.

"I don't want to be *alone* with him," I whispered. "What happened to not being a pawn?"

Alaric smiled wide enough to flash fangs, but kept his eyes on the blonde's back. "It is a game, Madeline. He will not openly confront you yet. He's simply testing the waters."

I hurried to keep pace with him, then whispered, "I'm not good at games."

"The mouse doesn't need to be good at games," he replied, "because she has a cat to protect her."

"I'm not a mouse!" I protested.

"It's good to be a mouse," he said almost cheerfully. "You can scurry out of harm's way." He stopped suddenly and looked at me squarely. "And that's exactly what I expect you to do."

He waited for me to nod, then continued walking to catch up to the blonde. She'd led us to the door of the comfortable sitting room that was attached to the throne room, then held the door open for me. I walked through, feeling vulnerable and nervous. Alaric gave me a nod of reassurance, then the blonde shut the door behind me.

I hesitated near the entrance, but the room appeared empty, so I took a step further in. There was a fire crackling happily within the stone fireplace that was the centerpiece for the seating arrangement. I walked toward the fire and reached out a tentative hand to touch the velvety fabric of the cushy, burgundy couch.

A hand suddenly alighted on my shoulder and I froze. Pulse thudding in my throat, I slowly turned my head to see Mikael, standing slightly off to the left behind me.

He'd exchanged his regal attire for silken pants and a smoking jacket. The outfit looked just as strange to me as the robe he'd worn earlier, but at least he looked more comfortable. I envied his comfort, because I was anything but.

He let his hand drop and walked past me toward the fire, taking the cushy chair closest to the heat and crossing his legs casually. One bare foot bobbed in the air as he turned his deep amber gaze to me.

I swallowed the nervous lump in my throat. "I wasn't aware that this was such a . . . casual meeting."

"Having a night cap is usually a more intimate event," he replied. He gestured for me to sit. His face remained impassive, so I couldn't tell if he was hitting on me, or if he'd used the word *intimate* in a more casual way.

Erring on the side of caution, I walked around the arm of the large couch and sat on the side farthest from him. Doing my best to avoid his too-intense eyes, I looked around the room. Everything was done in burgundy and other dark tones, and reminded me of something out of the late twenties.

I caught movement out the corner of my eye and whipped my head toward Mikael, suspicious of anything he might be doing while I was distracted. Instead of lifting some previously hidden weapon to kill me, he lifted a bottle of bourbon from a drink table beside his chair. In his other hand he balanced two glasses, each of which he filled effortlessly while his eyes remained on me.

He placed the bottle back on the table, took one glass in his now free hand, then held out the other glass toward me.

"No thanks," I mumbled, looking at the amber liquid like it might jump across the room to burn my skin off.

Mikael rolled his eyes at me. "This is kind of the whole point of a nightcap, and I poured both drinks from the same bottle, so I'm not trying to poison you."

I let my eyes linger on the glass, unsure of what I should do, then looked back at him. Alaric had said Mikael was just testing the waters, but still . . . "You could have poisoned the glass itself," I offered.

He rolled his eyes again, then retracted the offered glass only to then hold out his own. Out of a desire to get the strange situation over with, I stood and moved toward him to take the glass. He rose as I reached him, then pulled the glass close to his chest.

I eyed him cautiously, pretty sure by that point that he was flirting. When I didn't come any closer, he held the glass out to me again. I snatched it from him, then retreated to my seat.

He sat as well and sighed. "I imagine Alaric had many *wonderful* things to say about me."

I shrugged and took a sip of my drink, but didn't reply.

"He was but a child at the time, and had little understanding of what really happened," he continued.

"Living for one hundred years doesn't make someone a child," I commented, keeping my gaze firmly on my lap.

He chuckled. "And how old are you?"

I glared at him. "By your standards, I'm still inside the womb."

He laughed again. "You're quite hostile for one so young. Has the world been so very cruel to you?"

"Look," I snapped feeling defensive. Sure, the world had been cruel to me, but it was cruel to everyone. "I don't know what game you're playing, but it's not going to get you anywhere, so cut it out."

He cocked his head to the side as a strange smile crossed his face. "Okay, Madeline. What game would *you* like to play?"

"The one where you tell me what you want," I replied, then added, "*really* want."

He gave me an innocent look. "I want to help you, *my lady.*"

I snorted, slowly gaining confidence since he was yet to attack me. "Alaric told me who you're descended from, so I'm not inclined to believe anything you say."

"Then why even ask?" he countered.

I shrugged and took another sip of my bourbon. It was good, *really* good. "Wishful thinking?"

He laughed again. "I'm beginning to think this little game will be more fun than I'd imagined."

I glanced at the door, wishing Alaric would find some excuse to come barging in. "I told you games will get you nowhere."

He set his glass on the table beside him, then steepled his fingers in front of his face. "I was referring to this little war game you're playing."

Starting to get nervous again, I looked down at my drink. Maybe if I chugged it, the *night cap* would be over. Worth a shot.

I downed the glass, then held it up for Mikael to see. "Does this mean I can go to bed now?"

Instead of answering, he stood and walked toward me. I jumped up from the couch to get away so quickly that I stumbled, and his hand was suddenly there on my wrist, keeping me standing.

I dropped my glass in surprise and it thudded harmlessly to the thick rug. Mikael didn't release my wrist, and I looked up at him, feeling like a rabbit cornered by a snake. In my sudden burst of fear, I realized that I'd left my knife in my room, and I had nothing else to protect myself.

"I *will* help you," he said, face entirely serious.

"Let me go, please," I squeaked, feeling silly for being rude to the one-thousand plus year old Viking.

He obliged, but remained standing *way* too close. He towered over me, making me feel small, even though I was used to being one of the tallest kids in class.

"If Alaric told you that much of my history, I imagine he told you of my lineage," he said evenly as he stared down at me.

*Yeah, he told me you were a friggin Viking,* I thought, but what I said out loud was. "He didn't really tell me much."

I wanted to take a step back, but was afraid he'd grab me again. He saved me from making a decision as he sat on the couch, then looked up at me expectantly. Not knowing what else to do, I sat, then waited for him to get to his point.

"It doesn't matter," he sighed. "All you need to know is that I am not content here, hiding in a dark hole waiting for someone to come and take my small clan from me."

I cleared my throat uncomfortably, since that had been

my intent before he decided to cooperate with us. I glanced out the corner of my eye to see him smiling again.

"I will help you, Madeline," he stated again. "Not for you, or out of fear of the charm. I will do it for me, and for the look on Aislin's face when *I* take her clan from *her*."

"You want to rule," I stated, not knowing why it came as any surprise.

The barest incline of his head was my only answer.

I stood abruptly. "Then you want the charm."

He stood again as well, then reached out to move my hair away from my face. I jerked away, making him laugh. "Now Madeline, why would I try using the charm myself, when I already have the perfect tool to control it?"

I craned my neck upward to narrow my eyes at him, suddenly wishing I was wearing heels so I wouldn't feel so small. "I take it I'm the *tool*?"

He quirked an eyebrow at me. "Does that offend you?"

I shrugged, then took a step back. "A bit, yes. It seems that's how most everyone views me these days."

"Well if not a tool," he said as he once again closed the distance between us, "then how about a partner?"

I looked down to see his hand held out for me to shake, then looked up to meet his gaze. "I have no desire to rule."

"That simply cannot be true," he said with a hint of laughter in his voice.

"And why's that?" I asked, having the feeling that he was mocking me.

He grinned. "Because *Every-body-wants-to-rule-the world*," he sang.

Not expecting the joke, I inhaled to laugh so suddenly that I choked on my own spit. Mikael made his way back toward his chair, retrieved his still-full glass of bourbon, then returned to hand it to me.

I accepted it gratefully and took a sip to quiet my coughing.

"Now *that* glass was, in fact, poisoned," he commented as I took another sip.

I spat liquid all over the floor and began sputtering again, dropping the mostly full glass to the ground. It missed the carpet and shattered on the stone floor. I clutched at my throat in horror as I looked up at Mikael.

His face was impassive for a moment, then he burst out laughing just as the door to the room flew open. Alaric came rushing in, followed closely by the blonde.

Alaric glanced around the room, then took in Mikael and I standing way too close to each other. Laughter still coated Mikael's face, and I was pretty sure mine had turned beet red.

Alaric's eyes narrowed. "I heard a glass break."

Alaric and Mikael stared at each other, while the blonde crossed her arms in irritation.

"So that wasn't really poison, right?" I questioned weakly, feeling perfectly healthy now that my coughing had subsided.

Mikael turned his gaze from Alaric to me. "If I wanted to kill you, *mennskurð*, I would think of something much more fun than poison."

I swallowed the lump in my throat, then took a step back. "I'm going to bed," I stated.

Mikael was looking at Alaric as he said, "We haven't finished our discussion."

"So finish it," I demanded, completely out of patience.

He looked back to me. "I will help you because I want to rule. I will not be told by others that I must live in a hole in the ground. You will help me because you want to survive, and you need a ruler who doesn't give a rat's ass if you want to run off with your little kitty cat to live happily ever after."

Alaric cleared his throat at being called *my little kitty cat*, but didn't speak.

"And what do you plan to do as ruler?" I questioned, unable to agree until I knew if he was like Sivi, and wanted to *punish* everyone.

Mikael smiled mischievously. "I plan to eat a lot, *drink* a lot, and bed *a lot* of women." He placed a hand to his chin thoughtfully. "And perhaps I'll get back into politics. Much has changed since the *Thirty Years War*."

I blinked at him, a bit stunned. It was a lot better than what Sivi or Estus planned, and it seemed like he'd kill fewer people. Of course, many would have to die *before* he became ruler. The charm pulsed against my skin, excited by Mikael's plan. That made one of us, at least.

"I'll consider your proposition," I stated blandly.

Mikael bowed his head slightly. "Then we shall speak in the morning, *mennskurð*."

I inclined my head in return, then made my way toward Alaric as he held out his arm to me. I was quite tired of being escorted around, but if it meant I'd get to go to bed, I'd take it.

As we left the room arm in arm, the blonde began to yell at Mikael in that gutteral language that everyone except me seemed to speak.

"I have to ask," I whispered to Alaric as we walked,

leaving the sounds of arguing behind. "What is that language, and why do you all speak it?"

He smiled down at me, even though he still looked pale and slightly irritated. "It's Old Norsk. The Vaettir originated in these lands, and for many of us, Old Norsk was our first language."

I stopped walking. "Explain something to me. Everyone keeps mentioning that the Vaettir originated here, but most of us don't look very Nordic." I gestured up and down my body. "Especially me."

"We are not human, Madeline," he replied. "You must not hold us to human standards. The Vaettir were made in the image of the old gods from varying pantheons, and those genetics were passed down, but they are nothing like human genetics."

"Now when you say *made* . . . " I trailed off.

He shrugged and continued walking. "That is like asking humans the origin of their species. Some believe the old gods were embodiments of different aspects in nature, and that we came from that same energy. Others believe the gods created us themselves."

I shook my head, supposing it didn't really matter since we were here now. "So my ancestors are from this region," I concluded, "but since I never knew my parents, I'll likely never know any more than that. So, back to Old Norsk. Can you teach me?" I asked hopefully.

A look of surprise crossed his face as we continued walking down the stone hall. "You just finished making a deal with the devil, we're in peril, and your primary concern is learning a new language?"

I shrugged. "I didn't make the deal with him yet, and I

wouldn't mind having something a little more normal to focus my attentions on from time to time."

He waggled his eyebrows at me. "And I'm not *normal*?"

I laughed as the tension from my meeting with Mikael finally seeped away. "No, my *little kitty cat*, you are not."

"Can I have your attentions anyway?" he pressed jokingly.

I shrugged. "Once we get back to our room, sure."

Alaric dropped my arm, only to wrap his arm around my shoulders instead. "In that case, I'll teach you Old Norsk, if you'd really like to learn. It would probably be useful regardless if you're going into politics."

"I'm *not* going into politics," I pouted.

"Then I can kill Mikael?" he whispered conspiratorially.

I gave him a side-long glance, not sure if he was joking. "Let's deal with the creepy little key around my neck first," I replied slowly. "Then we'll worry about your centuries old vendetta."

Alaric leaned over to kiss the top of my head as we reached my room. "As you wish, *mennskurð*."

"Don't you start calling me that too," I groaned.

His arm left my shoulders to open the door in front of us. "How about my little *bani*?"

"That all depends on what that word means," I replied as I walked past him into the room.

He followed me in and closed the door behind us. "It means slayer, *one who kills*."

I turned and narrowed my eyes at him. "That's not exactly what I'd consider a term of endearment."

He paused, as if really considering his answer. "How about my *land-skjálpti*?"

I crossed my arms. "Let me guess, it means *destroyer* or something equally romantic."

He smiled, showing me his pointy little canines. "It means *earthquake*, since you came along and shook up my entire world."

I sighed as I walked over to drop down onto the bed. "You're not very good at this pet-name business," I observed, staring up at the stone ceiling.

The bed shifted as Alaric plopped down beside me. "I've just never understood why someone would want to be called *my little flower*, or *cupcake*, or something silly like that. Flowers have short life-spans and are easily crushed, and cupcakes are eaten without a second thought."

I reached my hand out to pat his arm. "When you put it that way, earthquake doesn't sound so bad."

"It's settled then," he said with a yawn. "Just don't let Sophie know. Growing up, our mother called her *veðr*, which means storm. She'll be jealous if she learns there's a new natural disaster in town."

I moved to lay my head on his shoulder, and he wrapped an arm around me obligingly. "Do you think Mikael will really help us?" I mumbled, fighting the call of sleep.

He turned his head so that his lips were near my forehead. "For now," he whispered against my skin, "but our plans will only suit him for so long."

"And what will we do then?" I pressed.

He was silent for a long while, and by the time he finally answered, I was drifting off to sleep. I could have heard wrong in my delirious state, but I was pretty sure that Alaric had replied with, "We'll kill him."

# 10

I woke up feeling like someone was watching me. At first I thought it was Alaric, but I reached out to find the bed empty beside me. I rolled over, forcing my eyes open, to find impassive hazel eyes staring down at me.

Mikael's blonde lackey pursed her lips and crossed her arms.

I sighed and sat up. "If we're going to be spending this much time together, I should at least know your name."

"Aila," she grunted in her thick accent as she continued to stare down at me.

Aila had been much more animated when she was taking us prisoner, but apparently having us as *guests* had put a giant bee in her bonnet. Wanting some distance, I scooted to the far side of the bed before standing. Aila stood immobile, staring at me across a sea of rumpled bedding.

"Where's Alaric?" I questioned. I wasn't sure at what

point he'd left me, and Aila's stoic expression had me worried.

"With Mikael," she said with a sneer, "*planning*."

I crossed my arms, allowing myself to get irritated now that I knew that Alaric was at least relatively safe. "I get the feeling that you don't want us here."

Her sneer deepened. "You should be killed for having our Doyen kneel before you."

I smirked. "He doesn't seem terribly upset about it."

She smiled suddenly, though it was more a baring of teeth. "If you say so," she hissed, then turned and walked toward the door, expecting me to follow.

"I need to get dressed first," I stated.

She looked over her shoulder at me. "Then do so. I'll wait outside."

She left the room and shut the door behind her, and I was able to let out the breath I'd only then realized I'd been holding. I also only then realized that at some half-asleep point during the night I'd lost the leather pants and black blouse, and was now only in my black bra and panties.

I sighed, thinking that Aila probably viewed me as a rather ridiculous creature, while wondering why I even cared. I started searching the room for my clothes, and eventually found them on the floor near the head of the bed. I struggled into the pants, once again cursing Alaric for his fashion choices. Who the hell buys leather pants for a vegetarian?

Fully dressed, but cranky, I went into the adjoining bathroom. Though the décor was spartan and somewhat medieval, there was a fresh toothbrush waiting with a full-sized tube of toothpaste. Vikings who appreciated oral hygiene, who'd of thunk it?

I brushed my teeth and tamed my wavy hair back into its braid. A shower would have been nice, but I really didn't want to leave Mikael and Alaric alone together any longer than necessary.

I returned to the bedroom, then opened the door leading out to the hall. Aila was waiting for me, as expected. She began walking almost instantly, and I had to practically jog to keep up with her, feeling like a dwarf next to her long, long legs.

After a few twists and turns down the hall, I suspected we were heading back to the little conference-style room with the big wooden table. My suspicions were confirmed as Aila led the way through the sitting room then stopped beside the interior door, gesturing for me to enter.

I raised an eyebrow, my hand halfway to the handle. “You're not coming?”

She moved her back against the wall, then stared levelly away from me. “I am *Merkismathr.* I have no say in matters of politics.”

I had no idea what a *merki-whatever* was, but Aila didn't seem terribly happy about it, so I didn't question her further. Instead, I opened the door and walked into the room without another word.

All eyes turned to me as I gently shut the door behind me. Alaric and Sophie sat together at one end of the table, frowns on both of their faces, and Mikael sat on the other end, his face unreadable.

Feeling awkward under the pressure of their gazes, I lifted my hand and waved feebly. “Um, hi,” I mumbled.

Sophie rolled her eyes at me. "Sit down, Madeline."

I did as she asked, taking a seat on the other side of Alaric.

"A message has been sent to the clan leaders," Mikael announced, his strange, amber eyes all for me.

My eyes widened. "Already? I never even agreed to a partnership."

Mikael smiled. "Well since I've used you as bait, you might want to make up your mind."

I turned to Alaric in shock, who sat stony-faced. He obviously already knew the score, as he didn't seem at all surprised. Sophie watched me, waiting for my reaction.

I turned back to Mikael. "I thought you said you were going to *help* me."

Mikael raised an eyebrow at me. "As I recall, this is exactly what you wanted."

"To be used as bait?" I questioned. "I don't think so."

He rolled his eyes. "How else did you intend to draw them out? Tell them that my tiny clan was looking for a fight?" He looked around the table to each of us, then settled back on me. "No. We tell them you have the charm and you know how to use it, and that you will side with the more powerful clan."

I clenched my teeth as I considered what he'd said. As a plan, it wasn't half bad . . . unless Estus just sent assassins to kill me quietly.

"Estus would never believe that I'd side with him," I argued.

Mikael quirked the side of his mouth. "Perhaps not, but he will also not allow Aislin to swoop in and claim you."

I opened my mouth to argue, but couldn't. He was probably right.

"So what do we do in the meantime?" Sophie cut in. "Just wait here while they kill each other?"

Mikael stood. "Not quite. We can't risk that either of them might send people to claim Madeline. We will need to remain on the move, always one step ahead."

Alaric finally looked surprised. "So you will just pack up your entire clan and abandon your Salr?"

Mikael's smile was more of a snarl. "There is no pride in hiding in a hole. A small group of us will remain together, while the rest of my people disperse. An entire clan is too easy to track. When the moment is right, we will come back together."

His energy was so ferocious in that moment that I almost didn't speak, but there was something we needed to get straight.

"I need to be near the battle," I stated.

Mikael's expression softened with slight confusion. "Why?" he asked suspiciously.

I couldn't tell him that I wanted to destroy the charm. His whole plan was banking on me using it to make him ruler, but I needed a lot of death in the same area to do what the Norn had shown me before she died.

"It's the only way the charm can gather enough power," I lied. "It draws its energy from chaos and war."

"And you draw yours from death," he added, still sounding suspicious.

I schooled my expression to be as cold as possible as I said, "Do you want to rule or not?"

He cocked his head. "I do," he answered finally, "but I

will require that you swear allegiance to me."

I cocked my head in return, doing my best to play it cool. "You offered me partnership. If any oaths are to be sworn, we'll *both* be swearing them."

Sophie and Alaric gave me identical approving nods, though I could sense they were surprised by my tact. Their reactions bolstered my confidence regardless, and let me know I was hopefully taking the conversation in the right direction.

Mikael on the other hand, was looking at me like he wanted to eat me. "Clever girl," he commented. "We will swear our oaths, then we will depart. I'll leave you to prepare yourself."

He walked around the table toward the door, then let himself out. I could hear Aila speaking frantically as they both ventured down the hall. Soon all was quiet.

I turned to Alaric and Sophie. "Um, what exactly does this oath require?" I asked, feeling nervous at the idea of needing to *prepare* myself.

Sophie smirked. "And here it sounded like you actually knew what you were doing for a moment. I thought perhaps the charm had taken over."

Alaric appeared solemn. "It is a blood ritual. Normally when fealty is sworn, the swearer will offer their blood to the Doyen. In this case you will both offer blood, and the ritual will be bound to the earth."

"Is it magic?" I questioned weakly, terrified of what the consequences of such an oath might be.

"Of a sort," Alaric replied. "A simple blood oath would not mean much, and would only serve to establish a connection. When an oath is bound to the earth, the terms are quite different. Breaking such an oath would result in the earth coming to claim you."

I gulped. "Claim me?"

"You would die," Sophie clarified.

My eyes widened. "You know, one of you could have stepped in before I put my foot in my mouth."

Sophie shrugged. "We're probably all going to die anyway. I'd rather be claimed by the earth than by the blade of my enemy."

I shook my head, not agreeing with Sophie's viewpoint. "What will the oath be, and what would I have to do to break it?"

Alaric stood and moved behind my chair so he could put his hands on my shoulders. He rubbed gently, attempting to sooth my panic. "I don't imagine it will be anything extreme, as Mikael will be swearing it himself. It will likely be an oath of no direct harm, which as far as I know, you aren't planning on killing him yourself, and it would be good to have such a promise for your own well-being."

I took a deep breath and let it out. An oath of no direct harm didn't sound so bad, though I was still a little shaken at the idea of *offering blood*. The Vaettir didn't do anything half-assed, and it would more likely be a pint than a thimble full. Not to mention that being bound to Mikael in any way gave me the serious creeps.

Alaric leaned down and kissed my cheek, startling me out of my thoughts. "We should prepare," he said softly.

I nodded a little too quickly. Things beyond my comprehension had been set in motion. I pictured Estus plotting within the confines of his Salr, vying for my blood, planning an assault on Aislin's clan so they wouldn't get to me first. So many innocents would die, and it was my fault. I flashed back to the scenes of bloodshed I'd seen the night Diana tried to sacrifice us, and tried to picture those same scenes as they'd apply in modern times. The thought made my stomach turn.

What was to come made one little blood-oath pale in comparison. After all, what was a little blood between acquaintances?

---

THE MEMBERS of Mikael's clan gathered around us as we stood in the woods outside the Salr. Fresh snow had fallen, blanketing the ground and making the world seem soft.

I stood across from Mikael with Alaric, James, and Sophie at my back. At his back stood Aila and two clan members I had only just met. The man's name was Faas, and the woman, Tabitha.

An elaborate design had been carved into the ground, deep enough to turn the soil underneath the snow. It looked a bit like a circular labyrinth, but with jagged edges making it imperfect, but no less mesmerizing.

Both Mikael and I held small, ornate knives in our hands as we stood mirroring each other. He'd traded in his robes for traveling clothes, and looked a little more normal in leather and fur attire that matched his clanmate's, though not as normal as he would have looked in street clothes. The four foot long sword strapped to his back seemed natural, and I had no doubt he knew how to use it.

The oath we had decided on was an oath against

betrayal. I was walking a thin line with it. Technically I had never said I *wouldn't* destroy the charm, so doing so wouldn't be a betrayal, but it still made me nervous. Alaric had assured I'd be fine as long as I didn't lie outright, or intentionally put Mikael in harm's way.

The preparation had consisted of me memorizing a few words in Old Norsk, that basically meant loyalty, honor, and truth. I had dressed in the leather pants with a new burgundy sweater. It felt nice to wear something other than black, but I wasn't really thinking about my clothes at that moment.

"*Hollr*," we both said in unison as we poised the blades above our open palms.

"*Mannvirðing*," we muttered as the blades slid across our skin, sharp enough to cut with only the weight of the metal as pressure.

"*Sannindi*," we finished as we tilted our palms to let our blood fall to the snow.

I could feel energy dancing around me as my blood trickled downward. A little shock went through me once the first drops hit the earth. I could sense the ground below me like it was something alive, and in a way, it was.

Our blood began to flow through the paths carved into the snow. There wasn't enough blood to build momentum, but it seemed to flow forward of its own accord. I watched in awe as the two streams of blood rushed forward, searching for one another, until finally they met in the middle of the design.

My eyes found Mikael's as our blood merged. He smiled, watching me with his head tilted slightly downward, framed by his loose auburn hair.

Something told me that I'd bitten off more than I could chew and then some. The moment our blood fully intermingled my ears popped with pressure, and the blood sank down into the earth. I watched as the design filled itself in, sucking soil then snow down into its lines. After a few seconds the only sign anything had happened were a few bloodstains on the pure white snow.

Mikael clenched his fist around the knife wound, then inclined his head toward me. I stared at him, resisting the urge to gulp. As he turned away to speak to his clan I stood frozen, looking down at the blood on the icy ground.

Alaric stepped forward and helped me into my coat, then began tying a bandage around my hand. I turned worried eyes to him, hoping for a little reassurance.

He shook his head with a small, bitter smile on his face. "He's mad that trusts in the tameness of a wolf," he quoted.

Unfortunately I knew my Shakespeare. I bit my lip before replying, "Things didn't exactly end up well for *King Lear*."

Alaric raised an eyebrow. "Yes, but who is the King in this situation?"

With that confusing question, he took my uninjured hand and led me forward to join the rest of our traveling party.

I still felt uneasy with Alaric quoting King Lear. Shakespeare either wrote comedies where most everybody lived, or tragedies, where most everybody died, and King Lear was a tragedy. It didn't really matter who was in charge if everyone still died.

If it was just a question of dagger, asp, or poison, we were all screwed.

# 11

THREE DAYS LATER.

I had to hand it to him, Mikael had eyes and ears *everywhere*. Given his Viking heritage, I had assumed we would be roughing it in the freezing forest, but Mikael had other plans. We would hide amongst the humans, where his network of spies could easily pass messages to us.

He'd also theorized that should enemy forces find us, they would be hesitant to attack within the confines of civilization. I'd argued that *his* people had attacked us in a hotel in broad daylight, but that ultimately only proved his point, because they had been *his* people, and unlike Estus and Aislin, he didn't want to preserve our secretive existence within the Salr.

Once we reached civilization, we'd learned that Mikael owned several houses, spread out across different towns, and some in different countries. He'd even changed into normal clothes once reaching one of the aforementioned houses, though it was obvious that he did so grudgingly.

We'd stayed at the house for several days, but would be leaving soon. To where was anyone's guess.

I peeked out through the heavy-curtained window, waiting for my turn in the shower. Our current hideout rested in a quaint, residential neighborhood. It was the kind of neighborhood where elderly people walked hand-in-hand, and children played in the streets without fear. The house was set back from the road, with large trees in the front yard, but I could still see a young couple walking happily down the street. I would have given a lot to be as carefree as they seemed, but my life had never, and would never be that way.

I suppressed goosebumps at the idea of Vaettir invading the small neighborhood in search of us with their cold and violent ways. The young couple would have plenty to care about then, if they even survived.

A hand touched down on my shoulder, and I turned to see Alaric smiling down at me, not sensing my worried thoughts.

"Our turn for the shower," he announced.

I blinked up at him innocently, pushing the feeling of dread to the back of my mind. "*Our* turn?"

Without answering, he scooped me up in his arms and carried me toward the bathroom, past floral couches, lace doilies, and other décor just as quaint as the neighborhood. Not exactly a house suited for a Viking, but I think the idea was to blend in more than anything else.

Sophie, with her long hair twisted up in a towel, and another towel wrapped around her body, rolled her eyes as she breezed past us. I turned and stuck my tongue out at her, unwilling to let her spoil my small moment of comfort amidst a sea of troubles.

We entered the cozy bathroom and Alaric used his foot to shut the door behind us. The bathroom was small, with a pedestal sink and toilet to the left, and a shower/bath combo to the right. There was still leftover steam from Sophie's shower fogging up the mirror. I hoped she had saved us some hot water.

As soon as Alaric set me on my feet I locked the door, pausing to listen for any movement outside.

Alaric grabbed my shoulders and gently turned me to face him. “Expecting an attack?”

I pursed my lips. “Something like that.”

More like I was expecting a Viking siege. Things had been weird with Mikael since we'd taken our oath. He had given up on hitting on me after his initial attempt during our *night cap*, but he was still giving me a strange vibe.

I knew he wasn't plotting, since he'd taken an oath to not betray me, and I didn't think he was wary of me or the charm. In fact, he seemed quite comfortable with *that* situation, unlike me. The vibes were more . . . portentous, like something big was coming and only the two of us knew it. Whatever it was had him excited, and it was like he was watching me, waiting for me to set events into motion.

Alaric brought me back to reality as he moved behind me, then pushed my hair aside to rain soft kisses down my neck.

“Focus, Madeline,” he whispered, his breath hot on my skin.

I sighed. “I'm sorry, it's just difficult to be in the present with all of the impeding doom.”

He kissed my cheek, then moved in front of me to turn on the shower. At some point he'd lost his shirt, and his dark hair cascaded down his pale, naked back enticingly. Always a sucker for nice hair, I reached out and ran my fingers through the velvety softness, marveling at its texture.

Faster than my eyes could see, Alaric whipped around and grabbed my wrist. He smiled wide enough to flash his little fangs. "Now that's the spirit."

My lips parted and suddenly I was no longer thinking about the war we had pushed into motion. My thoughts turned to the hot water running in the shower, and how nice it would feel for it to stream down both our bodies pushed together.

The warm feeling growing in my belly was only increased by the emotions Alaric was projecting. I could feel strong emotions the best, and his thoughts were just as filled with heat as mine. Our clothes were off quickly, little more than a secondary distraction.

Alaric took my hand, then stepped back into the shower, leading me to join him. I followed willingly. Although some might label what happened next as a sin, I felt less like I was stepping into the abyss, and more like I was stepping out of it.

---

WHEN THE WATER finally ran cold, we both hurried out of the shower, wrapping towels around ourselves to warm back up. I watched Alaric as I dried off slowly, not at all wanting to leave the bathroom to face the outside world. I would have stayed in that bathroom all day, but alas, our current abode was only a waypoint.

Mikael had alluded that we'd be traveling somewhere far different, though he wouldn't say specifically where. I imagined we'd be staying in Norway, but maybe a more densely populated city area where it would be easier to hide, and escape should we be found. The only thing I knew for sure was that we'd be meeting with a group of people that could help get us to where we were going.

Finished drying, I looked over at the new clothes I was supposed to wear. The house we were in had come equipped with all sorts of clothing. Mikael had planned for all contingencies, and all manner of companions. I'd originally gone for a pair of dark wash jeans and a plain tee-shirt, but Mikael had stopped me. I now looked down on neatly folded, Viking-style clothing, just like what most of Mikael's clan wore, except without the fur.

I reached out a hand to find that the steam of our shower had dampened the dark brown, tunic-style linen shirt, and lighter brown leather pants that sat on the closed lid of the toilet. Would I never escape leather pants? The clothing all looked like it was sewn by hand, but expertly so. Not wanting to put the strange clothing on, but also not about to leave the bathroom in nothing but a towel like Sophie, I frowned and crossed my arms. The now wet cord of the charm weighed heavily on my neck, one more annoyance to contend with.

"I don't feel like we'll fit in very well in these clothes," I remarked. "Isn't the whole idea to blend in?"

Finished dressing, Alaric walked behind me and wrapped his arms around my waist. "My only guess is that perhaps those we intend to meet with will expect more traditional attire."

I raised an eyebrow, though he couldn't see it. "This attire isn't exactly traditional, it's *ancient*."

Alaric kissed the top of my damp head. "I like it. It makes me feel like a young man again."

I turned in his grasp and pulled slightly away so I could observe his clothing, which was similar to mine. "I always forget that you're old enough to have worn stuff like this."

He quirked his lip into a half smile. "I can help you into yours if you like."

I nodded, then turned back to my pile of clothing. I had at least been given a modern day bra and panty set, which I was grateful for. While I slipped them on, Alaric unfolded the pants, loosening the ties that would cinch them around my waist.

He held them out to me. "One foot after the other," he said encouragingly.

I smirked at him. "I know how to put on pants."

He chuckled. "And I know how to take them off."

I took the pants from him and stepped into each leg. "I'm very well aware of that," I replied evenly.

Without another word he stepped forward and pulled the pants the rest of the way up my legs and hips. He criss-crossed the ties, then knotted them at the base of my waist.

"Shirt now," he ordered.

I reached back and grabbed the linen shirt from the toilet lid. I could have put it on myself, but I was having fun with the little game we were playing, so I handed the heavy fabric to him, then held my arms out.

With a lascivious smile, he slid each sleeve slowly over

my arms, then jokingly tugged the rest of the shirt haphazardly over my head. I ended up with half my damp hair caught in the collar, and had to pause my giggling long enough to tug the shirt straight. The hem fell half-way down my thighs, the fabric much more comfortable than it looked. The final touch was a pair of boots that would stay on with leather wrappings rather than laces or zippers. Alaric really did have to help me with those, as I never would have gotten them on correctly myself.

I turned to gaze in the mirror at my new attire, while Alaric retrieved my knife from my discarded clothes to hook it back at my waist. "Well it's much better than the clothes *you* picked out for me," I teased.

I watched Alaric in the mirror as he grinned, then stepped to the side and threw an arm around my shoulder. "We are a perfect pair of peasants," he commented. "Now I'll go till the field, while you stay home and raise our nine children."

I used my reflection in the mirror to glare at him. "You know, there has been a lot of speculation lately that some of the Viking warriors were women."

Alaric kissed my cheek, then turned to put his hand on the doorknob. "Perhaps that is why Mikael gave you pants instead of a dress, my little *land-skjálpti.*"

I grinned as I turned to follow him into the hall. I was liking the pet name of *little earthquake* more and more.

# 12

Sophie and James waited on the little floral couch, each glued to opposite ends.

"Why does he get normal clothes!" I exclaimed, looking down at James.

Sophie glared over at the man in question. "He's not coming to the mysterious *meeting*."

She was dressed in similar clothes to mine and Alaric's, except her linen shirt was deep blue, cinched close to her waist by an ornate leather belt as wide as my palm.

I turned as Mikael entered the room from the kitchen, followed closely by Aila. Mikael was back in his old-fashioned attire as well, only his had a little more leather than ours, and his sword had returned to his back. Aila was in street clothes like James, and didn't look comfortable with the situation at all.

"He cannot come because he is not involved in our plans," Mikael explained. "If he can't remember his own life, then he cannot choose a side,"

"He's practically an invalid," Aila commented, though judging by her clothes she wasn't coming to the meeting either.

I glared at her, but James didn't jump up to defend himself. Oh how the mighty had fallen.

"We must eat, and then we will depart," Mikael announced. "Faas and Tabitha will remain here with your . . . friend."

The two people he'd referred to were nowhere to be seen, and in fact, hadn't been around since we'd arrived at the house, unfortunately. I'd gleaned the information that Faas was Mikael's executioner, and I was dying to talk to him.

Aila stood rigid as a pole, glaring at each of us throughout the exchange. I wasn't sure what she was still so bent out of shape about, but she made sullen Sophie look like the Queen of Sunshine.

Mikael opened his mouth to say something further, but a knock on the door interrupted him.

Chaotic emotions hit me like a ton of bricks. "Don't answer that," I ordered, my eyes glued to the door.

I didn't know who was waiting outside, but I could sense their energy. Normally I'd have to be within touching distance to feel someone's emotions, but what I sensed was overwhelmingly strong. I shook my head. No, the emotions weren't *that* strong, they were just coming from more than one person. My heart raced as I picked up on the feeling of anticipation and something akin to bloodlust, coming from all around the house.

The charm, almost forgotten, began to thrum with

excitement. A battle was about to occur, and a battle would empower it.

James and Sophie both rose and came to stand near the rest of us. Everything was still and silent for several heartbeats. The metaphysical burning balls of excitement that were likely other Vaettir shifted around the house, preparing for the attack.

"They have us surrounded," I whispered.

I watched as Aila looked to Mikael. "Do we fight, or flee?"

Instead of answering, Mikael turned his perfectly calm eyes to me. "How many are there, Madeline?"

I frowned, not wanting any decisions to depend on me. The knock sounded at the door again. "Ten or so," I answered, "though it's hard to be sure."

"A scouting party then," Mikael commented thoughtfully.

If Faas and Tabitha showed up, we'd almost be evenly matched. Of course, having Alaric and Sophie on our side helped even the odds. I was yet to see Mikael or Aila fight, but something told me they would be proficient. James would do in a pinch, then there was *me.* I was useless in a fight.

The charm pulsed so rapidly it made my neck twitch. An indignant thought arguing against my uselessness echoed through my mind. The charm didn't view us as useless, and was offended I'd even question it. Alaric caught me as I swayed to the side, thrown off balance by the second presence in my head.

There was a loud thunk on the door, then another,

drawing my attention back to reality. They were going to break it down.

"Fight apparently," Mikael commented.

The charm shared Mikael's attitude. Both would always rather fight than flee. I felt compelled against my will to move toward the door, but Alaric shoved me behind him. Sophie suddenly had two long blades in her hands, and she tossed one to Alaric as she came to stand in front of me by his side.

I finally got to see the long sword that Mikael wore across his back as he drew it. The center of the blade was tarnished, but the sharp edges gleamed in the sunlight cast by the nearby window, belying its age.

James stood wordlessly, not needing a weapon, though in reality neither did Alaric or Sophie. Aila apparently didn't need one either as she stood next to Mikael empty handed, a deadpan expression on her face.

A much heavier thunk sounded and the door burst open. At the same time, the nearby window was shattered by a large rock, echoed by the sound of shattering glass in other areas of the house. Alaric and Sophie turned toward the first of our attackers. I was stunned to realize that I recognized one them, although last time I saw her she'd been missing a foot.

Maya now stood impossibly whole, framed in the doorway with several others standing behind her. More stood outside the now broken window, not entering, but the threat was there.

Maya's dark brown skin had all grown back to cover the burns James had given her, as had her curly deep umber hair. She quirked the corner of her mouth at me. "You're going to have to come with us, Madeline. Aislin would like you unharmed."

I stepped forward to stand between Alaric and Sophie, rather than behind them. Sophie was quivering slightly, and as I neared her I realized it was from rage. Sophie had risked everything to save Maya, and now I was pretty sure she was ready to kill her.

*We will not be taken prisoner*, the charm echoed in my head.

"No we will not," I murmured in reply.

Maya looked at me like I was crazy, and opened her mouth to say something else, but she didn't have time as Sophie launched herself forward and crashed into her, sending them both out into the sunlight.

"Well that makes *that* decision," Mikael quipped, stepping forward to meet the other Vaettir who now entered the doorway.

My vision went blurry as the charm started feeding on the small amount of energy generated by Maya and Sophie, fighting beyond our sight outside.

I had a moment of regret for ruining the peacefulness of the quiet, safe, neighborhood, then the real fighting began. I backed away as my companions met with our opponents. I knew I'd do more harm than good if I tried to fight and got in the way, but the charm's energy sent a shiver of bloodlust through me, something I'd never felt before. It was like it awakened some deep, primal part of my brain. Kill or be killed. The charm wanted to get closer so I could take the lives of our enemies as soon as they were weakened.

Pain hit me, bringing me back to myself as Alaric tossed

aside a man who'd almost made it past him to grab me. Mikael sliced another man nearly in half with his sword, and my pain increased. I doubled over, wracked with nausea, but the feeling was soon wiped away by the charm's excitement. It didn't care about pain, and wouldn't let me care about it either.

I shook my head over and over again, wanting to reach out to someone for help, but everyone was busy fighting for their lives. I watched as Alaric threw the same man he'd tossed before against the wall above the couch. The man thudded onto the couch cushions, then slipped down onto the floor. The entire backside of my body ached for a brief second, then the pain was once again blocked out by the charm.

I stared at his prostrate body, feeling oddly transfixed, then hands wrapped around me from behind, covering my mouth and lifting me off my feet. In all the chaos I had forgotten about the other Vaettir I'd sensed behind and around the house. They'd come in through a back door or window to get the jump on us.

My attacker carried me backward into the hallway, then toward one of the bedrooms at the far end of the house. The charm screamed in my brain, more because it was being taken away from the battle, than because I was being kidnapped, though it wasn't happy about either. The key's will warred to overpower mine. It wanted to free us, but at what cost? Would relinquishing control mean I'd never gain it again?

Internally fighting the key, I weakly thrashed about, dragging my feet across the carpet, but was unable to free myself of my own volition. Whoever held me was massive, and had arms like steel traps. I looked down the empty hallway in despair, screaming against the hand that covered my mouth, then Aila appeared.

She watched thoughtfully as I was pulled into the bedroom. I turned my head briefly to see the wide open window that I'd likely be going through, then I was whipped around and tossed to the ground. I scooted away on the floor as Aila launched her foot into my captor's chest. Other than his size and the way he flailed about to avoid Aila's kick, he looked perfectly normal with his bald, gleaming head and punk-style street clothes.

It was almost comical to watch him fend off the attacks of the lightning-fast, blonde Viking who whipped about like she could walk on air. Her movements were so fast, I almost couldn't follow what was happening. Then the man suddenly stopped defending himself, and Aila stood still a few feet away. In painfully slow motion his body slumped, then fell sideways, narrowly missing the area where I was crouched.

Now that he was on the floor, I could see the little knife sticking out of his neck. Blood welled up around the blade from the artery Aila had perfectly severed.

I looked up at her. "You almost let him take me," I commented, remembering her expression when she'd first come into view.

She sneered. "Mikael would not have forgiven me, now out the window you go."

My eyes widened in surprise. I could still hear fighting in the other room, and both the charm and I wanted to get back to it.

“Are *you* kidnapping me now?” I asked, distracted as I listened to the chaos just a few rooms away.

“I will get you to safety,” she stated. “Mikael will meet us.”

I glanced around the room for a means of escape, not liking how she'd only mentioned Mikael meeting us and not the others. I needed to get back to the outer room to make sure Alaric and Sophie were okay.

Knowing I wasn't likely to get past her to the doorway on physical prowess alone, I decided to stall in hopes that the fighting would end and the others would come to find me. I’d use the key before I’d let her take me.

A dull, throbbing pain, drew my gaze down the large, bald man, with a pool of blood slowly forming underneath him on the beige carpet. Maybe I didn’t need the key after all.

Misinterpreting my thoughts, Aila rolled her eyes. “Quickly,” she demanded.

I reached out to the mostly dead man and released his soul, feeling the usual rush. I drew my hand away like I'd been burned, a little shocked at how easy the process had become, and how little I thought about the fact that I was taking a life, even if he was already dead in the most literal sense of the word.

“Now go,” Aila prompted.

Police sirens wailed outside.

I stood. The sounds of fighting were cut through by a scream of anguish. “That was Sophie,” I breathed, terrified that something had already happened to Alaric if he wasn’t there to protect her. There was no way I was going out that window now.

Aila's eyes narrowed. "Don't even think about it," she warned, moving to block my way.

I shifted my weight from foot to foot, weighing my options. I had a little bit of power now, but I'd only have one shot at using it.

"Sorry," I mumbled, just before forcing the stolen energy in her direction.

It wasn't enough to send her flying, but it did knock her down. She fell on her butt with a surprised *yip,* then I launched myself over her long legs and out into the hall. With her speed I knew she'd only be moments behind me, but luckily I didn't have far to go.

Someone grabbed me as soon as I entered the room, and I realized with a start that it was Alaric. His pale face was dotted crimson with blood, and there were larger splashes on his clothes. "We have to go," he explained quickly. "Aislin's people fled at the sound of sirens, and we should do the same."

"Sophie—" I began, but then my eyes found her. She was hunched over, sobbing with her now-bloody knife held loosely in her hand. James was trying to help her up, but she kept swatting him away. The rest of the room had turned crimson, the work of Mikael's sword and Alaric and Sophie's blades.

I pulled away from Alaric and tried not to focus too hard on the bodies as I grazed my fingers across them, releasing that bit of energy that lingered in the Vaettir, even after death.

"Grab her," Alaric demanded of James as they both looked down at Sophie. He turned and guided me toward the kitchen and the back door as I wiped my bloody fingertips on my pants.

I looked back over my shoulder to see Sophie swat at James again, then Aila pushed him aside and picked Sophie up herself. She threw Sophie over her shoulder in a fireman's carry, ignoring the knife still clutched in Sophie's hand.

I turned to find Mikael already waiting in the kitchen, cleaning the blood off his sword with a dish towel. He stood grinning at us with crimson spatters in his hair and on his clothing.

"This is more fun than I've had in years!" he exclaimed.

"It won't be fun dealing with the human police," Alaric stated, pushing me forward.

The sirens closed in, accompanied by the sound of tires screeching to a halt.

"Shit," Alaric commented, tugging me away from the back door.

"To the tunnels!" Mikael exclaimed, a finger lifted in the air.

Aila shoved her way into the kitchen with Sophie hanging limply over her shoulder, still crying.

A megaphone screeched to life outside and we were flooded with the sound of a man speaking Norwegian.

I crossed my arms to suppress a shiver, looking to Aila. "Tell me he isn't joking and there really are escape tunnels in this place."

She glared at me. "He isn't, and there are."

She passed me to open a door into what I'd assumed was a laundry room, then held the door open and gestured for someone else to go first. Not wanting to be out in the open when the police stormed the building and saw the bodies, I obliged, finding myself in a small room with a washer, dryer, large basin sink, and tattered floral rug covering much of the linoleum floor.

His sword now sheathed, Mikael shooed me off the rug, then lifted the edge of the dusty fabric. He folded the whole thing back, revealing a trap door with its lid glued to the bottom of the carpet. It was quite clever really, as the rug would still cover the door once we escaped . . . *if* we escaped.

The megaphone had silenced and I could hear footsteps and shocked, murmuring voices in the living room. Not waiting for further instruction, I jumped down through the opening, barely catching my hands and feet onto the ladder inside. I made the short journey down, then waited in the near-dark as everyone else hurried down. Mikael came last, pausing on the ladder to shut the trap door quietly above him, leaving us in complete darkness. I heard a lock being slid into place, then lights flickered on.

We now stood in an old root cellar, complete with various jars of food and dusty barrels that might have once held apples or potatoes.

Aila, who'd carried Sophie down the ladder like she weighed nothing, now finally let her down to her feet to stand on her own. Sophie's eyes were red-rimmed and puffy, and her hands were still stained with blood. I wondered if it was Maya's.

"I tried to leave her to come back and help Alaric," she mumbled, "but she came after me. She came after me like I was just another enemy. She would have killed me if the sirens hadn't started. Even after I cut her, she wouldn't stop."

Alaric held a finger up to his lips to silence her as footsteps sounded above us. I cringed when I heard someone walk over the trap door, but they kept on walking normally, not noticing it.

Mikael went to open a door at the far end of the room, then waited for the rest of us to follow.

I hesitated, then put an arm around Sophie and guided her forward. "You know she's the enemy, right?" I whispered as everyone else waited on us. "You can't trust her."

Sophie shook her head. "I still thought she loved me, at least, but she would have killed me."

Not knowing what else to say, I gave Sophie's shoulders a squeeze as we walked through the doorway together. Alaric, James, and Aila followed us, then Mikael entered with an old kerosene lantern in hand. He shut the door behind him, and we were left with only the dull light from the lantern to guide our way.

Mikael took the lead and started forward while the rest of us formed a single file line behind him. What had started out as an extension of the cellar soon turned into a narrow tunnel like in a mineshaft. It had that damp, mineshaft smell too, making breathing unpleasant.

Sophie had walked ahead, directly behind Mikael, then came Aila, followed by Alaric. Their bodies blocked out most of the lantern light, leaving me blind. Luckily Alaric held my hand, guiding me with his superior low-light vision so I wouldn't be running into walls. James walked behind me, cursing to himself as he tried to keep up in the darkness.

"Where are we going?" he asked, out of breath.

"Away from the cops," Alaric replied sarcastically.

"Yeah, but *where*?" James asked, sounding annoyed.

It was a good question. I waited for someone else to answer, but no one did, so eventually I answered, "I don't know."

"How can you not know?" James asked, making me regret saying anything. "Doesn't that little key you wear make you the person in charge?"

I snorted, but Alaric gave my hand a little squeeze before I said anything. I was *so* not in charge. Mikael may have knelt before me, but we all knew who was calling the shots on this little adventure. Well, everyone but James apparently.

Some of us may have been more blind than others, but we were all being led by the mischievous Viking in front of us.

# 13

THREE DAYS LATER.

We walked for over an hour before we finally reached the tunnel's end. The sunlight streaming in through the small, cave-like opening was a welcome relief, as Mikael's lantern had begun to dim twenty minutes prior.

We climbed out one by one into a wooded area to find Faas and Tabitha waiting for us.

Faas crossed his well-muscled arms as he looked each of us up and down. "We came to meet you and saw the police," he explained. "What happened?"

I observed Faas as he spoke. He had similar coloring to Aila, blond and pale, but was a good eight or nine inches shorter than her, putting him at around 5'7". His pin-straight hair was long on top and shaved on the sides, a hairstyle I didn't find terribly becoming, but who was I to judge with the frizzy mess on my head?

Tabitha was taller, with hair so blonde it looked white. Unlike the others, she was more lithe than muscled.

"A scouting party," Mikael explained with a roguish grin.

Faas quirked his lip in reply, then looked at the rest of us one by one. His small smile disappeared when his eyes met mine, deflating my excitement about finally spending some time around another executioner.

Estus had once explained to me that when an executioner was born into a clan where the position was already filled, the child was dumped into the human world to be raised not knowing what they were. He'd said it was a needed precaution, as executioners tended to compete and often ended up killing each other. The remembered words sent a chill through my bones as Faas stared at me.

Tabitha cleared her throat, cutting the tension. "Will we move on with things as planned?"

I turned to Mikael in time to see him nod. "Indeed. Those of you not coming will join the others in hiding. You will come out for *no* reason. I will not have you harmed while I'm away."

Tabitha nodded, as did Faas, though he was still staring at me. I avoided eye contact, too worried about the implications of what Mikael had said to focus on Faas. He'd made it sound like we were going to be *away* for a while. As far as I knew we were just going to a meeting, so why would Faas and Tabitha need to join the others in hiding?

Alaric cast a worried glance at his sister, clearly sharing my concerns. Sophie didn't return the look, and instead stared forward like she was pretending she was somewhere else, maybe somewhere with a non-traitorous Maya.

Tabitha nodded in James' direction. "You'll come with us now."

"*Now*?" I asked, wondering why we would part ways before reaching the meeting place.

"The place we seek is not far," Mikael explained.

Alaric snorted. "You planned on leaving through that tunnel all along, didn't you?"

Mikael accepted a satchel that Tabitha had been carrying, then turned to Alaric. "I did, though I had not planned on leaving in such a dramatic fashion."

"And you couldn't have told us beforehand?" Alaric pressed.

Mikael shrugged.

"You offered Madeline a partnership," Alaric went on. "*This* does not seem like a partnership."

Mikael turned his amber eyes to me. "If Madeline would like to know my plans, she need only ask."

I raised my eyebrows in surprise. "Okay, what are your plans?"

Mikael's lips curved into a mischievous smile. "I will tell you everything after the meeting."

Aila smiled smugly at me.

I sighed. "Let's get this over with."

"I don't want to go with them," James interrupted, referring to Faas and Tabitha.

"You have no choice in the matter," Mikael replied.

"Well if we're partners," I interrupted, "then I have a choice."

Mikael raised an eyebrow at me. "You really want him along?"

I didn't, but I did want to assert myself in the situation before it was too late. "No," I replied, not sure if a small lie would constitute a betrayal that would break my oath, "but he's coming to the meeting anyhow. If Estus or Aislin got a hold of him, they would find out much more information than we want them to know. I feel better with him in my sights."

James seemed unsure of how to react to what I'd said. I *almost* felt bad since I was the only one that made any effort to be nice to him, but I once again reminded myself that he was still James, and I was pretty sure the real James was evil. I had the scars to prove it.

"He can come to the meeting," Mikael agreed.

I narrowed my eyes at him. "What's the catch?"

He lifted a hand to his chest. "Why Madeline, you wound me. You know I cannot betray you."

I let out an irritated breath. "Fine, let's go."

Faas gave me a final rude glare, then turned to Mikael. "We shall await your return, and guard our people while you are away."

Mikael nodded curtly, dismissing Faas, who walked away, followed by Tabitha.

He gestured to a narrow path through the looming, snow-speckled trees. "Ladies first."

It seemed silly for me to lead the way since I had no idea where we were going, but I was tired of standing in the cold so I obliged. The leather wrapped boots had thin enough soles that I was grateful for the loamy, well-cushioned soil beneath my feet.

The further I walked down the well-worn path, further from the scene of the crime, the more at ease I felt. Still, we were rather conspicuous walking through the woods together when most of us were covered in blood. If any humans saw us, they would likely call the police, but the woods were fortunately silent and empty. If I never had another close call with the cops, it would be too soon.

As the path widened, Alaric and James caught up to walk on either side of me, while the other three walked behind. I could hear a hushed conversation between Aila and Sophie, but they were far enough back that I couldn't make out the words. I could tell they weren't angry though, which was a surprise coming from either of them.

James cleared his throat, glancing at me. "Thanks for what you did back there."

I shrugged, not wanting to say that I hadn't really done it for him. "Sure."

"You did well, Maddy," Alaric commented quietly. "If you give him an inch, he will leave you with nothing."

"Are you speaking from your own experiences?" I asked.

He kept his gaze on the woods ahead of us as he answered, "I'm speaking what I know. We cannot rely on his oath to you alone. He will find a way around it."

"Well then perhaps we shouldn't be blindly walking into this *meeting* with him," I whispered.

Alaric shrugged. "I believe this *meeting* is only a means to take us somewhere far away, judging by the way his people spoke. If we're to carry out *your* plan, we must find a way to not go through with his. We will accomplish nothing if you are not near the bloodshed, correct?"

"Up close and personal," I confirmed, feeling a little sick at the idea.

"Remind me again what you will do once we get you there?" he asked, knowing full well I had no real explanation for him.

"I'm still not sure," I replied hesitantly, not really

wanting to discuss things around James, memory or no. "The Norn showed me pictures and emotions. I'm basing my plan more off a feeling than anything else."

Alaric pulled me close to him as we walked. "You know, Madeline, that is not at all comforting."

"It wasn't meant to be."

He gave me a squeeze and kissed my temple. "My offer to run away together still stands."

I smirked. "I'm pretty sure Mikael would view that as a betrayal, and I'd really like to avoid being *claimed by the earth*."

He laughed. "Pesky blood oaths, ruining all our fun."

I laughed in return, but it was cut short as the others increased their pace to catch up with us.

"We are nearing the meeting place," Mikael announced, moving past James to take the lead.

"I was expecting somewhere farther," I commented, feeling apprehensive and at the same time, a little excited.

Mikael looked over his shoulder and winked at me. "The location of my tunnel exit was not mere happenstance."

"Of course it wasn't," I sighed. "Will you at least tell us with whom we're meeting now?"

He stepped into a small clearing. "Nope."

The clearing didn't seem as touched by winter as the rest of the surrounding earth, and even boasted a few small purple flowers.

Mikael knelt to inspect the ground, then stood, took a few steps, and knelt again. "Madeline," he said, motioning for me to join him.

I only hesitated for a moment before moving to stand beside his crouched form.

"Lie here," he instructed, moving his hand across the grass to map out a specific area.

I crossed my arms. "Why?"

He looked up and rolled his eyes at me. "We're going to another Salr. This is the entrance."

I took a step back in surprise, making him sigh.

"What *now*?" he asked, clearly irritated.

I shook my head. "Nothing, just surprised you actually answered one of my questions."

He sighed again, then stood. "Lie down, *please*."

I did as he asked. The grass was cushy and comfortable, but there was no magic or extra energy that I could sense. If this was another Salr, it was very well hidden.

Mikael instructed the others one by one to lie in designated areas, then finally lowered himself to the ground. He was closer to me than I would have liked, but I didn't complain as the whole ordeal had already taken up a good twenty minutes, and I was ready to get it over with.

For a few minutes nothing happened, then the ground began to tremble. It took every ounce of my self restraint to not move as the soil shifted below us until we began sinking. Soon we were encased in the earth. I had a few horrifying seconds of thinking I might be buried alive, then we came out of a dirt wall, standing upright. I looked back at the wall, astonished to see it showed no sign of our entrance, then looked down at my miraculously clean clothing.

"I will *never* get used to Salr entrances," I commented,

glancing around at my companions. The only one who seemed as stunned as me was James.

"How did you enter the Salr in your homeland?" Mikael questioned.

"Vines," I replied, moving to stand beside Alaric and Sophie.

The room we were in was cellar-like, and reminded me far too much of the entrance to where the charm had been held.

Aila waited for us to fall in line behind Mikael before she brought up the rear. We left the cellar room through a short wooden doorway, then continued along a narrow passageway. Our surroundings slowly began to look more like the other Salr with stone ceilings, walls, and floors, only these stones were red and brown, as opposed to gray.

"Are we visiting another clan?" I asked curiously, hoping Mikael would continue to be forthcoming with answers.

He chuckled. "Of a sort. You'll see soon enough."

This Salr seemed smaller and less complex than the others. The halls of both Estus' and Mikael's Salr were like mazes, with countless twists and turns that were easy to get lost in. This one, though it had a few branches, had one long, straight hallway down the middle. I peeked around Mikael's broad shoulders to see a door at the very end of the hall. My heart jumped a bit when the door swung inward, but nobody emerged.

I gulped. "I take it that's where we're going."

"How very astute of you," Aila commented from the end of the line.

"You know what, Aila?" I said, finally getting irritated with her bad attitude. "*Shove it.*"

"Shove what?" she asked, truly perplexed and not at all offended.

"Nothing," I grumbled.

We reached the ominous door. Any other insults I might have tossed out froze on my tongue as I followed Mikael through the door and into a large room.

"Well I'll be damned," Alaric quietly mused, coming to stand beside me.

"I think we already are," Sophie replied, sounding awestricken.

I was fairly awestricken myself. In front of us stood seven Norns, all towering over even Mikael and Aila. They all looked similar to the Norn who'd guarded the charm, and all appeared female, but with slight variations. Some of their horns were deer-like, two had twisted goat horns, and one had horns resembling the long-horned cattle I'd only ever seen in pictures.

The Norns stood with no emotions playing across their angular, green-tinted faces. They all wore shapeless brown robes that made me wonder about the impossibly thin, tall bodies underneath. Hooved feet could be seen at the edge of some of the robes, some looking like goat hooves and some looking more like the hooves of a horse. They all clasped what passed for hands in front of them. A couple resembled the talons of a hawk, and the rest looked like paws of lions or tigers. The only thing all their hands had in common were razor-sharp, long claws.

"You could have given us some sort of warning," I said to Mikael in a strained voice.

Mikael shrugged. "I feared you would not want to come."

While I understood why he might assume that, I still would have come had I known what was in store. I had so many questions I would have liked to ask the Norn before she died, and now I was presented with seven more. If they truly were the weavers of fate, perhaps they could help.

Mikael began speaking loudly in Old Norsk, addressing each of the Norns in turn. In reply they each bowed their antlered heads.

"Old friends?" I questioned under my breath.

"Something like that," Mikael replied.

"Why is that one staring at you?" James asked over my shoulder.

I looked across the row of Norns to find that one was in fact staring at me. The cow-horned Norn tilted her head in thought, blinking large, almond shaped eyes at me. While Mikael walked forward to continue speaking to one of the other Norns in line, the one who'd been watching me held out a feline paw large enough to cover my entire face, with claws as long as my fingers.

I glanced at Alaric, then asked through clenched teeth, "What do I do?"

His brow furrowed with worry, he replied, "I wouldn't keep her waiting."

I looked back to the Norn. I'd just been wishing I could "speak" with one of them, but the long claws and sharp horns suddenly looked daunting.

She bobbed her paw slightly in the air, impatient for me to obey her request. I forced myself forward, step by step until I was only about a foot away from her. The

Norn closed that final gap herself, leaving me to either crane my neck awkwardly upward, or stare at her sternum. Before I could make a choice, she placed her heavy paw on my shoulder, and images began to play through my mind.

She showed me the place where the charm had been held, with the giant tree in the center and burial mounds surrounding it. Then she showed me an image of the Norn who'd watched over that place. The images were never quite still, and played more like glitchy videos in my mind.

I focused on the images and realized she was asking me what had happened there. I did my best to replay some of the scenes in my mind, unsure if the Norn would be able to see them like I could see hers.

She bowed her head as I pictured the Norn in my memory, ripping out her own heart and handing it to me. The Norn in front of me turned sad eyes to look down into mine, then placed her free paw on my chest so she could tap the charm beneath my shirt with one black claw.

I thought of the images the last Norn had shown me, but my memory had blurred them enough that they were difficult to convey. It was much more simple to picture things I had seen with my own eyes. The Norn tapped the charm again, not understanding.

Before I could think of a better way to convey what the Norn wanted to know, someone grabbed my arm and began pulling me away from the her. I lost contact with the Norn's paw, and turned to find that it was Alaric pulling me while Sophie waited by the door with a scared look on her face. What had happened while I was transfixed by the Norn?

I pulled against Alaric, scanning the room for the

source of his fear, only to find Mikael smiling and looking perfectly calm next to the Norn he'd been speaking with.

"They're going to send us away," Alaric explained before tugging at my arm more forcefully, throwing me forward.

"He doesn't want to take us to another place, he wants to take us to another *time*," he continued, finally motivating me to run.

Sophie turned in the doorway as we reached her, and I could see James already waiting further down the hall. There was no sign of Aila. Had I lost time while "speaking" with the Norn? My brain felt like it was filled with cotton.

We all ran, though I still didn't fully understand what was happening. Yet something was wrong. Mikael wasn't coming after us. I learned why as my feet suddenly went out from under me, I hit the ground *hard*, and Alaric landed beside me. I tried to crawl forward, but my limbs wouldn't budge.

Sophie looked back at us in horror, and began to run back toward us, then abruptly disappeared from sight, as did the floor beneath us and the walls around us. I closed my eyes tight in fear, grateful that Alaric's hand was still on my arm, though he seemed just as frozen as I was. We endured several moments where it felt like we were floating in space, then everything stopped. I felt rough grass beneath my palms, tickling my face.

I took a deep breath and opened my eyes. We were in an expansive yellow field, and I could hear the ocean nearby. A wild wind tickled strands of hair away from my face. Alaric's hand squeezed my arm. He got to his knees, pulling me along with him, only I felt so suddenly dizzy that I immediately pulled myself back to the ground.

"Where are we?" I groaned, fighting the urge to vomit from motion sickness.

"We are still in Norway," Mikael said from somewhere behind us.

"And what year is it?" Alaric asked coldly.

Mikael chuckled. His voice was nearer when he said, "It is the year 820."

I curled up into a ball on the grass, not wanting to open my eyes again. "That's not possible."

"The Norns are the keepers of time," Mikael replied happily. "With them, anything is possible."

I finally opened my eyes to see Alaric shake his head. "How did you make them do it?"

Mikael came over and crouched beside me, then looked down at me curiously. "Dizzy?" he asked.

I cringed and nodded. It felt like I had the world's worst hangover. "Why aren't you two sick?"

Mikael smiled down at me warmly. "It affected you more because you're pregnant."

# 14

I sat up so quickly my vision went black, and I had to huddle in a little ball again until I could refocus. "Come again?" I asked weakly, still on the ground.

"How could you possibly know that?" Alaric asked incredulously.

I opened my eyes to see Mikael shrug. "One of the Norns told me. I take it this was unplanned?"

I felt like I was going to faint. We were allegedly in the year 820, and I was . . . pregnant? Mikael had to be lying. He was descended from the god of deception for crying out loud.

Alaric stood and offered me a hand up. Not sure if I was ready to stand, I took the hand anyway. I looked to Mikael, unable to summon the glare I wanted to give him, but he inclined his head like he knew what I was thinking.

"I will give you two a moment," he stated, then moved away toward the edge of a long cliff, the ocean thundering distantly below.

Oh crap, we were on a *cliff*, not down on solid, safe ground. Suddenly the wind made sense. Another wave of dizziness passed over me. We weren't anywhere near the edge, but I'm not great with heights at the best of times, and this definitely wasn't the best of times. I leaned against Alaric, not sure what to say.

"We were careful," he stated, focusing on the more mundane problem, rather than what Mikael had done to us.

I nodded. "He has to be lying."

Alaric shook his head. "That would be a direct betrayal, and would break his oath. If he'd told *me* that you were pregnant, he could have lied, but he told you directly."

I shook my head, unable to digest the idea of a living creature forming inside me with everything else going on. "I really can't focus on the magnitude of both of these situations at once, so I'm just going to pick the more pressing issue. How the hell is time travel possible? I mean, I know the Norns have a lot of magic, but this is ridiculous."

He sighed. I could tell he wanted to discuss the *other* situation, but still he answered, "The Norns are meant to weave the fates we choose ourselves, but they are capable of giving things a . . . shove from time to time."

"The fates we *choose*?" I asked, wondering at his word choice.

Alaric smiled slightly with a faraway look in his eyes. "Fate might guide us," he explained, "but there is always a choice."

I shook my head, not sure if I even believed in fate at all. "If the Norns can *shove* fate, then why aren't they ruling the world?"

Alaric wrapped his arms around me and shrugged. "They aren't motivated by power like the rest of us. Plus, for *shoves* this grand, they'd have to all agree. Rarely do so many of them work together."

"So whatever Mikael wants here is important," I deduced, "or else the Norns would never have helped."

Alaric sighed and kissed the top of my head. "Or else they owed him a very big favor."

I buried my face in his chest. "I like the first option better."

"About the pregnancy," he began hesitantly.

I looked up at him, trying my best to keep the tears building up in my eyes from falling. "Can we please just worry about getting back to our own time for now?"

He gave me a soft smile. "That's probably wise."

We both turned to where Mikael stood near the edge of the cliff, looking quite picturesque with his warrior's garb, and long auburn hair whipping about in the wind.

Alaric pulled away from me, then took my hand before walking in Mikael's direction. I went reluctantly, not wanting to go anywhere near the cliffside. We stopped a few steps behind him, close enough to see the dark ocean several hundred feet below. The angry waves whipped about like a storm was coming, and sure enough, one was. The sky further out in the ocean was gloomy and ominous. I pulled my hand free of Alaric's to wrap my arms around myself against the cold wind, but it did little good.

"Why are we here, Mikael?" Alaric asked.

Mikael turned to us with a secretive smile. "To help Madeline, of course."

I glared at him, because it was better than looking over

the edge of the cliff. "If you really want to help me, you'll tell me what the hell is going on."

Mikael inclined his head in assent. "We're here to find one of the key's previous owners."

My eyes widened as I touched the key at my throat. It had been so quiet I'd almost forgotten it was there. "Why would we want to do that?"

Mikael chucked. "Because she's the only one to have used it to its full potential, and lived to tell the tale, at least for a time."

My mouth went dry. No one had ever said anything about the charm killing me. As far as I knew, it wanted me to use it, and would work to stay in my possession until I could, but what then? I honestly hadn't thought that far ahead. If I was actually pregnant, I wasn't sure I could go through with any of it. I also wasn't sure I had a choice.

Not waiting for my reply, Mikael turned and walked back toward where we had originally appeared. Alaric and I trotted to catch up, and I was grateful to find that my stomach did not protest the extra movement. Mikael led us past that spot, then onward.

We reached the first of many sparse trees populating the meadow as we walked, but as they were short with little foliage, they provided no respite from the wind. The storm on the horizon was gaining on us too, and the wimpy trees would offer little shelter.

"Why did Sophie and James get left behind?" I asked, my voice breaking through the soft howls of the wind. "And what about Aila?"

Alaric glanced at me, then his gaze joined mine on Mikael's back.

"James was always going to be left behind," Mikael replied, glancing over his shoulder at us. "And Aila departed before the spell began to return to my people. Sophie simply ran too far and ended up outside the boundary of the spell."

I glared at his back as he turned. "You said that James could come. You *lied*."

Mikael laughed. "I said he could come to the meeting, and he did. I made no promises after that. The Norns will watch over him until we return."

I bit my lip in irritation. I needed to improve my abilities at skirting around the truth if I was ever going to compete with Mikael.

"What about Aila?" I pressed. "Why did she leave? One would think you would have brought *her*."

"Someone must advise the troops while I'm away," he said simply.

I shook my head, irritated by his vague answers.

"So this person we're looking for," I began, hoping that a new angle would actually garner some useful information, "did you know her, you know, back in this time?"

"She was my wife," he replied

I stopped walking. "*Wife*?" I asked, really wishing I could see Mikael's expression. "You don't really seem like the love and marriage type."

Mikael chuckled, but kept walking, forcing Alaric and I to catch up. "You've got me there. Marriage in these times was more of a contractual obligation between two families, and this was a time when our people still lived amongst humans. We did our best to blend in."

"So the woman we're looking for is human?" I pressed, confused.

"No she is Vaettir, but to others it would have been strange if two youths from well-off families remained unwed."

"Did you have children?" I asked, then instantly regretted it. It was *so* not my business, and I really didn't want to think about the idea of children at that moment.

"Yes," he replied still not giving me any hint on how he was feeling.

His lack of emotion led me to suspect I'd hit a nerve. I had decided to just shut up when Alaric asked, "What happened to them?"

Mikael stopped walking, but his back remained turned. For a moment I thought he wouldn't answer, then with a tired sigh he said, "In this current time they are young men off to war. In our time, they have been ash for hundreds of years."

We were all silent then. Thunder rumbled behind us, pressing that we would soon be highly uncomfortable if we didn't find shelter.

We all kept walking. My hands absentmindedly went to my belly. With my particular . . . gifts, I'd kind of written off the idea of ever having kids. Wouldn't want to accidentally kill them.

I shivered. That could still be an issue.

The scent of distant woodsmoke filled my nose, and my shoulders relaxed. I'd never realized what a comforting scent smoke could be until that moment, when we were so far from anything we knew. The smoke smelled like civilization, and the comfort of others living with the same problems anyone else might face. In this case the *others* were likely fierce Vikings that would rather pillage the next town over than sit down for a nice cup of tea, but I'd take my comforts where I could find them.

We continued on as a path became clear in the grass. It seemed like Mikael knew exactly where we were going, even after all of the time that had passed since he'd last been there. I wondered if he would try to see his children while we were here, which led me to wonder how we were going to get back to our own era when the time came. I knew Mikael had to have a plan, but I really would have liked a preview.

I clenched my jaw, pushing uncomfortable thoughts about time travel out of my head, turning them back to Mikael. If he was feeling nostalgic or sad about his kids, I couldn't tell. He seemed better at shutting out his emotions than most, and I had a feeling he'd lived that way for quite some time, focusing on plotting and intrigue instead. It would have been interesting to meet him as a young, unjaded man. That particular thought led me to a question.

"We're not going to run into your past self, are we?"

Mikael slowed his steps to walk on my side opposite Alaric. "Past me has long since fled this place. Now correct me if I'm wrong, but you don't seem angry that I brought you here."

"*I'm* angry," Alaric interrupted.

I shrugged. "I don't appreciate the way you went about it, but I wouldn't mind speaking with someone who fought the charm and won."

Mikael smiled bitterly and looked ahead. "I said she lived, for a time, I didn't say she *won*."

With that portentous tidbit, an odd thought dawned on me. "Back when we first came to your Salr, the charm knew your name. When it spoke through me, it was as if it *knew* you."

Mikael glared at me. It was the first time I'd seen any real anger in his expression. "That was not the only time I was forced to kneel before the *Lykill*."

I veered away from that expression as we walked, putting me closer to Alaric. "If you hate the charm so much, why are you involving yourself in any of this?"

His mood changed so suddenly it was a little unnerving. "We're here because I want to beat it. I want to use it for my own advancement, and then I want to show it that it has no power over me."

Alaric snorted. "So this is all about your centuries long vendetta against an object?"

Mikael's expression turned sour. "And how much of this is about your centuries long vendetta against me?"

"If it weren't for Maddy," Alaric began calmly, "I would have already killed you."

"You would have tried," Mikael snarled.

I was beginning to feel overwhelmed with both men's emotions so close to the surface, a mixture of pride, aggression, and underneath that, regret.

"You guys are making me dizzy," I complained. "Please shove that anger back below the surface where you usually keep it and Mikael, tell me more about your wife."

Mikael clenched his jaw, but did as I asked. "Erykah was —*is* a telepath. The charm used her in more subtle ways, gleaning information from the minds of others to use for its own devices."

"What made her decide to get rid of it?" I asked, since I'd considered just ditching the thing countless times, but for some reason, had never followed through.

Mikael looked at me like I was being silly. "Deciding to get rid of it is one thing, actually doing it is quite another."

I scrunched my face in confusion, then immediately stumbled over a rock. Alaric caught me before I could fall. "I don't follow," I replied, righting myself.

"Have you tried?" he asked.

I shook my head and began walking again. "I've thought about it, but I don't want to risk it falling into the wrong hands."

"Is that really the reason?" he pressed.

The smell of woodsmoke was growing nearer, and I really wanted him to get to his point before we reached where we were going.

"Of course it is," I replied without really thinking about it.

"Try taking it off and dropping it to the ground," he advised.

I gave him a *you wish* look. "Why, so you can take it?"

He raised an eyebrow at me. "Now why would I take it, when I've set into action this elaborate plan to help you learn how to control it?"

I bit my lip. Hadn't he already proven that he wasn't trying to take it, and hadn't he sworn an oath that prohibited him from betraying me?

"The reality is that you *can't* take it off," he explained. "It has chosen you, and any time you think of taking it off, you'll find an excuse not to."

"Try it," Alaric prompted.

I stopped walking and reached a shaky hand up to my throat. Mikael and Alaric both stopped a few steps ahead and turned to face me.

I closed my eyes and touched the cool metal with my fingertips, but all I could think about was that if I took it off, it might get lost in the grass, and then where would we be?

I forced my fingers to close around it, and tried to make myself tug down on it to undo the leather cord . . . but if I broke the cord, how would I re-affix it? Wasn't this just a test anyway? There was no need to undo the cord when I would just put it back on. I didn't need to *prove* I could do it.

I looked back up at the men in front of me. "I don't think I can do it," I breathed.

Alaric looked momentarily stunned, then he walked up to me and grabbed the charm at my neck. As soon as his fingers made contact with the metal, a burst of energy emanated from me, throwing him off his feet to land in a heap where he'd started, and knocking me down onto my butt.

Alaric sat up and looked at me from across the expanse between us. "Oh *fuck*."

I blinked at him. "You can say that again." I turned my frightened eyes up to Mikael. "How did she do it? How was your wife able to get rid of it?"

Mikael offered me a hand up as Alaric rose on his own. "I believe it would be better for Erykah to explain. The village is not far."

I nodded shakily and removed my hand from Mikael's. I

had the urge to reach my fingers up to touch the charm, but I resisted. *That,* at least, I was able to do.

The first few raindrops from the storm pattered down around us. With a nervous look behind us, Mikael urged me ahead of him down the path. Alaric was soon at my side, and we continued onward with a storm licking at our heels, both literally and metaphorically.

## 15

We were soaked by the time we reached the village, and I was again awestricken by our situation. Many of the village structures were small, with wooden walls showing only on one or two sides. The other sides were covered by the green, loamy earth encasing the roofs, making it seem like the buildings had grown out of the ground like something straight from a fairytale. The layout of the buildings was circular, with the smaller buildings facing each other in a semi-arc.

While the small homes were enchanting in their own, rustic way, what really caught my attention was the longhouse. I'd taken enough history classes in college to know the longhouse was the main habitation in many ancient Scandinavian villages, and it definitely appeared to be the case in this village, judging by the size of the oblong structure. Animal skins covered the door of the wooden building, shielding whoever might be inside from the rain and wind.

The three of us stood together outside the village, but no one moved forward. I looked to Mikael, wondering what the hold up was. At first I thought it was just from the rain, since it had soaked his dusky red hair to drip onto his face and clothing, but then I realized his eyes held unshed tears. It completely caught me off guard, since his emotions were still shielded from me.

"Mikael?" I questioned softly.

He shook himself as if coming out of a dream. He laughed, but it came out more like a cough. "I had not considered what it might feel like to come back here," he admitted.

I glanced at Alaric, who watched Mikael suspiciously.

"Um," I began, not really sure what to say. "If you need a moment . . . " I trailed off.

I sincerely hoped he didn't *need a moment*, because my teeth were chattering so furiously I thought they might crack.

"Every extra moment spent in the past is a moment wasted," he announced, though the quiver in his voice betrayed the happy-go-lucky attitude he was trying to project.

I looked to Alaric again, who shook his head and looked back to the small village. His dark, loose hair was plastered to his back, but he of course still looked drool-worthy, if a little bedraggled. I really hoped the villagers didn't have mirrors, because I did *not* want to see what I looked like after our soggy, uncomfortable journey. If Alaric looked bedraggled, I surely looked something akin to a drowned rat.

Mikael finally walked forward without another word.

He approached the longhouse like he owned the place, leaving his previous hesitation behind as if it had never existed. We followed like good little minions.

Reaching the structure, Mikael whipped aside the pelts covering the entrance, then went inside. Alaric held the skins aside for me to enter ahead of him.

Mikael waited to my left. I moved to stand at his shoulder, the warmth and soft murmur of conversation a welcome relief. Several small fires lined the center of the building, filtering smoke up through narrow holes in the roof. Rain dripped in through the holes, falling in a sizzling cacophony on the flames.

Four women near the entrance looked up at us. They had all been doing needlework, aided by the light emanating from little pots of oil with cotton wicks. The women's copper needles paused mid-motion as they looked us up and down, then one stood and gave Mikael a toothy grin.

The girl couldn't have been more than sixteen, with dark, curly hair held back in a mess of braids and leather clasps. She began speaking quickly in Old Norsk as she stepped closer to Mikael. Judging by her tone she was excited to see him, but the words were all beyond me.

He gave the girl a sad smile, then spoke back to her. I recognized the name Erykah, and realized he was asking the girl where his wife was. I was suddenly nervous to meet her, especially since I didn't know what terms she and Mikael were on in the current time.

While Mikael spoke to the girl, the other women retreated further into the building, then returned to wrap animal pelts around mine and Alaric's shoulders.

I liked being wrapped in the pelt even less than I liked wearing leather, but not wanting to insult anyone, I accepted the musty skin gratefully.

Finally Mikael and the girl finished speaking, and she led us back out into the rain to slog through the mud. Though the animal pelt deflected some of the moisture from my shoulders, water still dripped steadily down my face.

"Are they all Vaettir?" I whispered to Alaric as we followed Mikael and the girl to one of the smaller structures.

"Can't you tell?" he asked back at a regular volume.

Feeling silly for whispering considering those in the village likely wouldn't understand us, I considered his answer. Come to think of it, I *could* feel it. It wasn't like I could just look at someone and tell whether or not they were human, but there was a distinct energy in the air that I'd become used to since I was first taken to Estus' Salr. Most, if not all who dwelled in the village were Vaettir.

"Do you understand what they're saying?" I questioned.

Alaric nodded. "Nothing terribly interesting yet. The girl believes Mikael has returned from a long journey, which I suppose in a way, he has."

We reached the small building, and Mikael knocked on a door of thin logs, the lightweight wood held together by intricately woven twine. There was a faint answer from within, then Mikael opened the door.

The girl left us, examining Alaric curiously as she walked by. Her eyes only met mine briefly, then she looked away and hurried back to the longhouse.

Not taking time to ponder the girl's strange reaction, I

walked behind Alaric as he entered the building behind Mikael.

I wrinkled my nose at the smell. I had expected another home-like environment, but the building was actually a cowshed. The cows inside were brown and fluffy, much smaller than the cows I was used to seeing. They were separated from each other by wooden bars, forming little pens. I covered my nose with my hand, but it was still hard to breathe.

A woman who had been feeding the cows turned toward us as she wiped her hands on the dark brown pinafore covering her lighter brown dress. She had yellow blonde hair, twisted in a messy braid falling all the way to her narrow waist. Large, aqua-blue eyes dominated a narrow, angular face.

At first she only saw me and Alaric and she looked confused, then she turned around fully and saw Mikael, standing almost meekly off to one side. At the sight of him she said something blandly in their language.

Mikael took a deep breath then began speaking rapidly back to her. Eventually both their voices raised to an uncomfortable volume.

"Translation, please?" I whispered to Alaric as we backed ourselves into a corner.

One of the cows reached out and nibbled at my damp sleeve as I waited for Alaric to answer me. He was quiet for a moment, listening to what was being said.

Finally he looked to me and answered, "Apparently we've arrived in a time where they have already parted ways. Erykah didn't expect him to return, and is quite upset that he did."

I opened my mouth into an *oh* of understanding. "I can't say I blame her for feeling that way," I whispered.

The cow nipped at my sleeve again. I shifted one hand to hold onto my pelt, then reached back with the other to pet it. Erykah eyed me sharply and I quickly retracted my hand from the animal's fuzzy forehead.

Erykah spoke rapidly as she turned away from Mikael to approach me. I tried to back away, but was blocked by the cow pen. Soon enough she had reached me. She lifted her hand toward my throat and I leaned away, scared despite the fact that she was much smaller than me.

She tsked and snapped her fingers at me until I straightened, then she gently pulled the charm free of my shirt. She tsked again, looking at the little key in disgust before letting it fall back against me.

She spoke to me again and I shook my head, not understanding.

"She asks if the key speaks to you," Mikael explained as he approached, looking sullen.

I bit my lip, unsure of how to answer. It didn't *speak* to me per se, but it did occasionally share its emotions, which sometimes translated clearly enough that I could tell what it was *thinking*.

"It doesn't use words," I explained, considering how I might convey what the charm's strange form of communication was like, "but I can tell what it wants, and when it's excited about something."

Alaric translated for me, and Erykah nodded, then said something else.

"She says if you can *hear* it, then you might be able to gain control over it, at least for a time," Mikael translated.

"Erykah was able to do so because she's a telepath, I believe you can do so because you're an empath."

The charm was silent against my skin. If I didn't know better, I would have guessed its sentient nature had left it, but I did know better. Life was never that easy.

Erykah said something else, and Mikael rolled his eyes. "She says she will help you, for a price."

I looked down at the fierce little woman in front of me, then thought of the life brewing in my belly, and what might happen to me and . . . it, should I refuse.

"Honestly, at this point. I'm willing to do just about anything." I looked to Alaric, remembering how I'd almost been forced to sacrifice him. "Within reason," I added.

Rather than translating everything I'd just said, Alaric nodded to Erykah. She nodded in reply, then said something else, ending with a sneer.

Mikael sighed wearily. "She says first there will be a welcome feast for me . . . though I deserve to eat with the cows."

I smiled, liking Erykah more and more. She quickly surveyed the rest of the cow pens, then led us back out into the rain.

I inhaled the clean air gratefully as Mikael shut the small wooden door behind us. Erykah led the way back to the longhouse amidst the scent of smoke. We all hurried inside out of the rain.

Erykah ventured away from us, while Alaric, Mikael, and I waited near the door, watching as two pairs of men hoisted cookpots over the fires. Mikael was drawn away, leaving Alaric and I to stand in the corner observing the scene.

Soon enough, savory smells filled the longhouse.

"This is *so* weird," I muttered, leaning against Alaric's damp shoulder. I glanced at him. "Well, I guess it probably isn't so weird for *you*."

He snorted. "I'm not *that* old, Madeline."

I laughed, feeling some of my tension easing away, then watched as several of the younger women carried stacks of wooden bowls toward the cookpots, then began filling them. One woman fetched a tray of hard little dinner rolls with dark brown outer crusts, which she began placing on top of each filled bowl.

Those already waiting near the fires seated themselves on long wooden benches, as more men and women filtered in from the rain. There were no tables that I could see, and those who already had bowls of food just held them in their laps.

One of the girls approached and handed me a serving of food, then took the slowly drying pelt from me. I looked down into the bowl to find several chunks of stringy meat, a few scrawny carrots, and one little loaf of bread that was too hard to soak up the thick brown gravy it rested in.

I gave Alaric a worried look. As a long-time vegetarian, the meal wasn't at all appealing to me, but my stomach was growling and there didn't seem to be any other options.

Alaric shrugged apologetically as the girl returned to hand him a bowl. Unlike me, he had no qualms with eating meat, and neither did Mikael judging by the way he began shoveling food into his mouth once he received his own bowl. He lounged on one of the benches next to the girl with the toothy grin, surrounded by several other teenagers speaking rapidly, begging him for stories of his adventures by the look of it.

Alaric nodded toward one of the less populated benches. Agreeing with the sentiment of relative solitude, I led the way over to the bench where we both seated ourselves.

Alaric began eating, then paused. "You could at least eat the bread."

I looked down at the hard little boulder in distaste. "It's all covered in the gravy."

"You don't know when the next meal will come along," he reminded me, "and you're eating for two now."

My pulse quickened at the thought. "So, are we talking about that now?"

"We have to talk about it sometime."

I looked down at the bread again. Before I could think too much about it, I snatched it up and took a bite. It was actually softer than it looked, but still took a bit of work to chew.

I swallowed, then looked to Alaric again. "Do you have any other children?"

He dropped his hunk of bread back into his bowl in surprise, then turned astonished eyes to me. "Why on earth would you think that?"

My face flushed. "I just thought, well, you've been alive a long time . . . "

He sighed and placed his bowl in his lap. "No, Madeline, I do not have any children. In fact, I was pretty sure by this point that I *couldn't* have children."

I took another bite of bread, feeling immensely relieved, and not really understanding why. "Is it common among the Vaettir?" I asked. "The not being able to have children?"

Alaric nodded. "Once bloodlines become muddled enough, it becomes easier, but if two from strong, yet opposing bloodlines try to conceive, the chances are very low. The different *tendencies* of each individual come from very different genetics, so a water spirit like Sivi would have little chance of conceiving a child from someone aligned with fire and heat, like James."

The thought of James and Sivi having a child made me shiver. I imagined Sivi's pointed teeth and translucent hair on James body, then quickly brushed the eerie thought away. Any child from those two would be an evil little bundle of doom.

"I've thought from the beginning that perhaps we are so drawn to each other because of our lineages," Alaric continued. "It would make sense that such a connection would make it easier to conceive."

"Yeah, death and war mix well, but that doesn't explain what we're going to *do*."

Alaric looked down at my stomach where this new creature allegedly dwelled. "Well, I'd say we're going to have a baby."

I raised an eyebrow at him. "We're going to have a baby, in the middle of a war, a war that we're at the center of, while I contend with a sentient key with a strong personality?"

"They're not the best of circumstances, but this is all happening whether we think it's rational or not."

I felt nervous again, because there was one more question I needed to ask. Okay, there were a million, but one was currently standing out above the others.

I swallowed the lump in my throat. "Do you want to get rid of it?"

Alaric dropped his bread again, and looked just as shocked as the first time. "Do *you*?"

Did I? It was a good question. The real question was, *could* I?

"I don't know what I *want* to do," I sighed, "but I don't think I could go through with anything that would snuff out a life inside of me. I have a hard enough time snuffing out the lives of others."

Alaric's shoulders slumped in relief. The fact that he was relieved made me feel infinitely more positive about the situation, even if the looming doubt that I'd even live through the entire pregnancy still nagged at me.

Someone plopped down on my other side. I turned to see Mikael, swilling something that smelled alcoholic out of an ornate silver cup.

He lowered the cup from his lips and smiled at me. "You've traveled through time for perhaps the only time in your life, and you two are sitting over here looking like someone ran over your cat." He winked at Alaric. "Pun intended."

"You're drunk," I accused.

He grinned. "No, dear Madeline, I'm just getting started. This might be the last time I see any of my kin alive, and I intend to make the most of it."

The thought was sobering. I was suddenly glad I had no kin to lose, at least not that I knew of. I looked around the room with a new perspective, realizing the happy, somewhat drunk people were all long since dead. Yet they somehow existed here in this time. The thought made me dizzy, and I suddenly felt like I might throw up.

I held up a finger, about to explain my situation to Alaric, but sensing I was running out of time, I shoved my bowl at him, stood, and hurried toward the door.

The chilly night air was like a slap in the face as I pushed the animal skins aside, but it was a welcome one. I fell to all fours and vomited what little food I'd eaten. As my queasiness subsided, I looked up at the sky, not quite ready to stand. The storm had moved away, leaving just a few clouds to partially obscure the moon. I felt a hand on my shoulder and turned, thinking it was Alaric. Instead of his welcome face, I got Erykah, looking stern and serious in the moonlight. Her yellow hair appeared white in the darkness, framing and equally white face.

Thoughts went through my mind suddenly, letting me know that she was aware of my pregnancy. Our language barrier was broken with this form of communication, just like with the Norns.

I groaned. I was really tired of being spoken to with no words, even if it was convenient.

Her return thought was that I was being childish. I had a gift and I should learn to use it to my advantage.

I attempted to climb to my feet, but felt so weak that Erykah had to give me a hand up. Her next thought was that I needed to eat. It was selfish to not eat when another life was depending on me.

She guided me away from the longhouse. I started to panic, thinking of Alaric.

Her thoughts assured me that he would join us soon, as

she had asked him to give us a moment. My panic dampened. I had no reason to trust her, but it was kind of hard not to when you were in each other's heads.

We walked over the soggy ground arm in arm to another one of the smaller structures. The doorway was covered with skins like the longhouse, which she held aside for me so I could enter.

The interior was small, but cozy, just three little benches covered in woolen cushions, and a large pelt over the center of the floor that I guessed once belonged to one of the little fluffy cows. Erykah held onto me until I sat on a cushions, then she began making a fire in a small pit in the back center of the room. When she was done, she sat on the bench beside me, rather than on any of the vacant seats, and handed me a small bowl of dried fruit. I munched on the fruit appreciatively until Erykah cut back into my thoughts.

*I will die soon*, she thought, though once again it wasn't with actual words.

I looked at her in surprise, and she conveyed that she had read her future in Mikael's mind. He was impeccable at shielding thoughts and emotions, but this one weighed on him enough that it leaked through.

My instinct was to comfort her in some way, to express my regrets, but as soon as I thought it, she already knew. She gave me a soft smile. She was glad she would at least die before her sons.

Not wanting to dwell on her impending demise, she reached out and once again pulled the charm free from my shirt. *This is the reason I will die,* she thought, sending a chill through my bones.

*I could not destroy it, only release it, and eventually it went on to another. Its new owner will send forces to kill me, not knowing I am their only hope of freeing themselves. All here will die.*

I stood up too quickly, thinking of the girl with the toothy grin, and everyone else having fun in the longhouse, worry free. "We have to warn them!" I blurted.

Erykah shook her head sadly. *You cannot change the past. No matter what you do, the same events will come to pass.*

I sat back down, defeated. I thought, *why are you telling me all of this?*

*You must agree to the price I've asked for helping you,* she explained. *You must swear to me the key will be destroyed, no matter the cost. It cannot move on to another owner. The destruction of the key will be my final revenge.*

I let my surprise project, not surprise at what she asked, but surprise she didn't already know my plans. I was going to destroy the key anyway.

She looked sad again. *You must promise me you will destroy it, no matter the cost.*

I nodded, thinking that it was an easy promise to make.

*The destruction will likely kill you, and your child,* she admitted.

My thoughts raced incoherently, which was good, because I didn't really want to share them with anyone at that moment. When they stilled, all I could think about was how she had mentally chastised me for not feeding my child. It didn't make sense if we were both going to die.

She patted my hand and smiled warmly. *Never give up hope. There is much to live for, much to fight for. I only wish I knew sooner.*

Someone knocked on the wood beside the door outside. Erykah said something in her language, then a moment later Alaric popped his head in.

"Is female bonding time over?" he asked, not sensing the weight of what had just transpired.

I forced a smile and nodded. "Erykah will teach me how to defeat the charm."

"And what of her price?" he pressed as he entered the room the rest of the way, letting the skins fall shut behind him.

I glanced back at Erykah, then returned my gaze to Alaric as I tried not to cry. "It will be paid."

# 16

As Alaric led me away from the little building where I'd sat with Erykah, her final thoughts echoed through my mind. *I will teach you at first light, then you must go. You cannot be here when we die.*

I shivered, and it wasn't just from the cold and my still damp clothing. The mud stuck to my boots uncomfortably, and I was overcome with the urge to just give up and lie down in the muck.

Alaric glanced at me every so often. "Are you okay? Did Erykah say something to upset you?"

I went over everything I'd learned, trying to figure out how to put into words that I might have to kill myself and our child, eventually coming to the conclusion that I shouldn't tell him at all. If he knew, he would try to stop me, but his efforts would be futile. There might be no other way. The charm would cling to me, and even if I managed to free myself like Erykah had, it would come back to destroy me. I *had* to destroy it first. If there was even the slightest chance I could survive that destruction, I had to take it.

I grasped Alaric's hand in mine and gave it a squeeze. "I'm just tired. This morning back in our time seems like it happened weeks ago."

Alaric squeezed my hand in return. "It's hard to believe that a mere ten or twelve hours ago we were having a nice shower without a care in the world."

I laughed, but it sounded forced, even to me. "I'd say we still had plenty of cares. They were just easier to shut out."

We reached the longhouse again, and Alaric let go of my hand so he could hold the skins aside for me. There was now music being played inside, melding with raucous laughter and conversation. I peeked in to see half of the Vikings dancing around the fires, while the other half sat and clapped along to the music.

The warmth of the fires appealed to me, but I would have rather just gone to bed. I didn't want to be around people having fun, especially when I knew all of them would soon be dead. I took a step forward and hesitated in the doorway, wondering if we could find somewhere else to go.

My decision was made for me as Mikael swung by the doorway and grabbed my hand, pulling me into the center of the dancing. He twirled me around to the music, clearly drunk.

I leaned away, reaching my hands futilely toward the edge of the room.

"Just one dance!" he begged. "Let us celebrate while we still can."

Underneath his revelry I could sense his sadness,

though I could probably only feel it because the alcohol had weakened his emotional shields. It gave me pause, and I shook my head at Alaric, who'd been coming to rescue me. He stopped and glared at Mikael, but didn't continue his approach.

Mikael pulled me close to him, swinging me in slow circles. Since he was eight inches taller than me, I had to crane my neck upward to look into his eyes. The same sadness I'd sensed from him was there in their amber depths.

He broke eye contact and leaned his face down to my ear. "She knows, doesn't she?"

"Erykah?" I whispered back.

He nodded, sliding his hair across my cheek.

For a moment I debated telling him, then not seeing the harm I answered, "Yes."

"You know you can't tell anyone," he whispered, still crouched so we'd be cheek to cheek.

"She told me I couldn't," I answered. "She said it wouldn't change anything."

He nodded again. "She was always wise beyond her years."

He pulled back and we both took in the people around us as we continued to dance half-heartedly.

"I came back when I heard what had happened," he explained leaning in, his arms loosely around my waist, "but I was several weeks too late. Since then I have been there each time the key was used, waiting for my chance at revenge. When it was sealed away, I thought it was over, then one of my spies brought word that the other clans were looking for it once again."

"You have spies among Estus' people?" I questioned.

He nodded. "Among Aislin's as well. I knew who you were before you even stepped foot in Norway."

I laughed despite the current mood of our conversation. "Of course you did. I'm sure you knew where the key was hidden all along as well?"

He let out a bitter laugh. "Just like many other things, the location of my chosen Salr was not mere happenstance. It was inevitable the charm would return, and I wanted to be near when that happened."

"And what about coming back here?" I pressed. "Was this all part of your master plan?"

He shrugged, and led me to dance in a more quiet part of the Salr. Alaric watched us like a hawk, ignoring the invitations he was receiving to dance.

"I had intended to come here on my own," Mikael explained, "once I knew the key might resurface. I wanted to speak with Erykah so that I would be prepared this time. I wanted to promise to avenge her."

"And when the key came to you, it just made things a little more convenient," I finished for him. "How did you get the Norns to agree to this?"

A wry smile crossed his face, reminding me of the less sad Mikael, hell-bent on becoming ruler. "When the Vaettir abandoned their old ways, they abandoned much of their magic, including the Norns. Under our new way of living, we were forbidden to shelter them."

I rolled my eyes. "And you suck at following rules."

He nodded. "The Salr were made for the Vaettir, and the Vaettir alone, but we can bring others there if we wish."

"You found them a home," I concluded, "and a trip back in time was your payment."

He pulled away from me, then led me to a vacant bench to sit. "A payment that took me several hundred years to call in. I've been waiting a long time for this."

Alaric finally took his cue to approach us as we looked out at the crowd. "You're sure we can't save them?" I asked, unable to let it go.

"I'm sure."

A group of young children ran in front of us, giggling as they shoved each other playfully.

I bit my lip, thinking of my own potential child. "How do you know?"

Mikael's eyes met mine just as Alaric reached us. "Because I've tried before. There are other magics that can alter time, and I tried to save them weeks after their deaths."

Alaric watched Mikael warily as he helped me to stand, then leaned down and kissed my cheek. "We should get some rest."

I nodded in reply, but felt unable to look away from the raw emotion in Mikael's gaze. Everyone he loved was about to die, a reality he'd already suffered twice, though I was sure he would suffer just as much the third time around.

It was all because of the little key around my neck. The key that chose that moment to buzz with energy against my skin, almost as if it wanted to remind me it was there.

I felt the key's satisfaction as the thought that I would never forget its existence danced through my mind. Our existences had been woven into one string of fate. When that string broke, we would both unravel.

# 17

"Are you telling me I'm stuck here with you?" Sophie growled.

James frowned. "I'm telling you that Aila ran off ahead of us, and everyone else has disappeared. Those creatures are standing in there like statues, just waiting. They won't talk to me."

"The Norns," Sophie mumbled as she rose to her feet. Whatever the Norns had done had knocked her unconscious. Now as far as James was saying, her brother, Madeline, and Mikael were *gone*, leaving her only the silent creatures to question.

"What do we do now?" James asked, sounding frightened.

Sophie hated hearing that tone in his voice. She'd take the overly-confident, easy-to-hate James any day of the week. He stood tall, well muscled, and imposing, even with his golden, angelic hair. At one point he had lived up to his looks, except the angelic part. An angel of sadistic destruction perhaps.

Sophie strode confidently back into the room with the Norns, flipping her long black hair over her shoulder, trying to hide the fact that she didn't feel entirely steady on her feet. She walked up to the nearest creature, one with little goat horns poking out of her head. The Norn didn't acknowledge her in the slightest.

Sophie jumped up and down, waving her hand in the air in front of the Norn's green-tinged face as James approached behind her.

"I already tried," he explained. "It's like they don't see us at all. I've been awake for hours."

Sophie ceased her jumping and huffed in irritation. "Why didn't you wake me sooner?"

James shook his head and backed away, seemingly frightened by her tone. "I tried. You were *out*, probably because you were closer to whatever happened."

"And what *did* happen?" she asked, hating the slight tremble in her voice.

James' gaze went distant, as if seeing the scene play out before him. "The air began to shimmer, ever so slightly, and the pressure dropped, like right before a storm. Then everything . . . shifted. The extreme change in pressure made it hard to breathe and I lost consciousness."

Sophie rolled her eyes. "Well that's of no help at all."

James looked truly apologetic.

Sophie grunted in frustration, wishing James would at least defend himself, then a thought came to her. "Aila," she growled, knowing she would likely get far more information out of the blonde Viking than she would the Norns. Without a word she left the room, heading toward the entrance of the Salr. Aila was Mikael's number two, and Sophie had no doubt he'd shared his plans with her. She'd known to run before the spell began.

James had to jog to catch up to her side. "But how will we find her?"

Not looking at him, Sophie raised a finger to tap her nose. "That won't be an issue."

James suddenly stopped walking.

Feeling increasingly irritated, Sophie spun on her heel to meet his astonished gaze.

"You're going to sniff her out?" he asked incredulously.

Sophie sighed, then turned to start walking again. The old James would have been useful in this situation. The new, impaired James was little more than dead weight. Maybe if she hit him over the head again, he'd regain his memory. If it didn't work, well, it would still be satisfying.

She reached the entrance of the Salr, and stared at a solid dirt wall. She shrugged, then pushed her fingers against the dirt, hoping this entrance was somewhat like the magical vines back in Estus' Salr. She held her breath as her finger sunk right through the wall. Next went her arm, and soon her entire body was encased in the earth. She panicked, unable to breathe, then she was lying on her back above ground, bathed in soft moonlight. A moment later, James rose up beside her.

Sophie was up in the blink of an eye, stalking off into the darkness with James trailing behind her. She'd find Aila, and she'd make her guide her to wherever Alaric had gone. For the past five hundred years, she and Alaric had always saved each other. She wasn't about to let him down now.

## 18

I woke up cold, even though Alaric's arm was still wrapped tightly around me. I could feel the line of his warm body against my back, perfectly still in the thrall of deep sleep. He had even remained asleep as Erykah, appeared for an early morning visit. Such deep sleep was unusual for him. We'd had a trying few days though, so his coma-like state was understandable.

I, on the other hand, hadn't slept at all since Erykah departed. She had promised to teach me to control the key at first light, and that was what she'd done . . . sort of.

She'd shaken me awake in what felt like the middle of the night, then led me outside to see the barest hint of sunlight peeking over the horizon. There was an unbearable chill in the air, but Erykah seemed unfazed.

The lesson hadn't taken long, in fact, she never even spoke, since I wouldn't understand her. Still, the moment she placed her hand on my shoulder, gazing intently at me with her aqua eyes, I was overwhelmed with information.

The images nearly knocked me off my feet, and I had to brace myself against her so I'd remain standing.

She showed me her entire struggle with the key, from when she first found it, to when she realized it was controlling her, to when she was finally able to rid herself of it. The whole ordeal felt akin to an abusive relationship, where the abused was so far in they believed their abuser when they said everything was for their own good.

I also saw some scenes with Mikael that made me blush. Erykah mentally tsked at my discomfort. He was her husband. What did I expect?

Erykah shook her head and got to the point. She had broken the key's hold over her by tricking it. She'd learned to shield her thoughts so the key couldn't convince her what she was thinking was wrong. The key was an effective adversary because it could insert thoughts into your mind until you couldn't tell the difference between your real thoughts, and the fake ones. Mentally shielding your thoughts meant the key would have nothing to work with.

I'd panicked at the revelation, because I hadn't learned to shield my thoughts, therefore the key would know I was planning to try. It would then manipulate me to keep itself fully in my mind.

At that moment, Erykah gripped my arms, conveying the thought, *If you are strong enough, it cannot stop you from shielding. It already knows you intend to destroy it. This game was begun when it first came into your possession. It may try to convince you otherwise, but all it will take is a moment of clarity, and the needed skills to defeat it.*

I nodded as her thoughts left my consciousness. She was right. It knew I wanted to destroy it, but wasn't willing to give me up as its host. I had to beat it at its own game by learning to shield my thoughts.

Then Erykah gave me what she thought was the answer to my problems. *Mikael can teach you. Shielding is one of his gifts.*

Understanding played across my face, then confusion. *If he can teach me what I need, then why did we travel back in time?*

Erykah smiled sadly. *He doesn't understand how he does it, or that it's what you need to survive this. He won't be able to show you willingly, but if you can break down his shields like I did, you can gather that information for yourself. I would try to show you myself, but my shields are not as strong as his, not as complex. If you are to truly best the key, best it in a way I could not, you must learn to shield from the best. You must see inside Mikael's mind.*

I shook my head. *I'm an empath, I feel emotions. I can't read minds.*

She sighed. *Thoughts and feelings are more closely knit than you believe. How else would we be having this conversation?*

I gasped. *I'm reading your mind?*

*Only because I'm letting you,* she explained. *It will be much more difficult with Mikael. He lets no one in willingly, even if he says he will.*

She hugged me suddenly, catching me completely off guard. *Thank you for your promise. I can march toward death with honor, knowing that my adversary will not win. I was only able to shield long enough to rid myself of it. You will learn to shield well enough to destroy it fully. I have faith.*

I hugged her back as a few tears slipped from my eyes.

They weren't tears just for her, as I'd only known her a short time. They were for the entire village. They would all die soon, even the children. I felt a pang of guilt for leaving, but in reality their deaths had occurred centuries ago. There was nothing I could do to stop them.

Erykah had left me then, and I'd returned to the small abode where Alaric still slept. I climbed silently back into bed with him, wrapping his arm around me like a life-line.

---

I COULD SENSE it the moment Alaric startled into wakefulness. His arm tensed around me, then relaxed as he maneuvered me more firmly against him.

"Good morning," he whispered in my ear, searching downward with his hand.

Realizing his intent, I pulled away and rolled over to face him.

He looked slightly hurt, then noting my expression, waited for me to explain.

I sat up, reluctantly pulling myself out of the warm bedding. "We have to go. Mikael will be here soon."

Alaric sat up, pulling free from the blankets to reveal his bare chest and the top of his dark brown, woolen pants. "What about the key? We still don't know how to destroy it."

I looked down at my lap as I tried to think of what to say. I knew I couldn't tell him the entire truth, that destroying the key might kill both me and our unborn child, but he wouldn't let me just brush him off.

"What is it, Maddy?" he said evenly.

I looked up to meet his dark eyes, then reached my hand out toward his black, silken hair.

He gripped my wrist softly, inches from his hair. "Answer me," he pressed.

I frowned, then shook his hand off my wrist so I could comb my fingers through his hair. He watched me cautiously with my hand inches from his face.

"I know what to do," I said finally, "but you're just going to have to trust me."

He grabbed my wrist again, but this time it was to press my palm against his lips. He kissed my skin gently, maintaining eye contact all the while. "I have ways of making you tell me," he said, only half-joking.

I pulled my hand away and let it fall to my lap, turning my head from him while I fought back tears. A moment later the bed shifted, and he wrapped his arms around me, bringing my face to rest in the crook of his shoulder.

We both jumped as the small, wooden door to our temporary home burst inward. Mikael stood framed in the doorway. His long, auburn hair flew forward in the cool morning breeze, but did nothing to obscure the intensity in his rich, chestnut eyes.

"It seems our manners have returned to medieval times as well," Alaric mumbled, but Mikael didn't seem to hear him.

Mikael's eyes met mine. He gave the barest of nods, which I returned without a second thought. We had to leave. There was no other choice.

"Meet me on the path," Mikael ordered, finally including Alaric in the scope of his gaze. "We don't have much time."

As Alaric and I disentangled ourselves, Mikael left us, leaving the door wide open behind him. I had kept on most of my clothing, so I only needed to put on the extra outerwear that had been provided by Mikael's village.

Alaric was dressed in an instant, and crouched down to help me with my boots while I secured the clasps on my short, leather and fur jacket, loose fitting with only half-sleeves. He had been given a wool cloak that swept down near his knees. I would have preferred a cloak like his, but I wasn't going to argue when I'd arrived with no coat at all. The furs were thick and warm, probably warmer than his cloak regardless.

Alaric pushed his hair out of his face as he began to wrap up my second boot. "Are you going to tell me what's going on, or do I have to guess?" he asked, clearly annoyed.

"I'll tell you as soon as we leave the village," I assured. "There's no time to explain now."

Alaric nodded as he stood, though it was clear by his expression he wasn't happy with the deal. He helped me to my feet, then placed his hand on my lower back as we squeezed through the doorway. He stayed protectively close as we made our way through the small village, likely sensing my nerves, but not knowing what they were about.

A few of the Vikings I'd met last night were already out and about, shaking out rugs and pelts, and moving in and out of the livestock huts. They paid us little mind, assuming we wouldn't actually be leaving them any time soon. Erykah was nowhere to be seen, luckily, as I wasn't sure I had the heart to face her. I was doing what she asked, but it still felt wrong.

I averted my gaze as a young girl walked by in front of us, oblivious to the peril that would soon befall her.

"You're shivering," Alaric commented, pulling me firmly against his side. "Do you want my cloak?"

I shook my head and looked down, unable to meet his gaze. It wasn't the chill in the morning air that was bothering me.

He let it go, though his expression remained concerned.

We neared the edge of the village without interruption. I could see Mikael further down the path, standing in a copse of trees with his back to us. His satchel looked bulky, likely stuffed with fresh supplies, but the rest of him appeared normal, at least to anyone who might be looking. To my secondary perceptions, he was brimming with a grief so powerful it leaked through his well-formed mental shields. His grief become more invasive as we neared his still form. At first it had been like a chill wind, but increased to the ferocity of an icy ocean wave as Alaric and I came to stand behind him.

He turned his face toward us, reddish brown eyes bland of emotion. I knew my face held just what he was feeling, and I knew he wouldn't appreciate that I knew, but I couldn't help it. I would have grieved even without his emotions helping me along. So many unnecessary deaths.

Alaric rubbed his tunic-clad arms like he had goosebumps, then looked over his shoulder at the now distant village. "Will someone please tell me what's going on?" he muttered, turning back to me. "We came all this way . . . "

I met his eyes and shook my head, urging him to stay quiet. Mikael was teetering on the brink, and I really didn't want to see what would happen if he uncaged all the emotion he was holding in.

Ignoring Alaric, Mikael turned to face me. "I trust you have the information you need."

Did I? What Erykah had given me was anything but clear, and definitely not what I *needed*, but I knew it was all she had to give. I nodded, and it seemed to be enough for Mikael. He turned from me to continue down the path. I grabbed Alaric's hand in mine and started forward, anxious to be away from the village before things started happening.

Alaric allowed me to pull him down the path, if a little reluctantly. He didn't ask any more questions, which got him major bonus points in my book. It was nice having someone actually trust that I knew what I was doing. Unfortunately, I didn't really trust it myself.

We'd only gone roughly a quarter of a mile when the first scream cut through the air. Mikael stopped in his tracks, forcing us to do the same on the narrow path.

"*What* is going on?" Alaric demanded, finally letting his anger seep through. His anger sent fiery sensations creeping up my hand where it rested in his.

Mikael didn't turn around as he answered, "It doesn't matter. It's ancient history."

Unsatisfied with Mikael's answer, Alaric turned to me. Another scream cut through the air, followed by the sound of metal on metal. I could sense his tension, and knew he was only moments away from pulling out of my grasp to run back toward the village.

"Ignorance is bliss," I explained weakly, clutching onto his hand.

Ire crossed his face. He pulled his hand away from mine, but didn't run. His gaze was on Mikael's back as he replied, "Only to those willing to play the fool."

Finally Mikael turned around and took a step toward us. I instantly felt like a dwarf with his 6'5" frame so near, and Alaric only a few inches shorter. "They're already dead," he hissed, daring Alaric to argue with him. "It is not for us to tangle the strings of fate."

Alaric stared at Mikael for a heartbeat, then turned his astonished expression to me. "You knew," he whispered as more screams reached us.

"Let us leave this place," Mikael said through gritted teeth, flexing his hands impatiently.

We both stared at him, knowing we had no choice, but unable to make the decision to move forward.

He spun on his heel and marched away, leaving a cloud of angry emotions in his wake. The decision made for us, Alaric and I began walking while I did my best to shut out the sounds of battle in the distance. Instead I focused on Mikael's back. His emotions were slowly sliding away, being shut back behind his normally impenetrable shields.

I didn't need to be an empath to know how much the move had cost him, and I didn't need to be a psychic to know I'd have a hell of a time finding my way past those shields again.

## 19

We continued walking as ominous clouds gathered overhead. The sounds of battle had faded long ago, leaving us with only the whistling of the wind to break the silence. Medieval Scandinavia might have been a blustery, rainy place in general, but as ice cold raindrops began to hit my face, it felt like the universe was mocking me. First, fate saw me kidnapped, then tortured, then nearly sacrificed to free the little key around my neck. As if that wasn't enough, Lady Fate continued on to see me shackled to said key, pregnant, and hunted by the majority of the Vaettir. Cold rain and no shelter was just icing on the cake.

The three of us continued on in silence, not remarking on the rain. Though it was uncomfortable, it was the least of our worries. I wanted to ask Mikael how we would travel through time without the Norns, and I wanted to ask him what we would do after that, but I was afraid to prod the beast. His raw emotions were still too fresh in my mind, though I felt nothing from him now as he walked beside me.

"What did she tell you?" Mikael asked suddenly, breaking the silence and making me jump.

Alaric and I both turned to watch him as we continued walking.

"I spoke to her after she met with you," Mikael went on, "but she wouldn't tell me. She simply said you knew what you needed to do."

I looked down at the ground ahead of us, still muddy from the previous day's rainfall, and bound to get muddier. My boots felt like they weighed a million pounds, and my clothing was beginning to take on the weight of moisture from the rain. I could at least unburden my thoughts and share everything Erykah had told me, but something stopped me. I had no doubt Mikael would allow me to sacrifice myself if it meant he would finally beat the sentient being that was the key, but Alaric would try to stop me. If not for my own well-being, then for our child's. I could just share the part about needing to break down Mikael's shields in order to learn how to build my own, but it might make Mikael close up even more. Still, I had no idea how to take down his shields without his help.

"I need you to teach me to shield my thoughts," I said finally, leaving out the implication that he needed to let his own shields down in order to show me.

Mikael stopped walking and turned to fully face me, while Alaric stood silently at my back. Mikael searched my face, as if to behold the importance of what I *wasn't* saying. Suddenly, he turned and began walking again.

Alaric and I had to jog to catch up with his long legs. "Well?" I pressed.

He wouldn't meet my eyes. "I don't know how. It's something that has always come naturally to me."

I grabbed his arm to halt his pace, then instantly regretted it. The angry look he gave me was nothing compared to the pain leaking through at my touch. My lips parted in surprise, and Mikael's eyes widened.

He shook my hand away and took a step back. "Stay out of my head," he growled.

I took a step back and bumped into Alaric's chest. "I didn't mean to," I replied instantly, feeling shaken.

I could almost *feel* Alaric smiling behind me as his hands protectively enveloped my upper arms. "But isn't that the whole point?" he taunted. "If she's to learn about your shields, you have to let her in. She must see inside your head, everything laid bare."

I was glad the look on Mikael's face was aimed above my head at Alaric and not at me. I *never* wanted to see an ancient Viking descended from a god glaring at me like that. Luckily, his expression softened as it dropped back down to my face. "Even if I *wanted* to let you into my head, I don't know how. Erykah broke my shields down without my consent. If you are not capable of doing that, then our plan has failed."

My head drooped. "Your shields come down in moments of extreme grief," I explained, avoiding eye contact. "In those moments I'm able to feel what you feel. If you can manage to rebuild that barrier more slowly next time, I might be able to learn how."

He gazed off in the direction we'd come. The village was miles away now. The carnage was likely over. He turned back to me. "The death of my people was the first and *last* grief I ever felt."

Alaric's hands flexed on my arms. "No grief for causing a woman's death after she helped to cover your tracks?" he snapped.

Mikael looked past me to Alaric. "I meant what I said," he stated, then turned and walked away.

I moved out of Alaric's grip and slid my hand around his waist. He obliged me by putting his arm around my shoulders. We gave each other a quick glance, then watched Mikael walk away.

Alaric's arm tightened around my shoulders. "He'll pay for his crimes before all this is over."

I watched Mikael round a bend in the wooded trail, disappearing from sight. Alaric and I had no choice but to follow. I wasn't so sure Mikael would be the one to pay. He was a survivor, after all. As we began walking, I could almost feel the noose of fate tightening around my neck.

"We're not going back in the direction we came," Alaric commented sometime later, as we continued to follow behind Mikael.

The Viking in question was still a good distance ahead of us, but occasional sightings of him let me know we were still heading in the right direction. I knew I should have been feeling a lot of emotions in that moment, but what I felt most was *hungry*. We had been walking for several hours, and were yet to stop to eat. Given Mikael was the one with a satchel full of supplies, and he didn't seem to be speaking to us, our prospects were not good.

"Does it matter?" I asked, narrowing my eyes as the trail straightened and Mikael once again came into view.

Alaric didn't seem tired or hungry in the least. In fact, he seemed at full alert, his eyes darting around the trail at the slightest hint of noise. The rain had subsided, but his dark hair still hung in wet clumps around his shoulders. "I had thought perhaps our way back to our time might lie in the spot we arrived, like a portal or some sort of vortex, but we've veered too far south. At this rate we'll miss that spot by several miles."

I shrugged. "Maybe we have to go somewhere else to get back."

"Or maybe we're not going back at all."

I stopped walking and faced him, feeling the barest hint of panic in my stomach. "Why would you say that? The whole point of coming here was for me to learn to control the key so we can use it to beat Estus. We can't beat him in a time where he doesn't even exist."

"Perhaps Estus is not Mikael's first priority," Alaric commented, grabbing my arm to guide me forward.

"B-but Mikael can't lie to me," I stammered, trying desperately to think of something that would mean Alaric wasn't right.

Alaric snorted. "And what has he told you of us being here? That you would gain information about the charm? Well, you have. He's told us nothing else."

I had the sudden urge to go running up the trail where I would violently shake Mikael until he told us what was going on, but I had a feeling it wouldn't turn out how I wanted. I thought back to the dance Mikael and I had shared the night before. He'd confided in me, and I'd felt bad for him. Was it all just manipulation? Did he intend to trap us here in a foreign time, where perhaps things were more to his liking?

I shook my head as I found my conclusion. "We're going back."

Alaric sighed. "And how do you know that?"

I smiled smugly. "Because Mikael hates to lose. Staying here would be too close to running."

Alaric stopped walking. At first I thought he was going to argue with me, but then I saw his expression. He held up a hand to keep me quiet while he tilted his head toward the twisting path in front of us, listening.

"I hear voices up ahead," he commented, face deep in concentration.

"Someone with Mikael?" I questioned, suddenly doubting my assertions of his intentions.

Instead of answering me, he continued to listen, though I couldn't hear a thing. I would forever be the feeble kid without any physical powers.

He straightened and turned to fully face me. "It seems like someone Mikael knows, but you should hide here just in case."

"I'm not going to stay here alone!" I rasped, taking a cue from Alaric on keeping my voice down.

Alaric quirked the corner of his mouth, revealing one of his dainty cat fangs. "Would you miss me?" he teased.

I glared at him. "I might miss you if a bear attacked me, but only then."

He grinned even wider and moved to put an arm around my shoulders. "Walk with me aways," he whispered, "but do not speak as we near their meeting place. You can hide out of sight before we reach them, far enough to not be seen, but close enough to not become bear food."

I nodded, too nervous to remark on the bear food comment. For all we knew, Mikael might be with more friendly people like those who'd perished in the village, but he also might have run into someone he didn't expect. Someone who might mean him, and by effect *us*, harm.

We continued walking. I did my best to be quiet, but my footsteps seemed thunderous next to Alaric's near-silent gait. Louder still was the groaning of my stomach. Back in the normal world I usually skipped breakfast, but I seemed unable to do that now. I wasn't sure if it was the pregnancy, or just stress, but my stomach was *not* happy with the situation.

Alaric chuckled softly at a particularly loud stomach growl, but didn't comment.

After a few more minutes I could finally hear the voices. Alaric stopped walking and gestured for me to hide. I glanced around for a good spot, but nothing jumped out at me. Finally, Alaric pointed to a bramble patch a few feet off the narrow path. I nodded, not liking the look of the plant's pointy leaves, but I could at least hide behind it and hope no one snuck up on me.

Alaric gave me a kiss on the cheek as I pulled away from him. With how he'd heard the distant voices, I knew he'd hear me if I screamed, and he ran faster than someone with a humanoid body should, so he'd reach me quickly. Of course, it would only take a few seconds for a bear, or other ancient woodland beast to break my neck. If I gave a bear in this time a hearty human meal, when it otherwise might have killed something else, would I alter the course of history? I shook my head at my thoughts as I crouched behind the brambles. I really needed to eat something.

I could still hear the voices as I waited in hiding. My clothes had nearly dried, but the ground was damp and loamy, making me not want to lower myself into a full seated position.

I heard the footsteps a moment too late. Before I could turn around, someone grabbed my arm and yanked upward. I was brought abruptly to my feet by a man roughly my height, wearing dirty wool clothing with leather bracers strapped over his forearms, and a wide, leather belt. His hair was even frizzier than mine, and its bright red color made it look like foamy fire.

He leaned his bearded face into mine and peered at me with one blue eye. Where the other eye should have been was nothing but a mass of scar tissue. He grinned, said something in Old Norsk that I didn't understand, then began dragging me toward the path.

Finally regaining my wits, I struggled against his grasp and yelled for Alaric. Though I was far from powerless, I couldn't steal the life from someone who wasn't weakened, and I hadn't taken the life of someone in a long time, so I had no pent up energy to wield. I cried out for Alaric, and moments later heard running footsteps thundering toward us.

The man jerked me violently forward, and I tugged back, screaming all the while. Before I knew what was coming, he had thrown back his arm, preparing to hit me.

Alaric, Mikael, and several other men reached us, just

as my captor's fist was about to collide with my face. Without warning, the key around my neck came to life, and a burst of energy knocked the man backward, leaving me unscathed. I stumbled backward and raised my hand to clutch the little key at my throat without thinking. As soon as I realized what I was doing, I dropped my hand, but felt no less shaken.

One of the men standing with Mikael and Alaric muttered something under his breath that sounded like *völur*.

"She's not a witch," Alaric mumbled as he came to stand near me. He took my shaky hand in his and gave it a squeeze.

I leaned in close to him before I spoke, even though no one there besides Alaric and Mikael would understand me. "I take it they're not Vaettir?" I questioned, since they seemed somewhat astonished by what had transpired.

Alaric shook his head. The man I'd knocked down got to his feet and shot me a venomous, if somewhat frightened look, then went to stand with his comrades. One of the other men barked something vehemently at Mikael while pointing to me. All the other men watched me cautiously. I did *not* like where this was going.

The man speaking, apparently the leader, judging not only by the way he took command of the situation, but by the style of his clothing, took a step toward me. He swept aside a vibrant blue cloak, held in place by an oval, bronze broach at his shoulder. His golden blond hair was held back from his face, gathered in a bun at the nape of his neck. His beard was neat and well trimmed.

He said something that sounded scathing while he

glared at me with dark gray eyes, his hand on the massive ax at his belt.

Mikael took a step forward and said something calmly, causing the lead Viking to turn and face him, a look of surprise on his face.

Alaric leaned in close to my ear. "Mikael revealed that he has sworn a blood oath to you, one that requires vengeance should anyone harm you."

I held my breath in surprise, then whispered, "That second part is a lie."

Alaric snorted. "And Mikael is the God of Lies."

I wasn't going to argue with Alaric, and I wasn't going to call Mikael out on his little fib. The men facing us all looked unsure now, including the leader. It was obvious they held a great deal of respect for Mikael, or at least knew his capabilities.

The leader gave me a final glare, then turned to Mikael and said something else.

"He says we will make camp with them tonight," Alaric explained. "But that the *witch* must agree to harness her powers."

The leader looked at me expectantly. I nodded, hoping the gesture meant the same thing in this time as it did in ours. It seemed to be enough for him, as he turned back in the direction most of the men had come from, expecting everyone to follow.

Mikael fell back in line beside me, while Alaric walked on my other side.

"Thank you," I muttered, hoping his sour mood had come to an end.

"I would have killed them," he replied, "but I fear the wrath of Lady Fate. I need you for my plans, so I had to protect you somehow."

His tone made it clear he was referring to me like a tool, just like many of the other Vaettir had done. I hated to admit it, but it stung. Until then, Mikael had at least treated me like a person. "And here I thought we were friends," I replied bitterly, unable to keep my emotions fully to myself.

"You are a means to an end, Madeline," he said coldly, then trudged on ahead to walk next to the lead Viking.

I looked to Alaric, expecting some sort of sarcastic remark, but his expression was serious as he turned his gaze from Mikael's back to my face. "He is a means to an end for us as well," he stated. "Let us not forget that."

I nodded, then looked down at the ground as we walked. Alaric was right, but I didn't like it. I wasn't used to using people like chess pieces. It was only in that moment that I realized how much I missed having friends. Alaric was the closest thing I had to a real friend, though our short history was obviously complicated. I considered Sophie a friend, but wasn't sure if she viewed me the same. I'd even somehow started to view Mikael as a friend, but he wasn't. It seemed all Vaettir would always view me as a tool first, and a person second, if at all. It was damn lonely.

I looked up at the cloudy sky, feeling numb and achy. No one would even care if I ever returned to the correct time. Sophie would be waiting for Alaric. Aila and the rest of Mikael's people would be waiting for him. For me, there was only Estus, waiting to kill me. I glanced over at Alaric. I was pretty sure *he* cared what happened to me. The child inside me probably cared too. It was more than I'd had a month before, and would have to be enough for me now.

I glanced up at Mikael's back with renewed determination. If the Viking wanted to play, the least I could do was give him one hell of a game.

# 20

"Slow down," James pleaded.

"We can't let them get any farther away," Sophie snapped. "I won't risk them entering another Salr where I won't be able to find them."

"How do you know that hasn't already happened?" James huffed, stomping up beside her.

She'd stopped to scent the wind. James' sweaty man-smell was confusing her senses. She glared at him, and knew her feline eyes were likely reflecting in the moonlight by the way he gasped.

"I hate it when you go all cat-like," he grumbled, looking down at his shoes.

"Says the man that can sear flesh with a single touch," she quipped before starting off again. They were close.

Sophie had retraced their steps back to the tunnel entrance where they'd parted ways with Aila and a few other members of Mikael's clan. It hadn't even been a full twenty-four hours since that meeting, so the scent was still fresh. With the distant wail of sirens spurring her on, she'd traced the scent all the way to where they now searched, a remote area of the woods, far northeast of the Salr where they'd first met Mikael.

Sophie stopped to scent the air once more, then perked up at the sound of far off conversation. The voices were speaking Old Norsk, letting her know they were Vaettir, and not the police who were likely looking for the villains who'd left several corpses in a quaint, suburban neighborhood. The only question was if the people speaking belonged to Estus, Aislin, or Mikael.

She continued listening as she crept near, gesturing for James to stay behind. She didn't need his lumbering steps giving her away.

As the camp came into sight, the first form she saw was very tall, and very blonde. Sophie's smile was more of a snarl. She shouldn't go charging into the situation with brute force, but it was the only way she knew how.

---

I SAT in a secluded area with Alaric, near the Viking camp. We were close enough to the sea that I could hear the waves crashing in the distance. A lot of people find the sound soothing, but it just made me nervous. I'd always been afraid of deep waters, even more than heights.

Not wanting to sit around while Mikael's human *friends* stared at me, Alaric and I had built a small fire of our own. We sat on a piece of driftwood, huddled near the flames for warmth.

I had a moment of wishing for our more comfortable lodgings of the night before. My heart lurched. Those lodgings were likely now burned to the ground. The people who had thrown Mikael a party the night before, dead in the cold night air.

"What are you thinking?" Alaric asked softly, startling me away from my morbid thoughts.

I jumped at his voice, then settled down to lean my shoulder against his. "What makes you think I was thinking anything?"

He put his arm around me and pulled me closer. "You had a look on your face like someone had just kicked your puppy. Were you thinking about the baby?"

I shivered. "It still sounds weird to hear you say that. We've travelled back in time, left a village full of people to their deaths, and were accosted by genuine Vikings, yet the pregnancy is the part that doesn't feel real."

He laughed. "I imagine it will begin to seem real as more time passes, and certain things begin to . . . show."

I turned my head and quirked an eyebrow at him. "You mean when I blow up like a balloon?"

He laughed again, using his free hand to push his tangled hair out of his face. "Something like that. Did you have enough to eat?"

I glanced over at the large wooden bowl we'd shared for our supper and wrinkled my nose. My vegetarian senses had not been pleased by the choice of fresh caught rabbit with hard, root vegetables, but I'd been so starved I ate anyway.

"More than enough," I replied, my distaste coloring my tone.

The sound of rustling branches and movement to our left caught our attention. Mikael appeared within the trees, then approached. I had no particular desire to share our fire with him, however, he might by slim chance tell us what we had to do to get home.

He looked right past me to Alaric. "I need to speak with Madeline."

Alaric didn't move. "No one is preventing you from doing so."

Mikael looked to me. I expected to see the harsh resentment I'd seen earlier, but there was an almost pleading feel to his expression.

I sighed, and looked to Alaric.

Picking up on what I wasn't saying, he frowned. "Are you sure?"

I smiled gratefully. "It's not like he's going to hurt me."

Alaric looked up at Mikael, then back to me. "If you say so." With that, he stood and walked off, not toward the rest of the camp, but further into the woods.

Mikael closed the distance between us, then took Alaric's vacated seat. I scooted away, but it was a small log. We still ended up shoulder to shoulder. I sat silently, partially turned away from him, waiting for him to speak.

He inhaled loudly, then exhaled with no words forthcoming.

I still didn't face him, feeling that it would somehow thwart his effort.

He finally spoke. "We can try working on the shielding thing."

The exasperated tone in his voice drew my eye to him. "What made you change your mind?"

He had the grace to look almost embarrassed. "If Erykah thinks—*thought* it's what needs to be done, then it will be done."

I knew it was a bad idea to say anything, especially with how he'd reacted earlier, but I couldn't help it. I placed my hand on top of his. "I'm sorry."

He didn't get angry, and instead smiled sadly. "Honestly, I was surprised you even told me the plan. Erykah manipulated my emotions and broke me down without warning. One would think it better to have me off guard."

I smirked. "Manipulate a descendant of Dolos, god of deceit and treachery? That seems like a losing battle."

Mikael laughed, and I suddenly realized that my hand was still on his. I withdrew it as inconspicuously as possible, though the act drew his gaze. "Dolos was simply misunderstood," he explained. "He was practically a slave to Prometheus, and copied his master's statue to show he was just as skilled. Prometheus stole the statue and claimed it was his own, and thus lies were formed."

I raised my eyebrows in disbelief. "Oh okay," I replied sarcastically. "So if deceit doesn't run in your blood, then how did you manipulate entire nations?"

He smiled, wiping away the rest of the sadness that had lingered on his face. "I see someone has been telling stories about me."

"That doesn't answer the question," I countered before he could change the subject.

He shrugged. "Through deceit and treachery."

I raised a finger in playful accusation. "But you just said that Dolos wasn't the god of those things."

Mikael grinned. "Did I? I'm pretty sure I just said he was misunderstood."

I frowned. He was playing games with me, and derailing the entire conversation from the original subject. "Misunderstood how?" I asked, giving in.

"By perceptions," he replied, holding up his hands to warm them by the fire. "Two men can commit the same *treacherous* act. One may be labeled a swindler, and the other, simply clever. There is no difference."

I stared into the fire. "The difference lies in how the man's actions affect others."

Mikael turned his gaze to me, and I suddenly had the feeling that I'd lost points in our verbal debate. "Oh?" he questioned. "And what about you? Should you be labeled a server of justice, a guiding hand, or a murderer?"

He was probably hoping to shock me with the term *murderer*, but I'd spent way too much time thinking upon it myself to be caught off guard. Without thinking, I replied, "If I was taking the life of someone who'd committed heinous crimes, then I'd be serving justice. If it was someone who wanted to die, a guiding hand. An innocent . . . well, I suppose that would be called murder."

"Yet each of those things depends on who you ask," he countered. "Say my best friend harmed someone in a crime of passion, and you took his life as justice. Most might call you the righteous executioner. I'd just call you a killer."

I grinned at him.

He leaned back slightly in surprise. "Whatever could have crossed your mind at that example?"

"I was just thinking that your example wasn't an accurate representation of the truth."

He seemed to think about my answer, then replied, "And why is that?"

I grinned even wider. "Because no one would want to be your best friend in the first place."

He threw his head back and laughed, obviously not offended. At that moment, a few flakes of snow began to fall. Mikael reached out a hand to catch them, seeming almost like a little kid marveling at the miracle of snow.

Seeing his good mood as an opportunity, I asked, "So where are we going now, *really*?"

He retained his smile as he replied, "We're going to seek a little more information, then hopefully find our way home."

"*Hopefully*?" I questioned, all of Alaric's observations rushing back to the forefront of my mind.

He patted my leg with his hand, and I shifted away, suddenly nervous. He sighed. "Everything in life is a gamble, my dear. The Norns in this time do not owe me favors like the ones in our present."

"Well I'm glad you've risked our lives, our futures, and the life of our child all in one fell swoop," a sarcastic voice called from within the tree line.

Mikael turned to me with a conspiratorial look. "Do you ever get tired of his kitty cat hearing?" he whispered.

Before I could answer, Alaric revealed himself and approached the fire. He seemed to fit right in with the surroundings in his dark, wool and linen clothing, and borrowed cloak. His loose, black hair had begun to gather snowflakes, little flecks of white amongst the solid darkness.

"Your lives, futures, and the life of your child were

already at risk," Mikael said happily. "Can you really argue that you had anything to lose?"

"We left my sister in that time," Alaric replied coldly, gazing off into the distance rather than at Mikael.

"It was my intention to bring her," Mikael replied blandly.

I realized his hand had come to rest on my leg again, and I scooted away, trying not to draw attention to myself. I had a feeling Mikael would find a way to flirt even as the fires of the underworld leapt up to drag us all to our fate.

"So we could all die together?" Alaric asked, taking a step closer.

Mikael laughed. "On the contrary. There are far fewer people who want to kill us in this time. We could easily live out our days here."

Before I could blink, Alaric was standing directly in front of where Mikael sat. "You *do* intend to keep us here, don't you?" he accused. "If you wanted to come live in this time, that's one thing, but why drag us into it?"

Mikael sighed, seemingly unintimidated by the fact that Alaric's eyes had shifted to feline, and he was flexing his fists like he might suddenly sprout claws. "I was simply pointing out that your deaths are not on my agenda," Mikael answered tiredly, "and I have no intention of trapping either of you in this time. There is nothing for me here."

"Things are just as you want them in this time," Alaric countered. "You have your freedom. You can manipulate others into following you without fear of being struck down by the other Vaettir."

"I have already lived this life!" Mikael shouted as he suddenly stood, placing himself inches away from Alaric. More calmly, he continued, "In my mind, everything here is already ash. It pervades my senses with its acrid stench, with every step I take, with every word I breathe."

Alaric was silent. The two men stood there, inches away from each other, with Mikael's head towering slightly above Alaric's. Their anger made my skin itch, muddling my thoughts with their opposing energies. Mikael was like the angry seas he'd traveled in his youth, and Alaric was like a cool, still, night, his rage contained beneath the surface.

I started to feel nauseous, and at first thought it was from the overwhelming energy, then a sharp, stabbing pain seared through my abdomen. "Uh guys?" I questioned weakly, clutching at my middle.

They didn't seem to hear me, too enthralled in their stare-down. The key started thrumming at my neck, though I had no idea why. The pain grew, and I fell from the log I'd been seated on to my knees.

"Guys?" I said again, and they both finally turned to look at me, identical, questioning expressions on their faces.

I couldn't answer their questions as the pain doubled. The key at my neck felt like it had been resting in fire. I was sure it was burning my skin, but I couldn't lift a hand to reach it. I fell to the side, but Alaric knelt and caught me before my shoulder could hit the ground. He sat and pulled me backward into his lap.

Seconds later, Mikael was by my side. The pain exploded into a wracking nausea. I would have vomited if my body were able to move forward. I looked dizzily past Mikael to the falling snow, with Alaric's arms wrapped around me. I was pretty sure they were both speaking to me, but I couldn't hear them. Everything had gone numb. All I could think about was how pretty the snowflakes were, and how nice they felt on my hot skin.

# 21

I woke up feeling warm. A little *too* warm. I could feel bodies pressed against either side of me. Something was wrong with this picture. I opened my eyes, recalling the pain in my abdomen, and the key burning at my throat. I freed my hand from being pinned by someone's arm around my waist, then reached up to my throat. The key felt cool to the touch, and my skin was unmarred.

I turned my head to the side to see Mikael's sleeping face, only inches from mine.

"What the hell!" I shouted, turning on my side to shove him away from me.

He opened his eyes with a start, just as I felt arms convulse around me from behind.

"Oh come now," Mikael mocked, making no move to get up. "I was having the most marvelous dream." He waggled his eyebrows at me suggestively.

The person behind me shifted, and Alaric's face came into view beside mine. We were in a small hide tent, with rough bedding encasing us. Alaric stared past me at Mikael as he explained, "After you fainted, your entire body went cold. I felt it pertinent that you were warmed, no matter the cost."

He was being very polite, especially with how Mikael was still grinning beside us.

"Thank you for your warmth," I said through gritted teeth while I glared at Mikael, "now please go away."

Finally he scooted out of the blankets and crawled toward the covered opening to the tent. "You kids sit tight," he instructed. "I'll be back soon."

Once the thousand plus year old Viking had departed, I rolled over to look at Alaric, who still had an arm around my waist. "The warmth *so* wasn't worth it," I said sarcastically. "He'll be going on about this for days."

Alaric frowned. "Maddy, we thought you were dying, or at the very least that you were losing the baby. If *I* could deal with being that close to Mikael, I figured you could too."

I frowned in reply, not liking his serious tone. The pain in my stomach was gone, though I still felt a little weak. I reached down toward my abdomen, as if somehow I could tell that the baby was still there, then quickly retracted my hand. It was too early to be able to tell just by touching. Heck, I hadn't even known I was pregnant until Mikael told us.

"Do you think . . . " Alaric trailed off, and I knew he was trying to ask about the baby.

I shook my head. "I'm not sure."

His face fell. I really hadn't expected him to become so invested in the idea of a child. He was a being of war. He *lived* for violence and chaos, both of which weren't exactly conducive to raising a child.

"I'm sure it's fine," I lied, wanting to wipe the hurt expression from his face.

Not replying, he drew me into a tight hug.

I felt guilty even just admitting it to myself, but part of me would be relieved if the child was gone. Not only had I not planned on having children, but I was terrified of what this child in particular might turn out to be. I wouldn't wish my calling upon anyone. The idea of having to teach my child to take the lives of others was horrifying. Even if it didn't end up just like me, we were still Vaettir. Our child would be destined for a life of violence and death regardless.

"What are you thinking?" Alaric asked with his face still pressed against mine.

"Nothing," I lied again. "Just wondering what supplies Mikael is off . . . procuring."

Alaric pulled away from me to flash a knowing smile. "Dating an empath is quite unfair. You always know what I'm feeling, but I cannot read you in return."

I cringed. "Sorry?"

Alaric kissed me softly before I could say anything else. I kissed him back, glad to put an end to the conversation. For the moment, we would just have to worry about getting home, then we could use modern medicine to determine if the child was still present.

I heard footsteps and a snuffling sound outside of the tent, moments before Mikael called out, "Knock, knock!"

Alaric and I pulled away from each other and sat up. He reached the tent flap first, pulling it aside to reveal a landscape dusted with pure, white snow. Amidst the near blinding white of early morning reflecting off ice stood Mikael, holding the reins of three stout, shaggy ponies.

I let Alaric help me out of bed, thanking my lucky stars that I had been left fully clothed. I searched the bedding to find that my coat had been draped over the blankets that had covered my legs. I donned it quickly, shivering as a cold gust of snowy air filtered into the tent, then took the boots Alaric handed me just as he finished wrapping up his own boots.

I put the boots on quickly, grateful to find that I finally had the hang of neatly wrapping up the strips of leather to anchor the boots around my ankles. Alaric left the tent, then offered me a hand out. I took his hand gratefully and stood, waiting for Mikael to make whatever sarcastic remark he was holding in.

I watched his face as he stood there, still holding onto the ponies, but instead of speaking, he offered me a *knowing* smile. A smile that said, *I just slept next to you all night, my body pressed firmly against yours, and there's nothing you can do to take it back.*

I scowled and gave Alaric's hand a squeeze, almost wishing Mikael would go back to being mad at us.

"Am I expected to ride that thing?" I asked, turning my attention to one of the ponies.

"It's likely not wise to exert yourself after what you experienced last night," Mikael explained.

I frowned and looked back to the animals. One of the ponies was pure white, looking innocent and pristine, while the other two were muddy brown in color. Guess which one I got.

I took the offered reins from Mikael and rubbed my chilled fingers across the animal's white neck. She bumped against me obligingly, so I snuggled up to her side while Mikael and Alaric packed up the tent and bedding.

When we were ready to go, I stepped back and put the reins over the animal's head, then prepared to insert my foot into the stirrup to climb onto the pony's back, only there was no saddle, only a rough blanket. I wasn't quite sure how to climb up without a stirrup to guide me. The ponies were fairly short, so maybe I could have hoisted myself, but I was feeling shaky enough that I was afraid to try. Finally, Alaric moved to my side and gave me an effortless boost, allowing me to climb onto the horse with little to no exertion on my part. Once seated, I steadied myself. I would still have preferred a saddle, but at least the pony was wide enough to make me feel secure in my seat. I looked down at Alaric with a reassuring smile, then he left me to take his reins from Mikael.

Before climbing atop the final pony still in his possession, Mikael came to stand beside me, digging for something in the satchel hanging from his shoulder. With his height, and how short my pony was, we weren't that far from eye level. He pulled his hand out of the satchel and offered me something akin to a pastry, only larger and round.

I raised an eyebrow at him. "Sweets for breakfast?"

"Aren't pregnant woman supposed to crave this sort of stuff?" he teased.

He'd meant it in a joking way, but my mood instantly fell. Was I even still pregnant? Did I want to be? With the threat of the key, I'd probably be better off without a child growing inside of me, but I'd also become attached to the little life.

Not commenting on my sudden change of mood, Mikael left me with the pastry in my hand, then climbed atop his pony while Alaric did the same. They both made their way to the main path while I followed shortly behind. I took a large bite of the pastry-like item. I *was* craving sweets, not that I was about to admit it. It was likely just a result of the long periods I've gone without calories.

Eventually the path widened into a road, and we were all able to ride side-by-side.

"Where did your friends go?" I asked, tired of the silence that had drawn out when the path was narrow.

Mikael startled, as if deep in thought, then glanced over at me, pushing a lock of hair away from his face. "Friends?"

"The ones that wanted to kill me for being a witch," I clarified.

Alaric snorted from my other side, but didn't comment.

"Well," Mikael sighed, "I had to defend your honor, so I killed them."

My jaw dropped. He had to be joking, right?

He let me off the hook with his laughter, then explained. "They invited me to sail with them, but I told them I had prior obligations. They departed first thing this morning," He was silent for a moment, then added, "While we were all nestled, warm in our bed."

I scowled.

He winked in reply.

"How much farther until we reach our destination," Alaric interrupted tiredly. Mikael had attempted to give him a sweet roll too, but he'd refused, and had seemed dejected ever since.

Mikael pointed off into the distance to a rising hill covered in the same sparse trees surrounding us. I could barely make out stone ruins near the top of the hill, but little else.

"Are there more Norns in our near future?" I asked, hoping the ruins would mean an end to our journey, and a return to modern times.

"Just one," he answered, gazing off into the distance ahead.

"*One*?" Alaric asked incredulously. "And that will be enough to send us back?"

Mikael chuckled. "Absolutely not, but she might have something that will aid us. She did it for me once before . . . " he trailed off.

He had to be referring to the first time he went back in an attempt to save his village, but I wasn't about to bring that up again. Before I could say anything, Alaric grumbled, "This better not be a waste of time."

Mikael smiled. I really wished I knew what he was finding so damn funny. "All will be revealed once we reach the crest of the hill," he explained cryptically.

*Yeah*, that's what I was afraid of.

## 22

It had started snowing again. I did my best to stay warm, huddled against the cold on my white pony. The animal's breath fogged the air near its muzzle as it labored onward. We'd nearly reached the top of the hill. The roadside, sprinkled with chunks of old stone covered in moss, was becoming quickly obscured in white.

Mikael rode ahead of us. He seemed unfazed by the cold, even as little white snowflakes began to cling to his loose, dusky red hair. He looked odd atop the little pony, especially with the intimidating touch of his great sword's pommel jutting over his shoulder.

I looked to Alaric as his pony caught up to mine. He looked worried. "Are you warm enough?" he asked softly.

My teeth were on the verge of chattering, but I nodded. It didn't really matter how cold I was, since there was nothing I could do about it.

Mikael's pony turned away from the path ahead of us. From our vantage point, and with snow obscuring our vision, it appeared he was riding straight into the mountainside on one side of the path. I had a moment of confusion before realizing he was riding into a cavern.

Alaric and I urged our ponies forward, anxious to get out of the cold.

The cave came into view, its entrance roughly eight feet tall. The opening would have seemed man-made if we were in a time where dynamite was used for mining. I could see Mikael inside the cave, dismounting his pony, but I could make out little else. Alaric rode in first, while I followed cautiously behind him.

Once inside, I observed the deceivingly large space until we reached Mikael and dismounted. The cavern was empty. No Norn. No signs of inhabitance. Nothing.

"What gives?" I asked, finally giving in and letting my teeth chatter.

Mikael calmly crouched down and began building a fire in the center of the cave. The ceiling was high enough we likely wouldn't get smoked out, and upon closer inspection, I could see that fires had been built there in the past, and there was even spare wood that Mikael was using now.

"Sit down," he instructed. "We may have to wait a while, and in the meantime, I'd like to tell you a story."

"We don't want to hear any stories," Alaric said coldly. "We want to know why you've led us to a deserted cave."

Mikael looked up from what he was doing to smirk at Alaric. "The story is for Madeline's benefit, and trust me, she wants to hear it."

I sat down with a huff as Alaric took my pony's reins. Arguing would be futile, so it was best to just get it over with.

Mikael stared Alaric down until he grudgingly sat beside me, trailing the ponies' reins in his left hand. The animals seemed content to be out of the snow, showing no hints that they planned to run. Mikael had released his pony completely.

As Mikael's fire caught, he sat down across from us and cleared his throat. "In the beginning," he began, "there was Yggdrasil, the World Tree."

"I've heard of that before," I interrupted.

Mikael rolled his eyes. "Yes, Madeline, many myths are founded in truth, though they become convoluted over time. Now no more interruptions." He eyed me until I nodded. "In the myths," he continued, "the Norns gathered around Yggdrasil's roots, and tended the tree. Really, they *were* the tree."

"I don't remember that part of the story," Alaric interrupted.

Mikael glared at him. "That's because you've been told the convoluted version that was altered to suit those in power. Now please, no more interruptions."

Alaric gave a sarcastic roll of his hand for Mikael to go on.

"The Norns are the weavers of fate," Mikael continued, his face illuminated by the fire to look somewhat sinister, "and Yggdrasil held them in place, merging time and fate. Within the bounds of time and fate, there is polarity. Light and dark. Life and death."

It wasn't the first time polarity had been mentioned to me. Like Alaric had said, life needed death, peace needed war, and so forth.

"After many centuries," Mikael continued, "the Norns

grew lonely. They plucked the strings of fate for humanity, watching people live and die, passing on their legacy to their children. The Norns wanted children of their own, and thus, the Vaettir were created."

I wrinkled my brow in confusion. So we were the Norns . . . children?

Mikael raised his eyebrows at me, daring me to interrupt him again. When I didn't, he continued, "The Norns embody all things in nature, as it is the divine force within us all. This energy also composed the old gods. Each of these new children embodied an aspect of the old gods the Norns missed so dearly, minor and major deities alike."

I glanced at Alaric, then back to Mikael, both embodiments of major deities, but not the highest tier.

"But the plan backfired," Mikael stated abruptly. "With each of the Vaettir embodying only one aspect of nature, they were far different from the Norns. The darker forces weren't directly balanced by the light. Forces of greed, the thirst for power, and stubborn independence led to the dismemberment of the World Tree."

I had become so enthralled in his story that I gasped, then held a hand to my mouth in embarrassment.

Alaric put an arm around my shoulder as Mikael flashed me a teasing grin.

*We were divided*, a voice said, but it wasn't Mikael speaking. The voice was in my head. I looked to Alaric to see if he'd heard it too, but he'd already turned to find the source of the voice.

I followed his gaze to a tall silhouette, blocking much of the cave's entrance.

The voice in my head continued, *Our children destroyed Yggdrasil, and separated us from time.*

The form stepped forward, revealing a Norn with the great antlers of a moose. I could make out little else of her figure.

*The separation created myself and my sisters as we are now,* she continued, speaking directly into our minds. *It let time dictate itself freely, while we remain in stasis. The division did little harm, but there was something else. There was the magic that held us together. Wild, chaotic magic, that had been tainted by the residue of those who dismembered the tree. It formed a key.*

This time I wasn't embarrassed when I gasped. I reached up to the key at my throat. Could it be?

The Norn took another step forward so that I could see her green-tinged skin and large, angular eyes clearly in the firelight. She had the paws of a wolf at the ends of her arms. Her thin lips offered me a confusing smile.

"I told you that you wanted to hear my story," Mikael mocked.

I shot him a glare, then turned back to the Norn, willing her to tell me what I needed to hear. Alaric had shifted his hand to my leg. He watched the Norn just as apprehensively as I.

*Are you ready?* the Norn's voice echoed through my head.

"For wha—" I began to ask, but it was too late.

The air of the cave pressed down on me. I felt like all of my bones were being crushed. I opened my mouth to scream, but there was too much pressure for me to even make a peep. Just when I felt like I might die, I was thrust upward. The cave was gone, and I was surrounded by darkness, speckled with lights that stretched oddly in my vision as I sped by them. Alaric had lost his hold on my leg, so I was alone in the dazzling emptiness.

Suddenly I thudded to the ground, and it was as if time and space were rushing to catch up to me. The scenery around me blurred with motion until it all came to a crashing halt, leaving me in my still surroundings.

Moist sand soaked into the knees of my pants, and I could hear the ocean not far off. The sky was a calm, perfect blue. I turned my gaze upward to what was towering over me. It was a tree, growing straight out of the beach, its roots twisting upward out of the sand to swirl in a dizzying pattern, forming the tree's bark. From the top, its branches spanned outward, obscuring the sky with their silvery, pointed leaves.

Somehow I knew the tree was an ash tree, and I knew its name. Yggdrasil. The Norn had transported me back in time to lie at the roots of the friggin World Tree, sometime before it was destroyed.

Even worse. I was alone.

---

Sophie sat on her butt in the dirt, glaring at those who surrounded her. James sat beside her, looking thoroughly cowed.

"What did you do?" Aila demanded, standing over Sophie like a Viking goddess of war.

Sophie frowned. She was descended from Bastet, a true goddess of war, not this, this *imposter*.

"You were supposed to go with Alaric and Madeline," Aila continued. "You shouldn't be back already. Where is Mikael?"

Faas and Tabitha stood behind Aila. Faas was short for a man at 5'7", and definitely short compared to Aila and Tabitha. He watched the conversation curiously, void of the venomous expression he'd had around Madeline. Sophie would never understand the rivalry all executioners seemed to hold to. She had little doubt Faas would kill Madeline, given the chance.

Noticing Sophie's gaze, he flipped the long portion of his blond hair to partially obscure his eyes. It would have worked better had all his hair been long, but the sides were shaved nearly to the skin.

Tabitha stepped up beside Aila, appearing slight near Aila's muscular form, despite their almost equal height. Tabitha's blonde hair was nearly white, a common color among Mikael's people. "Perhaps she escaped," Tabitha commented, not seeming to care much either way.

Sophie was growing increasingly irritated as those speaking continued to exclude her. She would have liked to stand, but the axes and spears of other Vaettir surrounding her and James kept her seated. She could probably take most of them on in a fight, but without her brother to watch her back, she didn't dare risk it.

"Where the hell is my brother!" she growled, interrupting the murmurs of conversation that had sprung up around her.

"See?" Tabitha replied, looking at Aila instead of Sophie. "She must have been left behind."

Aila replied with a sharp nod, then crouched down to

grab Sophie's arm, hauling her to her feet. Sophie was built more like Tabitha, and was only a few inches taller than Faas. She found Aila's size slightly intimidating, though she would never admit it out loud.

"You will wait with us until Mikael returns with the others," Aila stated. She glanced down at James. "Him too," she added.

Sophie shook out of Aila's grasp, then scowled up at the imposing woman. "I will remain for the time being," Sophie agreed, "but if it takes too long, I'll find my brother myself."

Aila gave Sophie a wry smile. "As you wish," she agreed. "Now come with me. There are many plans to be made, and I will not turn down the advice of a descendant of Bastet."

Sophie stood a little straighter, glad her heritage had been acknowledged. "Really, I don't know how you ever intended to go to war *without* my advice."

Aila smirked, then turned to lead Sophie back toward one of the many tents composing their camp. Sophie followed, leaving James where he sat, eyeing the Vaettir around him with apprehension. Sophie really would have to do something about his memory. Maybe she'd have Aila hit him. That amount of force would have to do *something*.

---

I STARED up at the massive tree before me in complete awe. I didn't know at what point in history the tree had been destroyed, but I knew it had happened a very long time before the time I'd come from, and an unfathomable amount of time before the time I belonged in.

I rose to my feet and brushed the sand from my clothing. The key was silent at my throat. If I didn't know any better, I might have guessed it was afraid.

I turned and surveyed the empty beach, unsure of what I was supposed to do.

"Alaric!" I called out.

No answer.

"Mikael!"

All was silent.

I trudged through the sand toward the sound of the ocean, which came into sight as I crested a large dune. I would have liked to think Alaric and Mikael had been sent back with me, landing somewhere out of hearing range, but not too far off, yet for some reason I doubted it. Some sort of internal instinct screamed at me that I was completely alone.

I gazed out at the calm ocean. It was warmer here. The short leather and fur coat I wore was almost too much. I continued walking, stripping the coat off as I went.

I reached the shoreline and gazed down at the frothy water as it lapped toward my feet, only to rescind with the tide. The water seemed normal enough. I found myself wishing I could see into its depths. If I was far back enough in time, all sorts of fascinating primordial creatures might lurk there.

I shook my head and stepped away from the water. I was back here to do *something*. Something important. I didn't have time to wonder about the mysteries of the deep.

I made my way back to the tree and stared up at it, not understanding how the Norns were *part* of the tree. I kept imagining them living inside of it, but I was pretty sure that wasn't how it worked.

I held my breath as the sound of hushed voices reached my ears, then suddenly silenced. I looked around, unsure of where they'd come from, then looked back to the tree. Not knowing what else to do, I reached up to the lowest branch and plucked a single leaf, then brought it close to my face. It looked like a normal leaf.

I gripped the leaf in my palm, then placed my other hand on the rough bark of the tree. The gentle ocean breeze pushed my hair back from my face, but everything else was still. I was about to remove my hand when I felt a gentle thrumming resonating from within the tree. The key at my neck echoed that resonance.

Excitement rushed through me, maybe I'd found what I was supposed to do. I felt the tree's energy flow up my arm as the key thrummed fervently. Wait. No! I watched in horror as the bark beneath my palm grew gray with death. The gray area spread, then pieces of the bark began to flake off, turning to ash before they hit the ground.

I tried to pull away, but my hand felt glued to the tree. The dead patch continued to spread. Hot tears streamed down my face. Panic crushed my chest. The Norn had sent me back to Yggdrasil to do who knows what, and now I was killing it. I was killing the World Tree.

I fell to my knees, but my hand remained firmly against the tree. I could feel the key's joy as we both filled up with energy. My thoughts turned to Alaric. What would he think if he could see me now? Killing the tree that gave life to his people. *Our* people.

Alaric's face filled my mind's eye as I focused all of my

energy onto getting back to him. I needed to get back. There was still so much to do. Suddenly my hand fell from the tree, and I was overcome with a feeling of vertigo. I kept my eyes firmly shut as the sand beneath me seemed to solidify into hard, cold earth. Someone wrapped their arms around me, but I struggled away. I was a killer. The only thing I could offer anyone was death.

My entire body buzzed with the energy of Yggdrasil. I was pretty sure I'd broken away before I killed the tree entirely, but the only way to know for sure was to look at it.

I opened my eyes, and there was no tree. Suddenly the arms around me made sense. I was back in the cave with Alaric and Mikael. The latter of whom was standing a short distance away, looking at me like I'd grown a second head.

I slowly unfurled one of my closed palms to see the leaf still in my hand, still silvery-green with life. With the energy of Yggdrasil, I'd traveled forward through time. I craned my neck back at Alaric as he put his arms around me once more.

"I'm back," I whispered in astonishment.

"You never left," he explained. "The Norn came and you fainted."

I looked down at the leaf in my hand again. "That's not possible," I said distantly. It had all felt so real, and the leaf *definitely* was real. I could feel Yggdrasil's power running through my veins. It echoed in the little leaf.

"Hold on to me," I demanded, though my voice came out as the barest of whispers.

Alaric's arms tightened around me, but Mikael still stood a good distance off.

"Hold on to me," I stated again, this time with more force as I looked up at Mikael.

I tried to steady my thoughts, but all I could feel was anger. Anger at the Vaettir for being so screwed up. Anger at the key for controlling me. Most of all, I felt anger at myself, for being an instrument of death and destruction.

Both of the men did as I bade them. I closed my hand around the leaf, crushing the remaining life out of it. Its energy zinged up my arm, and I was disgusted at the satisfaction I felt. I would have liked to blame it on the key, but I knew part of it was my own emotion. Emotion springing from that deeply repressed instinct that makes us what we truly are. I was death, and I enjoyed it.

I squeezed my eyes shut as the remaining power from Yggdrasil lit up my veins to make me feel all-powerful. Unstoppable. It was a wonderful yet sickening feeling.

I thought of the Salr back in our current time where the Norns were. This time the movement was barely jarring. Before I knew it, I felt cold stone beneath me.

I opened my eyes and saw blood. The floor was drenched in it, and the stone walls were painted with it. The cool liquid began to soak into my pants as I sat there, stunned.

Mikael and Alaric were both more quick to react, dragging me to my feet and away from the macabre scene. As my eyes fully focused, I saw the first of the bodies, its antlered head twisted at a strange angle, its bestial paw reaching out past its body, as if begging for mercy.

Alaric held me close to him. "You have to release them," he whispered in my ear.

His voice seemed like it was a million miles away. My

eyes darted around the room as I took in more corpses. "I can't," I replied numbly.

Alaric gave me a gentle shake as if trying to bring me back to reality. "Madeline," he coaxed, "you can't leave them in there. They're like us. They need to be released."

I shook my head. "No, I can't release them because someone already did."

It was the truth. I couldn't feel their pain, or their deaths. They were empty shells, nothing more. I recalled the amount of power I'd received from releasing a single Norn's life. Someone had come in here and released the lives of six. There were so many implications, but the one my mind honed in on was the fact that there was another executioner walking around out there with some serious juice.

Alaric had disappeared from my side without me realizing, and now returned to take my arm. "Sophie isn't here," he breathed, relief clear in his voice. "Neither is James."

Piecing things together, Mikael hoisted a small hand-ax up to his shoulder. "We need to make sure my people are alright."

I nodded, still feeling numb. I'd take numbness any day over the fear I knew would wash in eventually. "Where'd you get the ax?" I questioned.

Mikael smirked. "You didn't think I'd travel all the way back in time just to ask a few questions, did you?"

He turned on his heel and led the way out of the gory room. I did my best not to look at the corpses as we walked. If the Norns were, in a sense, our mothers, some serious matricide had just been committed. I felt a mixture of rage and guilt for their deaths. Rage, because they had been completely innocent, and guilt, because we had probably led the killer right to them. If we hadn't used the Norns to go back in time, they might still be alive.

Some might say pain and anger are the best fuels for vengeance, but in that moment, I knew better. Guilt fueled the fires of vengeance like nothing else. I had no doubt in my mind that taking the lives of the killers would be justice, not murder. I wouldn't be factoring anyone else's perspective into it.

There were many moments where I hated what I was, and what I had to do.

This moment was not one of them.

## 23

Sophie twirled around like a dancer, a long blade in each hand. This is what she lived for.

The attack came during the night. Aislin's people, by the look of it, given that Sophie didn't recognize any of them.

Sophie's blade met with flesh. She barely even registered whose life she had just taken, only that they were part of the enemy force. That was all that mattered. Aila had her back, swinging through the oncoming attackers with a giant ax.

To her left, Sophie barely registered Faas, releasing the souls from the fallen, and using that energy to injure or impede their enemies. With several attackers dead at her feet, Sophie took a moment to survey what had turned into a battlefield. Through the fighting, she thought she saw a glimpse of curly hair, and perfect, dark skin. Maya.

With a grunt of rage she rushed forward, leaving the ranks of Aila and the others. It was an unwise move as it left her back vulnerable to attack, but she couldn't help it. Maya had to pay for betraying her.

Sophie wove through the onslaught, darting around attackers like they were nothing. She knew her eyes and teeth had gone feline, and could feel her nails lengthening. She sheathed her dual blades at her waist as she ran. Killing Maya with her bare hands seemed a more fitting justice.

Just before she reached the area where Maya had been, something incredibly powerful knocked her off her feet. She fell to the bloody earth. There was a ringing in her ears, and she couldn't seem to move.

---

We raced forward as the first tents came into view. The sound of fighting was all around. Mikael had known exactly where to go. He let out a cry of rage as we reached the scene of the battle, and his people fighting for their lives. He rushed off, leaving me and Alaric on the outskirts, hidden in the trees.

We took a few steps closer, then the pain reached me. Bloodlust and fear were distant echoes, unable to rival the emotions of both physical pain, and the pain of losing friends and loved ones. It was all I could do to remain standing.

Alaric stayed back with me, though I could tell he wanted to race forward to find his sister. His resolve to protect me hung on a tenuous string, and I didn't blame him one bit. I would have rushed forward too if I could move.

Inside my head the key laughed, blocking out some of the pain. I stood a little straighter, grateful for the reprieve, but also fearful, knowing it was the key's influence that helped me shut things out.

I turned to Alaric, about to say we should move forward, then something swept across the battlefield like a shockwave. I watched in awe as the Vaettir in the distance were thrown like rag dolls.

Alaric stood immobile. "What was that?" he asked in disbelief, finally taking another step forward.

I shook my head. I knew, but seemed unable to speak. I had felt that type of energy before, coming from my own hands.

"The power from the Norns," I said finally, as if it explained everything.

Apparently it did. Alaric grabbed my arm and dragged me backward. "You need to hide," he demanded. "If there's another executioner here with that much power, they'll kill you."

I knew he was going to leave me to see if Sophie was alright. "They'll kill you too!" I gasped.

He kissed me on the forehead, then pulled away. Before I could grab him, he was gone. To hell with that. I threw my body forward and ran after him, letting the key take control enough to block out everything on the battlefield. It was a mistake, but I saw no other choice.

I ran through the dark trees. Branches snagged at my clothing, inflicting superficial cuts on my flesh. It didn't matter. My lungs burned with exertion. Luckily the fight wasn't far off.

Moments later, I reached Alaric's side. He turned to

scowl at me, but the moment was short lived as he returned his attention to more immediate threats. There were bodies all around us, many dead, but some still groaning in pain. It was like a giant wave had hit them, only there was no water. Judging by their clothing, it seemed like many of the victim's weren't Mikael's people. *Everyone* had been hit, with complete disregard for casualties.

At the center of the bodies stood a man, clothed in a form-fitting black coat, and matching black pants. Long hair that was either white or gray hung forward to cover his face.

Dark shapes milled about roughly twenty feet behind him. More enemy troops, ready to kill off any survivors.

Distantly I could feel death around me. It was enough death to attempt destroying the key, but what then? If I could absorb all the power, I might be able to focus it, but if the destruction didn't take out the other executioner, surely he or the Vaettir waiting behind him would kill us soon after.

Alaric tried to tug me behind him, but I refused. I didn't deserve to be shielded. The key was muttering in my mind, near incoherent thoughts of excitement. It knew I couldn't destroy it then. I needed it to survive, or so it assured me. It was right.

Someone stepped around the still form of the other executioner, a small woman in an out of place ballgown. She even wore a little sparkly tiara on her head, glinting in the moonlight. Her face appeared middle-aged. Her hair, its color indistinguishable in the low light, was done in soft ringlets like a little girl would wear. I could feel the centuries she'd lived echoing outward as her cold eyes found me.

"Aislin, I presume," I called out, sounding much more confident than I felt. I could hear fighting in the distance, but it was far off. Those on the ground around us were all still.

"Smart girl," Aislin replied, a hint of English to her accent.

The key thrummed around my neck, and I knew the next words out of my mouth were not my own. "It would be wise for you to bow to your new ruler, little Doyen."

Rage crossed her face, but the emotion was almost instantly wiped away. She raised one delicate, gloved hand up to the executioner at her side, gesturing for him to act.

He threw back his arm, then began to bring it forward for another shockwave. In the split second I had to make a decision, I knew I had no choice. I opened my mind fully to the key. Suddenly, all I could feel were the dead around me. The key sucked in their energy, releasing their souls without me even having to touch them. The power flooded me, just as the other executioner's wave of energy shot forward.

My hand raised in front of me of its own volition. I felt Alaric at my side, trying to move me out of the path of the shockwave, but I was like a mighty tree rooted in the earth. He couldn't move me, and if he stayed where he was the shockwave would hit him too.

Just before the wave would have hit us, energy shot from my hand to intercept it. Though the individual energies would be invisible to the untrained eye, the collision caused an eruption of static electricity. It crackled blue in the darkness, from the ground to a good twenty feet up in the air. As the energy dissipated, both Aislin and the other executioner stared at me in awe, unharmed, but so were we.

The other executioner looked down at Aislin. His voice sounded strained as he said, "Her energy calls to me."

I had a feeling I wasn't supposed to hear him, but all of my senses were heightened. The key was still sucking in the life of everyone around me. Alaric stood at my side, strong and immune to my vampiric powers.

Both Aislin and the other executioner were staring at me. "Now is not the time," Aislin said finally.

They retreated, and I let them. Not allowing myself to think, I reached up and snapped the cord holding the key around my neck. I focused all the energy I'd absorbed onto the key dangling from my hand, spinning and glinting in the moonlight. Its screams of rage echoed through my mind.

It fought against me. Our similar powers ricocheted off each other, much like what had happened with the other executioner. I had the energy needed to destroy it, but I only had one piece of the puzzle. I knew how to do it, but if the key could predict my every thought, it could counter my every move.

I lowered the key and grunted in frustration.

Alaric came up behind me, pressing his hands tentatively on my shoulders. "Maddy," he said softly, "there are many injured. Maybe you can help them. I have to find Sophie."

I looked out across the fallen, ashamed that I had momentarily forgotten them. I tied the key around my neck as it gloated in my mind. I tried to send my stored energy out to Mikael's people, but the key blocked me.

I hissed in frustration. "We can't have a war if half of our army is dead," I said out loud.

"What?" Alaric called out as he scanned the dark for his sister.

I shook my head. What I'd said gave the key pause. A moment later, I was able to send my energy outward, searching for those who could be healed. I felt sick as I realized all the bodies nearest me were fully dead. I'd taken their lives without a second thought, even though some may have otherwise survived.

With a muffled sob, I turned my attention away from them and back to the wounded. I may have given death, but I could also heal. I could feel wounds being knit in the distance as if they were my own. I could even sense each individual, which was something entirely new. I sensed Mikael, and knew he had been injured in the blast, but would live, and I sensed Sophie, cradled in Alaric's arms as he found her, already healed, but dazed.

I stood in the cold moonlight, feeling two dozen lives in my mind, yet I felt entirely alone. I could sense the key above all else. It knew it had me. It knew I would never survive any of this without it. There was only one final choice to make, and the key offered it willingly. Would I be its partner, or its slave?

# 24

We burned the bodies. The battle here had happened far from civilization, but some hiker would have discovered the grisly scene eventually. Heck, with the cops likely combing the land after we left them guessing back at Mikael's house, they might happen upon the scene sooner rather than later. We needed to minimize the evidence.

It felt odd to finally be back in modern times. The atrocities against Mikael's village would never be investigated. No one would ever be brought to justice. I had to say, I mostly appreciated the justice system of the modern times, even when it worked against me.

Hiding bodies was an anxiety inducing prospect, but wasn't the matter at the forefront of my mind. I'd missed my first chance to destroy the key. The whole purpose of starting a war was to give me enough energy to destroy it, but how do you destroy something that can see into your head? The answer, you don't. Erykah was right. I had to learn to shield my thoughts, else all was lost.

Aislin's people had retreated after I had neutralized her executioner. Aislin knew exactly what the key was, I was sure of it. She knew she didn't stand a chance against it. I briefly wondered if she knew I'd killed her sister, or if she knew that her great-nephew James was among those her people had injured. He was fine now, except for the missing memory.

Alaric walked up beside me, stinking of smoke from burning the bodies. "We're done here."

I couldn't bring myself to meet his eyes. If only he'd known how close I'd come to losing myself entirely to the key. It was quiet now, but I was certain it could flood my thoughts again whenever it chose.

Sophie joined us, fully healed. Mikael and his people had marveled at the effect of my healing energy, since most executioners caused only destruction, but Sophie had merely been irritated. Maya had escaped her again, and that was all she had to express.

Mikael walked up out of the darkness, followed by Aila. Most of his people had been sent on ahead of us. "We need to move far from this place," Mikael stated. "I'm without many of my contacts, and can't cover up anything that's happened any more than we already have. The human police will likely be on a terrorist hunt quite soon."

I nodded, but didn't speak, thinking of the burned bodies. So much death had transpired, and only more would come.

"What will we do now?" I asked distantly.

Mikael gazed up at the moon. "Once we are safe, we

plan the next battle. This time, it will be in a place and under terms of our choosing." He turned to Aila. "Scout the way ahead. Make sure no one waits in ambush."

Aila nodded sharply.

"I'll join her," Sophie volunteered, then looked to Alaric expectantly.

He waved sarcastically. "Have fun!"

Sophie placed her hands on her hips. "We have better eyes and ears than most. We'll be able to see any scouts before they see us."

Alaric grunted in reply, then glanced at me.

"I'll keep her safe," Mikael assured.

Alaric looked over my head at him. "Somehow, I don't find that comforting."

A moment later, Alaric, Sophie, and Aila slipped away. I felt the barest caress of Alaric's hand on my back as he left, leaving me with shivers as I stared back up at the moon.

"Your ability to heal . . . " Mikael trailed off.

I continued looking up at the sky. "Pretty good for a creature of death, eh?"

Mikael chuckled, then gently guided me forward as the few members of his clan left with us began walking.

Mikael glanced at me. "What exactly did you do right before that?"

Before I could answer, Faas walked past us, glaring all the while. He probably hated me even more now that I'd saved his life.

"Hmm?" I asked, watching Faas walk away. "Before what?"

"I've been told you defeated the other executioner. How?" he clarified. "He was a force to be reckoned with."

I winced, uncomfortable with what I'd done. Not only with *how* I'd saved us, but with the wary looks Mikael's people now gave me. They might be alive because of me, but it wouldn't stop them from being cautious. If I was a threat to Aislin, I was a threat to everyone.

I bit my lip, feeling uneasy about what I was going to admit. "The key took control. I let it."

At that moment I really wished I could sense Mikael's emotions, but he was giving me nothing. His face remained passive. "That was unwise, Madeline," he said finally.

Well, *duh*. "I tried to destroy it afterward," I explained, "but it knew my every move. I had the energy to do it, but the key had the energy too. When I attacked the other executioner, our energy collided. The same thing happened when I tried to attack the key. It fended off my every attack. I couldn't have even dropped it to the ground in that moment, that's how powerless I was."

Mikael sighed. "I suppose all of this is my fault."

I gave him a surprised look and almost tripped on a branch. He grabbed my forearm to keep me from falling, then let go as soon as I'd righted myself. "How so?"

"If I had taught you to shield when you first asked me, you might have been able to destroy the key."

I shook my head. "I doubt it's something I'll be able to learn in a day."

Alaric appeared in the woods ahead of us, then made his way toward us as we continued walking.

"All clear ahead," he explained upon reaching us, then fell into step beside me. "Sophie and Aila are looping back around to ensure we are not followed." He looked over my head at Mikael. "I'll scout further once you tell us where we're going."

"We'll need to split up again," Mikael explained. "We're too easy to track in a large group. We will only come together when we're ready to attack. There is another house at my disposal where we may hide."

"My sister stays with us," Alaric said instantly.

"Agreed," Mikael replied, "As will some of my people."

"What about James?" I interrupted. I hadn't even had a chance to talk to him since we'd gotten back. It seemed cruel to just leave him with a bunch of people he didn't know, even if he deserved it.

Mikael nodded. "Three for Madeline, and three for me."

"Aila, I'm assuming," Alaric guessed, "but who else?"

"Faas and Tabitha," Mikael answered.

I tripped again, and both men dove in to steady me. I seriously needed some rest. I was going to end up impaling myself on a branch. "Faas?" I questioned, feeling a nervous ripple in my chest. When I'd first met him, I'd been dying to ask him a ton of questions. Now, I would have preferred to be anywhere but near him.

Mikael gave me a knowing look. "There are few I would trust more."

I raised an eyebrow. "Do you trust him to not try to kill me?"

Mikael laughed.

Alaric grunted in irritation.

"I trust him to do as I command," Mikael replied.

I supposed that would have to be good enough. Really, with the forces currently gunning for me, one executioner with a bad attitude shouldn't worry me. I should be more worried about one who would kill the beings that created us just to ramp up his power, or about the two rulers hell-bent on gaining control over all. Still, it was Faas' cold, angry eyes that would haunt me that night.

# 25

When Mikael had said *house*, I'd assumed he'd really meant a house. Something similar to the quaint little home we'd stayed in before being chased off by the police. The living room where our group now stood was as large as my entire little house back in Spokane.

The house's owners, an elderly couple, watched us excitedly from the entry room. The woman wore a classic sheath dress and pearls that made her look like an elderly version of Audrey Hepburn. Her husband was a little less dapper with his wrinkled plaid shirt and green trousers.

"Who are these people?" I whispered, leaning in close to Mikael's shoulder.

With us were Alaric, Sophie, James, Aila, Faas, and Tabitha. I thought again how I could have done without the latter three, or really, the latter four, but I hadn't chosen the arrangements. Mikael's people stood near him, and mine near me.

"They're my fan club," he answered mischievously, too far away for the old couple to hear.

I walked a few steps further into the living room. The furniture was all over-stuffed, done in floral fabric heavy on the gold thread. The rug beneath our dirty boots probably cost several grand.

"Fan club?" I questioned softly as Alaric went to marvel at one of the painted landscapes on the wall. James stood near our hosts, seeming to prefer their less aggressive company.

"They're historians of mythology, more specifically of Dolos and Prometheus," Mikael explained. "They're quite fond of me."

"But they're human," I argued. I didn't really know that for a fact, but it seemed a safe guess considering how they were gawking at us.

Mikael snickered. "Some humans are more informed than others, choosing not to look blindly past what is right in front of their faces."

"But we haven't been right in front of their faces," I argued. "We've been hidden away within various Salr."

"Your beau and his little sister, perhaps, but not I," he said with a waggle of his eyebrows.

"I can hear you," Alaric said tiredly as he slumped across the cushy couch uninvited.

Sophie lowered herself to sit primly beside him. Mikael's people stood waiting near the entryway, silent like good little minions.

"Can we get you anything!" the elderly woman finally burst out, waving one of her frail hands in the air to gain our attention.

The old couple's excitement was palpable, yet there was no twinge of fear or anxiety. They trusted Mikael, though they probably shouldn't have.

The Viking in question gave a slight bow. "Dinner would be lovely."

My stomach growled at the mention of food. More pressing still was my need for a shower. Between the time we'd spent in a livestock shed back in Viking days and the burning of my victim's bodies, I stunk.

Our hostess hurried off to the kitchen, dragging her husband behind her. James watched them forlornly as they disappeared down the hall. With our hosts' advanced age, and the size of the house, I knew they likely had help with the upkeep, but I saw nor sensed anyone else.

Sophie, still seated on the couch with her spine ramrod straight, aimed an icy glare at Mikael, "You should not let them worship you."

With Sophie's superior attitude, I was surprised she cared. It made me feel a little more warmly toward her. I didn't like taking advantage of the sweet old couple either, and I liked even less that our presence might be endangering them.

Before Mikael could make whatever sarcastic remark he had in mind, I cleared my throat. He turned his gaze away from Sophie to land on me. "Yes, Madeline?"

"I agree with Sophie," I stated, "but right now I'm more worried about someone finding us here, and our hosts getting caught in the crossfire."

"No one will find us here," Mikael assured.

"They found us last time," Sophie cut in before I could point out that fact.

Mikael suddenly looked angry, but he stored it away quickly. "We had a, what is the modern term?" He held up a finger. "Oh yes, a *mole*."

"Not exactly a modern term," I muttered.

Alaric stood abruptly. "One of your people gave us away?" he hissed.

Mikael tilted his head and gave a slight nod, remaining calm.

Alaric looked past Mikael to where Aila, Tabitha, and Faas stood. "And how do you know they will not do so again?"

Mikael glared at Alaric. "No one else knows we're here. Those who have accompanied us have been by my side longer than you've been alive. I trust them with my life."

"I hope so," Alaric replied, his voice low, "because you're trusting them with *ours*."

Tabitha shifted uncomfortably under Alaric's gaze, while Aila remained indifferent. Faas glared at *me*. I glared right back, wanting to flip him off, but knowing we were all close enough to a fight as it was.

"I need a shower," I grumbled. I looked to Mikael, "I trust our *hosts* won't mind?"

He gestured toward a hallway further into the house. "Up the stairs, third door on the left."

"Great," I muttered, then turned and walked away.

Alaric followed me out of the room, with Sophie close behind. We both stopped and turned questioning looks at her.

"Well I'm not staying with *them*," she explained, gesturing behind her at the Vikings.

"Whatever," I grumbled. I turned to continue walking, leaving James to take care of himself.

Mikael's directions held true. Up a very wide set of stairs covered in the cushiest carpet I'd ever felt, and past several closed doors, we found the bathroom.

Sophie leaned her back against the hallway wall and slid downward with bent knees until she was slumped into a seated position, her legs pulled up against her chest. "Don't take too long," she advised. "I reek of blood and burnt flesh."

Ignoring Sophie, Alaric followed me into the bathroom. Though some alone time would have been nice, I didn't mind the company. Somehow having Alaric close made me feel less frightened, as if his very presence could ward away the impossible task of destroying the key.

Once the door was locked behind us, he cranked up the hot water in the shower. The place we were supposed to bathe was one of those huge, glass-walled contraptions, big enough to fit five people. There were multiple shower heads angled down from the ceiling in different directions. The shower didn't go well with the rest of the house. It was the epitome of modernity, nestled in a house filled with old-world, wealthy charm.

I stared at myself in the massive mirror above the double sinks as Alaric began to undress. My dark hair was matted and dirty, hanging limply nearly to my waist. My face was just as dirty, the mottled colors of soot and grime blending in with the bags under my eyes. I stared at myself, and wasn't sure if I recognized the girl in the mirror at all.

Alaric moved to stand behind me, fully comfortable in his nude state. His hair was somehow in better condition than mine, but it was also pin straight. It didn't tangle as much as my wavy mass.

"We don't have any clean clothes," I muttered miserably, only then realizing it.

Alaric turned me away from the mirror and helped me out of my tunic and pants, bending to undo my boots to remove the pants fully from my legs. He stood again, and stared down not at me, but the key around my neck.

"I brushed it when I was removing your shirt," he commented, "but it didn't knock me away. Not like last time."

I sighed. "I'm an empath and it's linked to me. It can sense your intent. It had no need to exert the energy to repel you when you were simply trying to undress me."

Alaric raised a dark brow at me. "You speak as if you can read its thoughts."

I stared up at him, letting all of my worry shine through in my expression.

"Oh, Maddy," he said softly. He wrapped me in his arms, understanding what I was trying to tell him. I *could* read the key's thoughts, and it could read mine. We became closer every time I used its power.

"It tolerates you because it knows you'll protect me," I whispered against his shoulder as the first of my tears fell.

He stroked my matted hair. "You make it sound almost benevolent."

As my tears fell faster, I began to shake. The hot water from the shower was filling up the entire bathroom with thick steam, making it hard to breathe, or maybe it was just my anxiety. Either way, I felt so suffocated I could hardly keep my feet.

"Sometimes I forget it isn't around to help me," I sobbed. "I don't know how to block it out, and sometimes its thoughts seem like they're mine. Sometimes I can't tell our thoughts apart at all."

Alaric rubbed small, comforting circles across my bare back. The touch of his skin on mine was the only thing keeping me grounded, and I dreaded the moment I'd have to step away.

"We'll insist that Mikael teaches you to shield tonight," Alaric assured. "Once you can block it out, your thoughts will be your own again. You're strong enough to do this, Maddy. I know it."

The key laughed in my mind. Shielding wouldn't work. I didn't really want the key out of my mind, did I? It was a part of me. I should want it as close to me as I wanted Alaric. *Closer*.

Alaric, unaware of my thoughts, at least I thought they were *my* thoughts, guided me gently into the shower. I couldn't seem to stop crying. Once the hot water hit me I felt like I couldn't move. My entire body was exhausted, as was my mind. The idea of keeping my thoughts separate from the key's was always in the back of my head, and in that moment I realized just how much energy I'd been expending on that goal. It was a constant battle, whether I realized it or not.

Alaric began to wash my hair, gently combing out the tangles with his fingers. I could feel his worry, and his sadness. Underneath that was fear, though whether it was fear for my sanity, or something else, I wasn't sure. I did, however, get the impression he thought we'd lost the baby.

My empathy at times was becoming eerily close to telepathy.

I shivered, despite the hot water running down my body. I had no definitive answer to soothe Alaric's mind either way. Part of me felt like I was maybe still pregnant, but I hadn't been sick or felt any other signs. It was just a feeling I had. I didn't want to get his hopes up based on a gut feeling. I could sense what the eventual disappointment might do to him.

Once Alaric had finished helping me wash, he positioned me so I'd be kept warm under the falling water, then moved to stand under one of the other shower heads so he could get clean. I watched as the water made his black hair even darker, cascading down his pale skin. Normally the sight would have put *other* thoughts in my mind, but all I craved was a good cuddle, and a long night's sleep.

I watched as he washed his hair, using the same shampoo he'd used in mine, something that looked and smelled pricey, and had probably been placed in the shower just for guests. As the foamy streaks washed down his body, I felt the sudden need to go to him. After all the scary crap that had happened, he was still here, doing his best to protect me. At some point I'd forgiven him fully for past betrayals. He had become my partner, in both name and action. It was a feeling I'd known little in my life.

I moved toward him and wrapped my arms around his waist, startling him since he'd closed his eyes to protect them from the shampoo. He responded seconds later, wrapping me in his embrace.

"Thank you for still being here," I said softly, huddling to share the single shower head with him.

"Thank you for existing," he replied.

I laughed, and it felt strange with all the emotions welling up in my chest. I pulled away slightly so I could look up at him. "That's not exactly something deserving of praise."

He pulled me tightly against his chest. "Yes it is," he whispered against my wet hair.

We stayed like that for a long while, until finally we had to admit we should probably get out of the shower. After shutting off the water, we stepped out and made use of the fluffy white towels stacked on a shelf near the door. With the towels wrapped around us, we both looked down at our dirty clothes with distaste.

"Any day now!" Sophie shouted from outside the bathroom door.

I frowned. "I can't decide if I'd be better off with dirty underwear, or no underwear at all."

Alaric gave me a mischievous grin. "I like the idea of no underwear."

I sighed. "You go without underwear in wool pants and tell me how much you like it."

Alaric chuckled and picked up the offending black panties. "Dirty underwear it is."

I grabbed them and put them on my clean body before I could think about it. I didn't care that we were in hiding. Tomorrow I'd be procuring some clean underwear, or else.

Sophie cleared her throat loudly.

We finished getting dressed and let ourselves out into the hall amidst a veil of steam. Sophie looked up at us from her seat on the carpet. "It's about damn time. It smells like dinner is ready."

Sophie rose to her feet and stalked past us, shutting herself in the bathroom. Alaric took my hand and gave it a squeeze before we prepared to head downstairs. I didn't fancy the idea of eating at the same table as Faas, but it was the least of my worries. When your life, free will, and perhaps your very soul were hanging in the balance, what was dinner with a mortal enemy?

## 26

Our meal was blissfully uneventful. Afterward, I found myself wandering the house alone while everyone else talked strategy. I'd never been involved in a war before, so my opinions weren't exactly valuable.

Our hosts, who I'd found out were named Clive and Marie, had dined with us. They were expats living in Norway, and they'd spent their lives tracking down the strange and unnatural, trying to find proof the old gods existed. Mikael had met them whilst drunk in a human bar, and had told them the story of his entire life. They didn't believe him, but remained friends. After twenty or so years of friendship with their eccentric comrade who thought he was a Viking, they started to realize he hadn't aged a day. The rest was history.

I shook my head as I trailed my hand up the gold-patterned wallpaper of the hall. I didn't blame Clive and Marie for searching for something magical. I'd done my fair share of wondering after accidentally killing Matthew, but had never come to any real conclusions until the Vaettir came for me. Luckily, Clive and Marie's initiation into Vaettir society had been a little more pleasant than mine.

I padded barefoot further down the upstairs hall, wondering if I'd find anything strange, or if our hosts, who had retired for the evening, were actually as normal and friendly as they seemed. Even James had stayed for the war planning, so I had no one to speculate with, leaving me only with the option of snooping. Okay, I could have just tried going to bed, but I knew I'd have trouble sleeping, and snooping seemed like a lot more fun.

One room in the hall drew my attention. It was guarded by a set of white double doors, one slightly ajar. I lifted a finger and pushed the door open a little further to reveal a large study, though all I could make out was a large desk in the center. Wanting to see more of the room than the hall light allowed, I flipped on the switch inside and quickly entered, then shut the door gently behind me.

The desk in the middle of the room looked antique, but that wasn't what held my attention. What caught my eye were the books. Lining both walls on either side of the desk were books that looked hundreds of years old. Some spines were cracked and fraying, while others, made of thick leather, held together a little better. Closer observation revealed the books were all on the occult, mythology, or ancient history. The collection had to be worth thousands, if not more, though I'm no book appraiser.

My fingers skimmed the shelves until a title caught my eye. I removed the book simply titled, *Norse Mythology*, figuring with everything that had happened, I could stand to brush up on the subject. I was glancing around for a comfortable place to sit when the door opened. I dropped the book in surprise and cursed, then bent down to pick it up.

Mikael beat me to it, crouching in front of me to cradle the book lovingly. We both stood.

"Doing some light reading?" he asked as he closed the heavy tome to look at the cover.

"I wasn't really needed down there," I said defensively, taking the book back from him. I took in his fresh clothing and damp hair. He must have snuck away from the group to take a shower. His clothing was just as Viking-esque as ever, making me worry that perhaps he was planning another visit to olden times.

He gestured to the book. "You won't find much of use in there," he explained, "just the human versions of the myths."

"You've read it?" I asked, unable to picture Mikael snuggling up contentedly with a good book.

"I've read them all," he answered, sweeping his hand to encompass the books surrounding us.

I smirked. "Is that why you've spent so much time with Marie and Clive, their books?"

He snatched the book away from me and thudded it onto the shelf, obviously offended.

"I didn't mean—" I began, realizing how bitchy my comment must have seemed.

"It's fine," he grumbled. "Spend several centuries using people for your own gain, and eventually that's all anyone will see."

I went silent, not sure what else I could say.

Mikael sighed and his anger leaked away. He gave me a

knowing smile. "Your little kitty cat was quite insistent we work on your shielding tonight. It quickly became clear that we'd accomplish nothing else until I attended you."

I sighed. I had been hoping for a good night's rest before tackling *that* issue, but it probably was wise to do it sooner rather than later.

Yet, there was still a more immediate matter. "Where did you get a change of clothes?" I asked, shifting uncomfortably in my dirty tunic.

He looked me up and down and laughed. "I keep supplies anywhere I might end up. *Your* wardrobe will have to wait until the morning. Now back to the shielding . . . " he trailed off, as if he didn't really want to talk about it, but knew he had to.

"Go on," I urged, wondering if Mikael's temper would resurface at the previously touchy subject.

"I've been thinking," he began, moving away from me to pace around the room, "it's going to be a difficult task for me to let down my shields. Deceit is in my nature, and it's a trying task to fight one's nature."

"I didn't think it was going to be a cakewalk," I commented, not seeing his point.

He paused his pacing to smirk at me. "What if we try it while I'm asleep?"

I opened my mouth in surprise, then paused to think about what he'd said. It made sense. We were all at our most defenseless when we slept. "It's worth a shot," I agreed.

He smiled, but it was strained. If I didn't know any better, I'd say he was nervous. For someone like Mikael to be showing his nerves, they had to be pretty extreme. The only question was, what did the ever-confident Viking not want me to know, and would he forgive me if I found out?

He leaned in close to me, reaching his arm around me to retrieve the mythology book once more. He handed it to me.

I frowned. "I thought you said it wasn't any good."

He smiled, looming over me. "I said it wasn't accurate, not that it wasn't any good."

My frown deepened. I wasn't sure if he was just covering up for his nervous display, or if he was somehow mocking me. Men were complex enough to begin with. Give them a thousand plus years and they only got worse, like ever-growing labyrinths of smugness and bravado.

Mikael was the most complex labyrinth of all. I had a feeling he possessed many dead ends, and probably more than a few dark abysses. I sensed I might be seeing into one of those abysses when I tucked him into bed that night. I could only hope I'd find my way out again.

---

ELEVEN O'CLOCK FOUND me in Mikael's room. I had waited in the study alone, reading the mythology book, until Alaric appeared, looking for confirmation that Mikael had spoken with me. Alaric had warned me to be careful. Careful with what, I wasn't sure. Could a sleeping Viking really be so dangerous? Don't answer that.

When Mikael hadn't answered my knock, I'd let myself into his room, hoping he was already asleep. No such luck. He was, however, drinking straight from the bottle of some hundred year old bourbon. He leaned against the padded headboard of his bed as I stepped into the room, his lower half obscured by the blankets, but his bare chest plain for all to see. His deep, reddish hair was pushed back from his face, trapped between his back and the headboard.

He paused to regard me with the bottle's opening hovering near his lips. "No kitty cat?" he questioned, then immediately started giggling.

"You're drunk," I accused, still standing near the doorway. I would have told him to put a shirt on, but I knew the comment would only get turned against me.

Nervous, I looked around his room. It was just as grand as the rest of the house, with plush, beige carpeting and a queen-size, four-poster bed. A cushy chair had been placed beside the nightstand for my convenience.

"It helps with the defenses," he explained as he lifted the bottle, slightly slurring his words. "Plus, I doubt I'll be able to fall asleep whilst you're staring at me awake without it. I'd offer you some, but—" he glanced down at my belly.

"Yeah, yeah," I said tiredly, shutting the door behind me before approaching the bed.

"So he let you come alone?" he asked, looking up at me.

I sat. I didn't like the way he said *let*. Alaric hadn't wanted me to come alone, but he'd seen the logic in it. Mikael's defenses would be difficult enough to penetrate as it was. We didn't need someone that he disliked, and who hated him in return, in the room to make matters more difficult.

"You should probably close your eyes if you're going to fall asleep," I said sarcastically, knowing Mikael would go to sleep when he damn well pleased, if at all.

He took another deep swig of the bourbon, then

lowered the bottle to his lap. "Perhaps it would help if you sung me a lullaby."

"I don't sing," I grumbled.

"All women sing," he stated matter-of-factly. "They just don't all admit it."

I glared at him. "Well if we never admit it, then how do you know that we sing?"

He crooked the corner of his lip into a half smile. "Well do you, when no one else is around?"

I did, but I wasn't about to admit it, and I sure as hell wouldn't make the admission for the entire female race, allowing Mikael to lump us into some antiquated stereotype.

"Do you have any advice?" I asked tiredly, attempting to change the subject.

"About singing?" he asked, before taking another deep swig of the bourbon.

"About what I should do," I clarified. "I've never tried to read someone's emotions while they're sleeping. I never really *try* at all. It just happens."

"Do the Erykah thingy," he suggesting, seeming more drunk by the second. I glanced down to see there was an extra empty bottle beside his bed. "The one where she puts her hands on either side of your face," he continued, "and suddenly knows everything you're thinking."

"She was a telepath," I sighed. "I read things a little differently than she did."

"*Was*," he sighed, suddenly sad. "Sometimes the past seems like it was just yesterday."

I smiled softly. "Probably because yesterday we were in the past."

"Oh yeah," he replied, still gazing forlornly across the room.

I took the bottle from his hands and placed it on the floor beside the empty one. "You know, you're a terrible drunk," I teased.

He turned to me and grinned. "Perhaps, but I'm awful good at most everything else."

I smirked and pushed my hair behind my ears. "Not good at sleeping, apparently."

Suddenly he was somber again. His mood swings were jarring, especially with my fatigue setting in.

When I just stared at him, he explained, "Sleep becomes a tiresome thing after a few centuries. You can only see so much evil before all of your dreams turn ugly."

It was an interesting thought. I only had twenty-some odd years of experiences to dream about, Mikael had centuries. "I'm sure you've seen a lot of good," I countered, "and beauty."

"I'm staring at some beauty right now," he said lasciviously, leaning forward to playfully leer at me.

I snorted. "Add flirting to the list of things you're bad at."

He sighed dramatically and resumed his comfortable position against the headboard. "If you keep up with the scathing remarks, I'll be up all night nursing my wounds."

I slouched back into my chair. "My guess is my remarks don't affect you in the slightest."

He smiled softly. "Words wound more fatally than swords my dear, for time may dull a blade, but words will never fade." He hiccuped and chuckled at his rhyme.

I rolled my eyes. "At least lie down properly," I

instructed. "You're never going to fall asleep like that." I gestured to the headboard he was still propped against.

"It would be more comfortable if you laid with me," he teased. "Of course, a lullaby might warm me just as much."

He was being manipulative, but his past few days had been almost as rough as mine, and he'd been pretty nice to me about it. *Mostly*.

"Shut up and I'll sing you your damn lullaby."

He grinned. "I promise I won't tell anyone you sing. It will be our little secret."

"It better be," I grumbled, as I wracked my brain for something to sing. "Now close your eyes."

He did as I bade him, scooting down so his head rested on his pillow. I cleared my throat and began to sing the only song I could think of. It was a song I'd made up for myself as a child, because I didn't have a mother to sing it for me. I briefly wondered if Mikael had known his mother, and if she'd sung to him at night. I couldn't imagine it, but since I was about to dive into his head, maybe I'd find out.

# 27

"Pregnant?" Sophie balked, letting her surprise and disdain show through in her voice. "Traveling back in time I can believe, but *you* being a father?"

Alaric put his arms behind his head, resting comfortably on the soft mattress. "You'd think you would be happy about being an auntie."

Sophie paced across the room. These cushy interiors were making her claustrophobic. "I'm more worried about what it might do to *you*," she grumbled.

Alaric snorted, increasing her ire. "Like what?"

"Like making idiotic decisions," she snapped. "Like trying to put yourself between Madeline and that executioner." This blasted pregnancy was going to get him *killed*.

The widening of Alaric's eyes gave her a great deal of satisfaction.

"Yeah," she went on, "I heard about *that*. Not everyone was unconscious when they had their little showdown."

"I would have done that, baby or no."

Sophie felt her expression soften, just as her resolve wavered. She took a seat beside her brother. "You do have a penchant for stupid decisions."

Alaric shoved her playfully. "Luckily I have my practical sister to do wise things like rushing off in the middle of battle to chase after a certain little woman who somehow replaced her missing foot."

Sophie's mouth formed a hard line. She was still intent on killing Maya. Next time, she wouldn't get away. "I'm not ready to talk about that yet."

Alaric raised an eyebrow at her. "Remember, the longer you hold it in, the more your rage will get the better of you."

Sophie smirked. "Well then we'll both have something to inspire stupid decisions."

"That we will," Alaric mused.

Their conversation died off, but Sophie had a feeling Alaric still had something to tell her. She poked him in the arm, then looked at him expectantly.

He sighed. "You're almost as perceptive as Madeline."

She chuckled, her brother often brought out her better moods, though he just as often brought out her worst. "Tell me."

Alaric raised his hands to rake his hair away from his face. Hair that was just like hers. Many might mistake them for fraternal twins, though Alaric was actually several years older than her.

"She's hiding something from me," he said finally. "Something that has her frightened."

Sophie stroked her chin in thought. "She has plenty to be frightened of. It doesn't mean she's hiding something."

He shook his head. "It's worse than she's letting on. I'll watch her when she doesn't see me, and her eyes look so . . . haunted."

She frowned. She had noticed Madeline's mood after the battle, but that was just Madeline. She was emotional about everything, and probably felt bad about sucking the life out of the injured at her feet, even though she used it to heal everyone else.

"She did just travel back in time and leave an entire village of people to die," she commented, repeating the information Alaric had told her while they scouted the woods.

"Exactly," Alaric replied. "She was shaken after that, but this new fear came after what happened with the other executioner."

Sophie pursed her lips. "What could have changed?"

Alaric shook his head. "She told me the key is in her thoughts. That sometimes, she cannot tell which thoughts are hers. I think the battle made it worse."

Sophie felt a small tickle of panic at the base of her spine. She didn't wish Madeline any harm, but she feared even more what it might do to her brother. "We need to destroy it," she said firmly, referring to the key.

Alaric smiled sadly. "I know. I would not have her alone in a room with Mikael if it could be any other way."

Sophie gave him a knowing look. There was some reason Alaric had it out for Mikael, though he wouldn't tell her why. She planned on figuring it out, no matter how adamantly he kept it from her. She laid her head on his shoulder, doing her best to belie her thoughts.

"I'll try to talk to her," she offered finally. "Perhaps she'll tell me how bad it really is."

Alaric laughed. "You might give her horrid flashbacks of when you were her social worker."

Sophie lifted her head to glare at him. "I was a damn good social worker, thank you very much."

He patted her shoulder. "If you say so."

They both laughed, then their conversation ebbed once again. Sophie knew better than to leave her brother alone while Madeline cozied up with the Viking. He would go barging in there eventually, unable to take it anymore. Sophie would simply have to wait it out with him until Madeline broke down Mikael's shields and found what she needed.

"You love her, don't you?" she asked suddenly.

The idea of her brother in love was a little jarring. Sure, he'd dated, but love was neither Sophie's nor her brother's strong suit. It wasn't what they were made for.

He leaned forward to rest his chin in his hands, bracing his elbows against his knees and shielding his face with his hair. "I have from the start."

Her jaw dropped. She hadn't really expected him to admit it. "Why her?" she blurted out.

Alaric turned to her, looking slightly offended.

She bit her lip. "I didn't mean it like that. It's just, you've had plenty of opportunities to fall in love. What was different this time?" Her heart was racing, and she wasn't sure why.

Alaric shrugged, disappointing her. "It could be our similar natures," he explained, "death and war go together nicely, and I'm sure that's why she ended up pregnant. But—" he cut himself off, seeming deep in thought.

"But what?" she pressed, feeling elated once more. She was quite sure what she'd previously felt for Maya was love . . . or was it just affection? Attachment from knowing someone for long enough? She wasn't sure.

Alaric sat up straight and flexed his hands in the air, as if grasping at the words that would not come. "She cares about *everything*," he began hesitantly, but then the words began to tumble out of his mouth like a mudslide, just a few rocks at first, leading to an almost frantic downpour. "The Vaettir abandoned her with no knowledge of who she was, and our treatment after reclaiming her wasn't much better, yet she still cares what happens to us. She forgave me for letting James haul her off to a cell, and for letting him stab her. It's like she *understands*, even though she's only been a part of our world for a short time. She balks at even killing one of her enemies, but can accept the fact that I've killed thousands. She wants to save us all, even though none of us deserve it."

Sophie stared at him, surprised by his outburst. "So you love her because she's a martyr?" she asked skeptically.

He grunted in frustration. "It's more than that. How do you explain why you love someone? It's not just their smile, or the way they laugh, or how they look when they sleep. It's all of it. It's seeing that burning humanity inside them, a single light that's like no other. It's irreplaceable."

If Sophie was surprised before, now she was completely dumbfounded. Jaw agape, she watched her brother, waiting to see if he'd say more, but he didn't. He buried his face in his palms and sunk into a fugue.

She placed a hand on his back. She might not know romantic love, but she knew familial love for her brother. She hated seeing the pain of worry on his face. "We'll protect her," she assured. "You'll see."

He nodded, but not like he believed her.

"I'll talk to her," Sophie offered again. "We'll get to the bottom of her worries, then we'll find a way to fix them."

Alaric nodded again, seeming slightly hopeful this time. Sophie took a deep breath, sincerely hoping there was a way to help Maddy. She didn't like to think how her brother would be affected if there was not, and she had no doubt he'd do something stupid, even if he had no chance of coming out alive.

She didn't like the idea of living alone in such a painful world. It simply wasn't an option.

## 28

The song did the trick. Eventually Mikael's breathing slowed as he drifted off to sleep. I looked down at his passive face, illuminated only by the small amount of light given off by the bedside lamp. His dark lashes formed perfect crescents below his eyebrows. It was odd to see him in such a relaxed, almost helpless state.

Really, I was shocked he'd managed to fall asleep at all with me in the room, though the alcohol had definitely helped him along. Still, you don't survive for a thousand years by trusting people enough to fall asleep near them, especially people you'd only known for a little over a week.

I shook my head. Who was I kidding? If someone burst into the room to murder us, I had no doubt Mikael would be up in two seconds flat, skewering them with his sword.

Thinking of the sword, I searched around the room for it, finding it resting against the wall near the closet. The ax he'd brought back from the past was nowhere to be seen.

I took a deep, shaky breath. I was stalling. I really didn't want to see inside Mikael's head. I didn't want to see inside *anyone's* head. I looked back to Mikael's still form. I *had* to do this, and it was now or never.

I leaned forward in my seat, then placed my hands gently on either side of his face. His skin was soft and supple, not like what you'd expect after so many years of existence. I smoothed my hands up so they rested partially in his hair. It was an oddly intimate gesture, and I was glad he wasn't conscious for it.

As if sensing my thoughts, his eyelids began to flutter open.

"No, no," I soothed, my voice barely above a whisper. "It's just me."

Not fully waking, he lifted one of his hands to cradle my palm against his face for a moment. Either realizing it was just me, or perhaps thinking it was someone else he wished was there, his arm fell back to his side as he drifted back into drunken sleep.

I tried to focus on any emotions I might pick up on, but Mikael almost waking up had me panicked. It was well past midnight, and my thoughts were muddled with my need for sleep. My empathy wasn't something I used on purpose, which made it difficult to hone in.

With another shaky breath, I closed my eyes and thought back to my *conversation* with Erykah. It had been effortless, but then again, she had been purposefully projecting her thoughts for me. Mikael was projecting nothing but bourbon breath. I would have to *take* his thoughts, giving nothing in return.

I scrunched my eyes tightly shut and focused, internally begging and wishing, but nothing happened. I opened my eyes and was about to pull away, but something stopped me.

As if seeing a moment of weakness, the key came alive at my neck. Reading the key's intent, I tried again to pull away from Mikael, but seemed unable to move. It was like a voice inside my head was saying, *You want to see inside his head? Oh, I'll show you inside his head*, only there were no words.

My outward sight went blind as scenes began to play inside my mind. I was powerless to stop them. I saw Erykah and the village we'd left behind, but felt none of the guilt Mikael felt in the present. It was a time before the key destroyed them all. His lovely wife was yet to be twisted into the hard, calculating woman she'd become. A woman that would climb inside his head without permission.

I turned to the side in the vision, and it felt as if my actual body was turning. I turned from Erykah and saw Mikael's sons, running in and out of the livestock huts, frightening the cattle, then laughing maniacally as adults tried to catch and chastise them.

I felt my lips curve into a smile, and realized I was seeing through Mikael's eyes, inhabiting his mind during the memory. There was something in my arms. I looked down to see a baby girl. She smiled up at me with bright, reddish brown eyes, her delicate skin alabaster perfection. I felt a tear come to my eye. The scene blurred, and changed.

I was standing in the same spot, but was surrounded by corpses and ash. All the structures had been burned, and the people murdered. It was many years later. My daughter had long since been killed, now Erykah had joined her. My sons were far from that place, safe for the time being, but they would want revenge.

Fast forward again. Entire empires crumbling at my feet. I didn't care. Let them grieve as I'd grieved. The world was not a kind place.

I felt dizzy as Mikael woke. He'd realized what was happening, and was trying to force me out. I felt his shields raising, and the key fought them for control.

The struggle seemed to last for ages, but its end was sudden. Mikael forced his shields up, shutting me out. It was like iron gates slamming into place. The impact rattled my teeth. Mikael's eyes shot open, meeting mine as I still gripped the sides of his face. At some point I'd moved closer, my mouth was only inches from his.

Words that were not mine trickled from my lips, "You are a more worthy adversary than we thought, Agnarsson.
"

Then I fainted.

---

I SHOT UP IN BED, panting as my breathing tried to catch up with my heart. The room was pitch black, and arms wrapped around me from behind. I screamed.

"Maddy, Maddy," a voice soothed. "Shh."

Part of me recognized that voice, but I didn't understand where I was.

"Madeline," the voice said again, then it clicked that it was Alaric. In my sleep I had been seeing images I never should have seen. They'd all happened long before I was born, in places far away.

As reality set in, a new panic hit me. "Oh my god, Mikael. I practically raped his memories."

A light flipped on at the bedside. I noted a sliver of sunlight at the window, though the curtains were heavy enough to block most of it out. I turned around and was able to see Alaric's face. It helped bring me the rest of the way into reality.

"He carried you here after you fainted," Alaric explained. "He would not say what happened."

I shook my head over and over again. "This is *not* good. He's going to kill me. I shouldn't have seen all of that."

Alaric scooted behind me and rubbed his hands up and down my arms. "If he was going to kill you, you wouldn't be sitting here. Whatever it is, it's okay."

I took a deep, shaky breath. "You don't understand. He wouldn't have wanted anyone to feel his emotions like that."

Alaric continued to rub my arms. "He knew the risks."

I nodded, but it didn't make me feel any better.

He hugged me against him. "Did you at least get what you needed?"

I pulled away, only then remembering my initial intent in reading Mikael's thoughts. I recalled the moment he shut me out, and how his shields felt going up. It was quite literally a physical barrier in his mind, created by sheer force of will, and a desperate desire to hide his emotions.

"I think I did," I whispered, feeling somewhat astonished by the notion.

In my mind I thought, *You didn't expect that, did you?* but there was no reply. The key had delved into Mikael's memories, thinking he wouldn't have the will to shut it out, but he did. Mikael had managed to catch the key off guard. I briefly wondered if he'd be able to do it again, now that the key knew what it was up against.

"What are you thinking?" Alaric asked softly.

I shook my head. "Ugly thoughts. I need to talk to Mikael."

"I'll go with you," he offered.

I nodded. It was probably a bad idea to take Alaric with me, but I wasn't sure I possessed the bravery needed to face the scary Viking on my own.

We left the room and walked down the hall as the first hints of dawn chased us through the window. I did *not* want to do this. I remembered how Mikael had felt when I'd picked up on just an ounce of his grief. Now I'd seen his memories first hand, instead of just focusing on his shields. He was going to be *pissed.*

We made our way to the room where I'd sat with Mikael. Maybe he would still be asleep and we could delay the inevitable conversation. I knocked on the closed door.

No answer.

With a deep, shaky breath, I turned the knob and peeked inside, with Alaric hovering over my shoulder. The room was perfectly clean, the bed made, with no sign of its inhabitant.

I turned wide eyes to Alaric as I pulled the door shut, leaving us out in the hall. "Do you think—" I began.

Alaric shook his head. "He wouldn't be able to abandon you. It would be too close to a betrayal, which would break his oath to you."

My strength left me as I leaned against the wall. Alaric was right. Part of me would have liked to think we'd be better off without Mikael, but that part wasn't very wise. Like it or not, we needed him, and we needed him not mad at me.

Movement at the end of the hall caught my attention. Mikael became fully visible as he ascended the last few stairs. "I'm surprised to hear you speaking on my behalf," he commented, eyeing Alaric as he approached us.

Alaric glared. "I was speaking upon your oath to Madeline, nothing more."

Mikael smirked, though it was half-hearted. "Of course," he said quietly.

I stayed where I was standing, waiting for Mikael to address me, but he was yet to meet my eyes. As silence engulfed us, I leaned more heavily against the wall. I was exhausted, and felt like I might lose the bile in my stomach.

Finally Mikael looked at me. "Are you well?" he asked, his eyes focused somewhere in the vicinity of my mouth rather than further up my face.

"Are you?" I breathed. Yep, I was going to have to find the bathroom.

Alaric reached for me, but I sprung from the wall and rushed past him. I really didn't want to mess up Marie's hallway carpeting. I made my way down the hall and burst into the vacant bathroom, slamming the door against the wall as I threw it open.

I made it to the toilet and began heaving, though nothing came up. I hadn't managed to turn on the bathroom light, but I was grateful for the darkness. It felt somehow safe as I huddled over the toilet. I heard Alaric and Mikael speaking in the hallway, then Sophie's voice was added to the mix. A moment later someone was behind me, sweeping my hair back from my face just as another wave of nausea hit me.

"It seems you're still pregnant," the man holding my hair mumbled once my dry heaving had stilled.

I jumped when I realized it was Mikael.

"Where's Alaric?" I groaned, feeling like I might heave again.

"I requested that he allow me to tend to you," Mikael explained.

I wanted badly to turn around and look at him, but I was afraid to move away from the toilet. "And he listened?" I asked skeptically, my voice barely above a croak.

"No," Mikael said, a hint of laughter in his voice, "but his sister intervened."

I shook my head, then instantly regretted it as my stomach did a little flip-flop. "No offense," I began slowly, closing my eyes to still my dizziness, "but holding my hair while I heave really is a job for the father of my child."

Mikael was silent for a moment, but continued to hold my hair. Little tugs of movement let me know he was twining it around his fingers. "You stole your way into the memories I hold most dear. The least you can do is let me sit here with you."

I sighed. It was time to have *that* talk, apparently. I would rather have had it somewhere other than the bathroom, with me able bodied and ready to run away, but I wouldn't deny him answers now.

"I didn't mean to," I explained. "It was the key."

I expected a wash of anger, or an accusation that I was making excuses, but Mikael just silently kept playing with my hair while I hovered over the toilet. Feeling slightly more steady, I moved away from the bowl and sat back to lean against the wall. I tugged my hair out of Mikael's grasp, then brought my knees to my chest.

He took a seat beside me, mirroring my position. "How much control has it gained?"

I turned my neck to look at him, feeling slightly stunned. "You're never angry when I most expect it."

He picked up a lock of my hair and started playing with it again. Not meeting my eyes, he explained, "I *was* angry, but my anger will do us no good now."

I sighed and slouched further down the wall, giving up on keeping my hair to myself. Not knowing what to say in response, I decided to answer his original question. "Even now, with the memory of how you build your shields in my head, I'm not sure I can fight it. At times, I'm not even sure I want to."

"What did Erykah really tell you that night, right before we shared our dance?" he asked softly.

The bathroom darkened, letting me know that clouds were moving in outside to obscure the sun. "I don't know what you mean."

His hand found its way to my knee, but it was more attention-getting than flirtatious. "Yes, Madeline, you do."

I placed my hand on my belly, wishing I could somehow feel the small life inside. I knew I shouldn't tell anyone what Erykah had told me, or if I did, Alaric should be the first to know. It was his child too, after all.

Still, the words began to tumble from my mouth. "I know how to destroy the key, and I think I might be able to shield from it," I began, just as a tiny voice in my head argued both of those points, "but in all likelihood the effort would kill me . . . " I trailed off, then patted my belly and added, "and *it*."

Mikael's face went slack, the shadows in the room emphasizing the subtle change. "Why would you not say anything?"

I shrugged, wondering where Alaric had gone, and hoping he wasn't close enough to hear anything I was saying. "It would do little good."

"Then why tell me now?" Mikael pressed.

I closed my eyes, suddenly feeling excruciatingly tired. "Because I can't tell Alaric. Sometimes I consider Sophie a friend, but I can't tell her either."

When Mikael didn't reply, I opened one eye to see him smiling. "Does this mean that *I'm* your friend?" he teased.

I smirked. "You don't have friends."

"No," he replied, "I don't. Yet somehow you're wiggling your way in."

"Your daughter," I began, remembering how he felt looking down at the baby girl in his arms.

"Gone," he said simply.

"Was she . . . " I trailed off, hoping he'd catch my meaning so I wouldn't have to say it out loud. She wasn't around when we visited the village, at least I didn't think . . .

He shook his head. "She wasn't in the village the day they all died. She was lost to us long before that."

"I'm sorry," I said, unsure of what else to say.

He nodded, looking suddenly determined. "I will not allow your child to suffer the same fate."

I cringed and smoothed my fingers over my hair, turning my head to hide my expression. "I shouldn't have told you," I whispered. "I thought you of all people would understand I have to do this, no matter the cost. If I cannot destroy it, the key will find a way to destroy me regardless. If dying is my only choice, you can bet your ass I'll be taking the key down with me."

I turned back to Mikael to see his jaw set in a firm line. I could tell he wanted to argue with me, but before he could I said, "You know I'm right. Erykah escaped it without destroying it, and look what happened. I won't let the key come back for us all with a new owner. What if it ends up with Aislin or Estus?"

Mikael sighed, signaling that I had won the argument. "Nothing is ever truly written in stone," he said finally, "and I will do everything possible to keep you alive."

"Because of our oath," I added. "Letting me die when you could save me would probably count as a betrayal."

He sighed again, and looked somehow sad. "Yes, Madeline, because of our oath."

He stood and offered me a hand up. I wasn't sure if I was ready to leave the bathroom yet, but it was worth a shot. Mikael took hold of my hand and lifted me effortlessly to my feet.

I felt more steady as I followed him out into the hall. The key had been silent during our entire exchange. I wasn't sure if it was a bad sign, or a good one. Did it fear Mikael, or was it simply lulling us into complacency?

Sophie was coming toward us down the hall, but I didn't see Alaric anywhere.

"We need to talk," was all she said as she reached us.

Mikael handed me off to her without a word.

"Where's Alaric?" I asked as Sophie led me away. I

wanted to be the one to tell him that I thought the baby was still there. I didn't want to miss his reaction.

A look crossed over Sophie's face that I didn't quite understand, making me apprehensive. What did she want to talk about that she couldn't say in front of Mikael? I looked back over my shoulder to see that the Viking in question had disappeared down the stairs.

I went willingly with Sophie as she guided me the rest of the way down the hall and into the study. I felt oddly energized. Mikael's assurances were still hanging in my mind. I was probably just delirious and hormonal, but as Sophie shut the door of the study behind us, I was overcome by a strange surge of energy.

I opened my mouth to ask why she needed to talk to me in private, but what came out was, "Get me out of here."

I reflexively wanted to lift my hand to my mouth, surprised by my words, but my hand lifted toward Sophie instead. A dome of energy encircled my palm, though I wasn't sure if it would be visible to the naked eye, or just mine.

I tried to lower my hand as Sophie's dark eyes widened in shock. My heart should have been racing, but my body was no longer my own. I'd been pushed into the passenger seat as the key took over, but I couldn't tell its intent. I might have learned to shield my thoughts, but so had the key.

# 29

"Put your hand down, Madeline," Sophie scolded, not quite getting how serious the situation had become.

I wanted to call out to her, to warn her somehow, but it was like sitting in a dark projection room with my hands tied. I could see the scene playing before me, but was powerless to stop it.

"We are leaving this place," I said against my will.

I tried to shake my head, but it wouldn't work. I couldn't imagine why the key wanted to leave now. Its host was protected, and we were starting a war. It was getting everything it wanted.

Sophie took a step back toward the door. "We're not going anywhere," she said calmly.

I reached my arm back and threw the energy collecting in my palm at her. She dove out of the way gracefully, rolling across the plush carpet, only to rise to her feet near one of the book cases. The energy hit the door harmlessly, dissipating to spread back into the environment.

I turned, stalking Sophie like a predator, ready to anticipate her next move. I threw another ball of energy just as the door opened behind us.

"I apologize—" said a woman's voice before cutting off, realizing the situation she'd just walked into.

I didn't hear her approach, but suddenly my body was leaping aside right before Aila could wrap her arms around me from behind. I landed back near the door, slamming it shut to trap Aila and Sophie inside with me. The two moved to stand shoulder to shoulder, ready for my next attack.

"The key seems to have taken her over," Sophie explained, keeping her eyes firmly on me as she partially crouched, ready to move.

Worry crossed Aila's face. "I don't know what to do," she admitted.

I watched the exchange between the two women while my mind was screaming at me to do something. I still couldn't sense any of the key's thoughts. I had learned how to shut it out of my mind, but not my body.

"Get—" I managed to force out through gritted teeth, but the key sent a searing wave of pain through my brain. It dizzied me enough I couldn't see for a moment.

When I opened my eyes again, Sophie and Aila were flanking me. I could hear footsteps running down the hall. The women exchanged a subtle nod, then leapt for me at once. Sophie was going to reach me first, and the key turned my body to fend her off. At the last moment, Sophie side-stepped and Aila crashed into me from behind, knocking us both to the floor.

Energy coursed through me, attacking the weight on

my back. Aila screamed, then I was free. I rose shakily to my feet, just as Alaric and Mikael came rushing into the room, followed by Faas, Tabitha, and James. With so many of us, the study became suddenly claustrophobic. A small measure of the key's panic leaked into my mind. I had thought it was completely in control of the situation, but it was scared. We didn't have much energy left, and wouldn't be able to fend our captors off for long.

Involuntarily, I backed away toward the large window that sat behind the desk, opposite the door to the room. Horror overcame me as I realized the key might try making us jump out the second story window to escape.

The key held up my hands in front of me as I continued backing away. Both of my hands were glowing, and I was pretty sure I wasn't the only one who could see it, given James' awestruck expression. However, no one else seemed surprised.

All at once, the room exploded into movement. Energy shot from my hands as I was attacked, harming some, but not enough to get them away from me. We hadn't received any new energy since we'd used it all up on the battlefield, and fighting Mikael had pushed us past our limit. I looked around frantically. No one here was weak enough to drain. We were too weak.

Just as I realized the key was no longer shielding its thoughts, Alaric and Sophie simultaneously tackled me, knocking me onto my back and pinning my arms against the carpet. Faas moved to stand over us, his blond top knot of hair falling forward to cover half his face. He reached his hands toward me, but didn't close the distance. At first I couldn't tell what he was doing, then my last bit of energy began to drain away. He was stealing it from me, like I could do from a corpse, but I wasn't a corpse, and I wasn't weak enough to die.

"Get it off of her," Mikael demanded, stepping into view beside Faas.

"We can't, remember?" Alaric growled. I could hear his voice, but couldn't see his face. All I could see was Faas, and blearily, Mikael.

"They're both weakened. Try," Mikael demanded.

Not arguing, Sophie kept my arm pinned with one hand, while she used the other to lower the collar of my shirt, revealing the key. Alaric mirrored her pose, using his free hand to reach for the key itself.

Before Alaric's hand finished its descent, I was overcome with pain like I'd never known. It felt like the key was tearing apart the flesh and bones it laid upon.

"It cannot be," Faas said in shock as he hovered over me, struggling to keep the key from using me to lash out.

I had a moment to take in the awestricken faces around me, then I was out.

---

I WOKE up lying on cold stone, or maybe I wasn't awake. I didn't feel awake. In fact, I didn't feel real at all. I propped myself up into a seated position, then instinctively reached for my throat. I gasped. The key wasn't there.

Elation filled me, but it was brief. Why could I still sense its presence? I looked around the shadowy room. It was oddly familiar, but somehow not. Something shifted in the near-darkness and I leapt to my feet.

I let out a sigh of relief as a Norn came into view, the same one we'd met when we'd travelled back in time. Suddenly I realized where I was. I was in the cave where the Norn had sent me back to the World Tree.

"Am I really here?" I asked, though I knew I didn't need to ask out loud for the Norn to hear me.

*Not entirely*, a voice echoed in my head. *You are here visiting me, just as much as you were present in your visit with Yggdrasil.*

"Where is the key?" I asked shakily.

The Norn took a few steps forward to tower over me, then lowered her wolf-like paw to my chest. *You are one.*

I gasped and pulled away. That wasn't possible. "Why am I here?" I asked, feeling almost angry in my desperation.

*I did not bring you here,* the Norn answered.

I shook my head. The key could have brought me, but that wasn't right. It wouldn't want to be here, but I wasn't capable of any sort of subconscious travel myself, was I?

I took a shaky breath. How I'd gotten there wasn't important. There were far more pressing matters. "What do you mean, the key and I are one?"

The Norn approached me again and put her massive paw on my shoulder. *I can feel its energy, intermingling with yours. It was not always an object, but pure energy made when Yggdrasil was torn apart. It has reverted to that state, within you.*

The Norn caught me as I almost fell, holding on to my arms until I became steady once more. At some point I'd began to cry, but the tears didn't feel wet. I knew they were there, but they weren't entirely physical, just like I wasn't entirely physical.

"How do I get rid of it?" I sobbed.

*You and the key may both die,* she explained, *releasing your energies into the universe.*

My thoughts jumped from Alaric, to Mikael, to the child inside of me.

*There may be another way,* the Norn thought suddenly. She crouched to lower her paw to my belly. *Perhaps the foreign energy could be focused into your child, giving the wild magic human form.*

I pulled forcefully away from the Norn. "How dare you!" I gasped. "I won't sacrifice a child just to save myself."

The Norn didn't seem offended, and instead continued to look down at me impassively. *Then you all shall die.*

I closed my eyes and shook my head over and over again. I needed to get out of there. I knew my body was still back in the present time, but I didn't know how to reach it.

*As you wish*, the Norn thought sadly. I lurched backward as she shoved me, then sat bolt upright in a cushy bed, laboring to catch my breath.

Alaric had been in a hunched, seated position next to me, silhouetted by the moonlight peeking in through the window. As soon as I woke, he turned to face me and gripped both my arms in his hands, searching my face for some sign that I was myself.

He looked scared, and whether it was of me, or for me, I could not tell.

I was trying to think of how to explain everything to Alaric, when there was a knock on the door. Neither of us told the visitor to come in, but the door opened anyway.

There were several visitors I would have expected at that moment, but Faas wasn't one of them. He looked almost like a kicked puppy as he pushed the door aside and slowly entered the room to approach the bed. I would have glared at him if I'd had the strength.

"What do you want?" Alaric asked, his anger at the interruption clear in his voice.

Faas raked his swatch of blond hair away from his face, unperturbed by Alaric's tone, then turned his gaze to me. "I wanted to apologize."

If I'd been shocked by his appearance, now I was doubly shocked. "Come again?"

"I thought you unworthy to be the bearer of such a power as the *Lykill*," he explained. "For lack of a better word, I was jealous. Now I see what a burden it truly is. I pity you."

I wasn't sure I liked his explanation, but at least he was trying. "Thanks, I guess," I conceded. "And thanks for keeping me from killing anyone."

He replied with a sharp nod. "Before you lost consciousness, the key seemed to melt," he went on. "It slid across your skin like molten metal. Is it gone?"

I held my breath. I hadn't yet figured out how I would explain things to Alaric, but it looked like now was the time, whether I liked it or not.

I exhaled. "It's inside of me—part of me . . . or something."

Alaric inhaled sharply, then turned to meet my eyes. "Are you sure?"

I nodded. "While I was . . . out, I visited the Norn back in time, just like what happened when I visited Yggdrasil."

"Yggdrasil?" Faas hissed.

I waved him off and continued to speak to Alaric. "She told me the key was part of me now."

"I must inform Mikael," Faas interrupted again.

"*Go*," Alaric ordered, clearly not desiring any more interruptions. As Faas left, Alaric turned back to me. "Did she tell you how to undo it?"

I shook my head. I felt like I should be crying, but I was oddly calm. I couldn't help but wonder if it was the key exerting its influence over me. "She said the key and I could die together, or perhaps we could put the key's energy into our baby, thus giving it a physical form. I refused either option."

He took my hand in his, lifting it to kiss my knuckles. "Good," he breathed.

I closed my eyes, reveling in the simple sensation of his lips on my skin. Just that morning I could have killed him. I might still. I shivered.

"Is it good?" I asked softly. "I'm a danger to everyone. Perhaps I should have let the Norn end things for me right then."

Alaric squeezed my hand and gave me a dark look. "Your risk is more than ours. At least we can choose to put ourselves in harm's way. This was all thrust upon you."

Movement caught my eye, and I turned to see Mikael standing in the doorway, his head nearly reaching the moulding. "How do you feel?" he asked.

I laughed, though it was more of a bitter grunt. "I'm sharing my body with a force of corrupted, wild magic that could take me over at any time. How do you think I feel?"

"There may still be a way to defeat it," he stated.

"How?" Alaric asked instantly, before I could close my gaping jaw.

"The key is an ancient power," Mikael began as he approached the bed. "It is a concentration of the forces of chaos and corruption that destroyed Yggdrasil, the dark to balance the light. The old gods left this world long before Yggdrasil, and that is why the Norns created so many of us in their image."

I clenched my fists in impatience. We needed an answer and Mikael was just standing around talking about long dead myths. Yggdrasil and the old gods were gone. There was nothing they could do to help us.

Mikael looked at me like he was reading my thoughts, then gave me a slightly mocking smile. "The power of Yggdrasil is still within the key, just as it still resides within the Norns. The power to jump through time, and to different worlds. That power is now within you."

"Please don't tell me your plan is for me to travel to a different world to find the old gods."

Mikael scoffed. "Of course not. That would be ridiculous. My plan is for you to bring the old gods to us, using the power of Yggdrasil, and the connection of our blood to draw them forth. You have a direct link to Bastet sitting right beside you."

Alaric looked stunned. "You're mad."

Mikael smiled at Alaric, then knelt on the floor in front of us to take my free hand in his. "And what about you, Madeline? As someone who has touched Yggdrasil itself, as someone who has tasted the power of the Norns, and in effect, of the old gods, do you think me mad?"

Fear tickled down my spine, but it wasn't my fear. I

opened my mouth to speak, then closed it, feeling more than thinking about what he'd said.

After a moment, I smiled. "Quite the contrary, I think you're on to something."

Alaric turned to me in disbelief. I really didn't know if Mikael's plan could work, but the key seemed to think it might be a possibility. It shivered again. It was afraid of the old gods. Something about this new closeness let me sense its emotions more keenly. We were one in the same now, after all.

# EPILOGUE

I finally obtained new clothes. The dark wash jeans fit me like a second skin, complementing the magenta silk blouse. It felt unbelievably good to be back in normal clothes, and even better to have clean underwear. Tabitha had done the shopping, though I could have trusted any of the women with us to get me jeans that were long enough. They all knew the tall girl struggle.

We were all packed up and planned to leave Clive and Marie's home later that evening, under the cover of night. According to Mikael, we were heading North, *far* North. Someplace remote, where police weren't looking for a group of murderers, and where another altercation with our enemies might go unnoticed. The only other hint I'd been given was that it would be cold. Full winter gear was laid out across mine and Alaric's bed.

We'd all gotten a full night's sleep, and the key seemed to be lying dormant within me. I knew it would resurface eventually, especially once it gained access to more energy, but hopefully by then we'd be able to fight it. We'd just have to keep me away from any dead bodies in the meantime. I didn't like the idea of weakening myself to weaken the key, but it was our only option until we could summon the old gods.

I laughed at how silly my thoughts felt as Alaric walked up behind me. "What is it?"

I shook my head and leaned forward to finger the sleeve of my new winter coat. It was one of those expensive, micro-down numbers, thin and light, but extremely warm.

"Just amusing myself with the fact that we actually think we stand a chance of summoning *gods* to help us," I explained.

Alaric kissed my cheek. "You're the one that encouraged the idea, my dear."

I smirked, though he couldn't see it. "We travelled back in time, I touched Yggdrasil, and now an ancient magic is housed within me. I'm pretty sure anything is possible at this point."

Alaric spun me around and kissed me, but as he pulled away, a dark look crossed his face.

"What is it?" I questioned, still wrapped in his embrace.

He half shrugged. "After what I've seen, I wouldn't put it past you or Mikael to summon the old gods. The real question is, will they want to help us once they're here?"

I quirked an eyebrow at him. "What do you think Bastet will say?"

He frowned. "I'm not sure. We can choose between Bastet and Dolos. War and deceit . . . not the most magnanimous pair."

"Freyja too," I added.

I got the reaction I was hoping for as surprise crossed Alaric's face. It wasn't often I got the jump on him. "Freyja?" he questioned.

I nodded. "Aila is her descendant," I explained. "She told Sophie while they were waiting for us to return from the past."

Alaric seemed thoughtful. "A goddess of war and death," he mused, "but also love and fertility. Perhaps a goddess that would fight to save an unborn child."

I smiled. It was a slim, jagged, tenuous ray of hope, but it was hope nonetheless.

Alaric lifted me in his arms, then carried me to the bed, laying me down gently atop our winter clothes. "We have hours to kill until dark . . . " he trailed off, his voice gone low with seduction.

I raised my eyebrows as I looked up at him. "I can think of a thing or two to pass the time."

He kissed down my neck. "Name them slowly, please."

I stated my first suggestion.

Alaric lifted his gaze to mine, a dark grin on his face. "Now that's my little *land-skjálpti.*"

---

HOURS LATER, as the sun began to make its slow descent from the sky, we prepared to leave. Still in our room, Alaric helped me into my new coat, taking the time to zip it, and button the clasp that would hold the collar close to my neck.

He pulled the hood up over my head playfully, then used it to draw me in for a kiss.

"I love you," he breathed.

I pulled away, surprised. "Come again?" I asked with a wry grin.

He tilted his head downward and eyed me like I was a misbehaving child.

"No," I said innocently, "I really didn't hear you, I need you to repeat yourself."

"You know," he teased, "I don't even say that out loud to my sister."

I crossed my arms and looked up at him. "You know, I'm an out loud kind of girl."

He grabbed me and lifted me effortlessly into his arms, cradling me like a baby. He kissed me fiercely. "Madeline," he began, "you are incorrigible, head strong, you care far too much about everyone else, *and* I love you."

I laughed. "Alaric, you are single-focused, impulsive, and perhaps a bit wily, but I love you too."

He kissed me again, then walked us toward the door. "I'm holding you to that," he joked. "You can't take it back now."

I smiled up at him as we prepared to go join the rest of our group. "War is capable of love," I teased.

He returned my smile, flashing his little fangs. "And death has a heart."

## NOTE FROM THE AUTHOR

I hope you enjoyed the second installment in the Bitter Ashes Series! For news and updates, please sign up for my mailing list by visiting:

www.saracroethle.com

## SNEAK PEEK AT BOOK THREE

ROCK, PAPER, SHIVERS

The cold wind stung what was visible of my face, and my hands and feet were numb despite the thick gloves and heavy duty winter boots. As far as the eye could see in any direction was crisp, pure white, almost blinding as the sun made its slow descent toward the horizon. I stood alone, musing over everything that had gotten me to this point, camping out in a frozen wasteland, contemplating summoning gods.

It had taken us weeks to get to our location. Weeks of hiding from our enemies while we traveled through the larger cities. Weeks of plotting our next step. Weeks of waiting for the key to rear its ugly head in an attempt to possess me again. We'd made it all this way without conflict. I shouldn't have been surprised since we'd taken so many precautions, but still, by this point, I expected things to go wrong at every turn. More surprising than our success so far, was that the key had remained dormant within me.

Mikael appeared by my side, staring out at the cold

landscape ahead of us as the breeze played with his long, auburn hair. "Are you ready?"

I shook my head. "No."

I rubbed the slight bump of my belly, still not fully believing I was growing a child inside me. My winter clothing was all cinched up around me, so my pregnancy didn't show, but the entire group knew regardless. Sophie had a big mouth.

"Freyja is, among other things, the goddess of childbirth," Mikael reassured, placing a hand on my shoulder. "She will not harm you or your child."

I turned and raised an eyebrow at him, though my eyebrows were mostly covered by the black hood of my jacket. While I wore a top of the line, full-length, micro-down coat, plus many layers underneath to keep me warm, Mikael had only added a heavy, fleece lined, knee length coat to his normal Viking-esque gear. His dusky red hair whipped about freely in the icy air, yet he seemed unfazed. I was freezing even with all the layers. Camping out in the Arctic Circle was no joke.

"She's an ancient goddess," I countered, "one who left our people long before you were even born. You have no idea what she'll do."

Mikael smirked. "No, I don't, but you know I wouldn't tell you that your child will be safe if I didn't think it was true."

"Because of our oath," I agreed.

Mikael rolled his strange, amber eyes. "I wouldn't lie to you about such a thing, even with a blood oath hanging over my head."

I sighed, not because I thought he was misleading me,

but because I believed him. The past few weeks had been trying. I'd finally been reported missing back in the States, but luckily still had fake identification from Diana. Many of Mikael's people, living safe within the Salr, had never possessed any real forms of identification, so we'd had to purchase a batch of fake IDs for them. Never mind that Mikael already had *a guy* in place to make the transaction go smoothly, and had around ten different personas in place for himself, all with passports, bank accounts, and backstories. Some even owned property.

We'd done much of our traveling by train, with me gritting my teeth the entire time, waiting for the cops to storm in and take us all away. Mikael had been the one to keep me calm through it all, oddly enough, and I'd really come to depend on him to keep the panic away.

Alaric and Sophie had been there for me too, but they were both a little more blunt, a little less tactful. They said exactly what they thought, which usually wasn't very comforting, though I appreciated it in a whole other way.

I turned to see Alaric waiting in the distance near our camp. He wore a more modern coat like mine, and a stocking cap over his long, black hair. Even from the distance I could tell he was smiling at me, I could *feel* it. Alaric might not be the best with comforting words, but he offered me partnership. We could both be worried together about ourselves and our child, and we could both be brave together. At that moment, if I didn't have Alaric's bravery helping me along, I probably would have called off the whole thing. I wasn't fit to summon gods . . . but then again, who was?

Mikael walked by my side as we started back toward the

tents. The dense snow beneath our feet crunched, but didn't give way. I'd slipped and fallen on my butt on some of the harder-packed patches more times than I'd like to admit, far less graceful than any of my companions.

As we reached Alaric, Sophie and Aila came into view, both in full winter gear with their hoods pulled up. Aila looked gargantuan, but dangerous with the added layers on her already tall, muscular physique. I just looked like a fat penguin.

The other members of our small group, Faas, Tabitha, and James, waited inside the large tent that was our main base. The snow mobiles we'd used to reach such a remote area were parked around the tent, covered by fitted tarps, but otherwise ready for a fast escape.

We hadn't wanted to risk bringing any more of Mikael's people into our plan, so it was just the eight of us. We needed to be as unfindable as possible.

Many had voted against even bringing James. He was the weakest link without his memories. The arguments had ended though as Mikael pointed out that James was the only one who could create heat from nothing. It was a useful backup skill when camping on the frozen tundra.

I reached Alaric and stepped into the cradle of his arms, feeling some of the tension leak out of my body at his nearness. If Freyja didn't work out, we'd be using Alaric and Sophie to summon Bastet. I really hoped Freyja worked. I had no desire to meet a cat-headed war goddess.

I looked to Aila, who we'd be using to summon Freyja. All we needed was a bit of her blood. Aila looked nervous, her eyes a little too wide, and I knew it wasn't the prospect of slicing her arm open that had her worried. She'd suffered countless injuries over her long life, but it wasn't every day you met your patron deity.

Faas appeared from within the tent, just as bundled up as me. As executioners, denizens of death, we were much stronger in the magical department, but slightly lacking in the physical. In other words, we were a lot more prone to the elements.

Faas' white hood covered his blond swatch of hair and eyebrows, leaving only his eyes and nose visible. His eyes no longer held intense hatred for me, but they were still wary. His job was to step in and drain my energy if the key took over again, and I didn't blame him for being nervous about it, and I was still just as nervous around him. Even though he was built smaller than any of the other men, and tended to be less aggressive, he'd mastered skills I'd only recently found out I even had, and he knew how to use them to kill, maim, and control. He couldn't heal though. That little quirk was mine alone, but he had a little quirk too. He could drain energy from those who were uninjured. I could only steal from someone who was already near death, or from a weakened human. Faas had been draining my energy for weeks, keeping me weak enough to prohibit the key from using me to murder everyone.

We'd also kept me away from any corpses so I couldn't get a quick boost, just in case, but the key was still a force all on its own. Even without anyone to drain, it could do a great deal of damage before running out of juice, despite Faas draining my energy.

Still, the key hadn't been present in my mind, except for the occasional emotion leaking through. It was deep in hiding, which made me even more nervous than when it was trying to take over. At least when it tried to take over, I knew what it wanted. When I had learned from Mikael how to shield my thoughts and emotions, the key had learned too. It had built a brick wall between us, letting me know that if I wouldn't let it in on my plans, it wouldn't let me in on its plans either. Of course, I had a feeling it could still *hear* everything that was said, so it probably knew what we were planning with Freyja. Either it agreed with the ritual, or it was waiting for the right moment to pop in and cause chaos.

"Is everything prepared?" Mikael asked as Faas went to stand near him.

Faas nodded, though the gesture was almost imperceptible in his thick coat. "We'll begin the ritual as soon as the sun sets."

We all nodded in agreement, because there was nothing else to do. We were about to use my connection to Yggdrasil, the World Tree, to pull one of the old gods through into our world. If we succeeded, we would ask for her aid. It would be her choice whether she helped us, as there was nothing we could really do to compel her.

We were banking on the small chance that Freyja was a magnanimous goddess. My hopes were not high. I couldn't claim to know much about the old gods, but I knew one thing for certain. No one does anything for free.

Printed in Great
Britain
by Amazon